# *The* EAST END

**Center Point
Large Print**

**This Large Print Book carries the
Seal of Approval of N.A.V.H.**

*The*

# EAST END

# JASON ALLEN

CENTER POINT LARGE PRINT
THORNDIKE, MAINE

For my mother and brother

I've been absolutely terrified every moment of my life—and I've never let it keep me from doing a single thing I wanted to do.

—Georgia O'Keeffe

# *The*
# EAST
# END

# COUNTDOWN TO MEMORIAL DAY:

# THURSDAY

# ONE

After sunset, Corey Halpern sat parked at a dead end in Southampton with his headlights off and the dome light on, killing time before the break-in. As far as he knew, about a quarter mile up the beach the owners of the summerhouse he'd been casing for the past two weeks were busy playing host, buzzed from cocktails and jabbering beside the pool on their oceanfront deck, oblivious that a townie kid was about to invite himself into their mansion while they and their guests partied into the night.

Smoke trailed up from the joint pinched between Corey's thumb and forefinger as he leaned forward and picked up a wrinkled sheet of paper from the truck floor. He smoothed out his final high school essay, squinting through the smoke-filled haze to read his opening lines:

> In the Hamptons, we're invaded every summer. The mansions belong to the invaders, and aren't actual homes—not as far as the locals are concerned. For one thing, they're empty most of the year.

The dome light flicked off and he exhaled in semidarkness, thinking about what he'd written.

13

If he didn't leave this place soon, he might never get out. Now that he'd graduated he could make his escape by taking a stab at college in the fall, but that would mean leaving his mother and brother behind, which for many reasons felt impossible, too abstract, the world outside this cluster of towns on the East End so unimaginably far away.

His keys jangled as he slipped them from the ignition column and the dented pickup door swung wide with a whine at the hinge, and even after he'd pressed the door shut, tendrils of smoke continued seeping through the slim space where he'd left the driver's-side window cracked. He walked past the Dead End sign and over the hard-packed sand of the shallow dune with his sweatshirt hood raised and hands balled up in the front pocket, head bowed like a monk, hooking left to trudge down the beach against the stiff ocean breeze.

A few minutes later, he let his hands fall to his sides and paused at the wooden stairs that connected to the seventh house down. On the other side of the dunes he'd need to be on his game, but he didn't feel quite ready to break in yet. For one thing, the weed he'd smoked had been much stronger than he'd expected and kept creeping up on him, his mouth perceptibly dry and cottony while he faced the miles of light sparking against the ocean. Standing on the beach, drifting from shore, he imagined thousands of broken necklaces slowly unraveling between ropes of white water, the scattered diamonds bobbing and blinking like tiny stars or Fourth of July sparkler heads. Wave after wave crashing and coming to rest, while the sand all around him, blanketed by moonlight, looked frozen, like a wide shelf of Antarctic ice, the dunes like a series of icebergs all huddled together.

If only he could write as he saw things, maybe this place wouldn't be so bad, though each time he'd put pen to paper and tried to describe these solo hours at the ocean, or anything else, the words remained trapped behind locked doors deep inside his head. Sitting on his heels, he reached up and pressed the faint bruise below his right eye, recalling the fight last weekend with that kid from North Sea and how each of them had been so quick to throw punches.

His reason for being there on the beach returned to him. He couldn't wait any longer, so he turned and slogged over the deeper sand at the foot of the dunes with his favorite line from a black-and-white Bruce Lee interview playing in his head at full volume: *Be water, my friend,* Bruce was saying, *be water* . . . These few simple words ranked as just about the wisest he'd ever heard, the best mantra to hold inside his head right now as he reached the dunes, dropped down and began crawling elbows-first with his chest as low as possible.

He crested the soft hill and slid like a lizard down the other side, his shirtsleeves and the belt line of his jeans filled with sand by the time he entered a copse of beach grass waving in the wind. The mansion's deck came into view. He wriggled forward another few yards with an arm out to protect his face from the grass blades slapping like whips against his hood with each rush of wind, and squinted up at the vaulted oceanfront windows of the vacation home. The glass wall loomed like a movie screen reflecting the moonlight. He stared at the dark balcony, his muttered curses the only sound aside from the backdrop of crashing waves. Despite overhearing the homeowners say last weekend that they'd be hosting another party tonight, by the looks of things now, the night might turn out to be a total bust.

Just to make sure, he rose to a crouch and crept alongside the three-story east wall and its series of dark windows, on high alert for any signs of neighbors or headlights out on Dune Road as he turned the corner and went scrambling up the front steps on all fours. He cupped his hands to one of the glass panes beside the door and immediately saw what he'd hoped not to see. The red light on the security system wall panel told him all he needed to know. The house was locked down, and breaking in with no one here to hide from, or to narrowly avoid, defeated the purpose.

He stood and looked out at the quiet road, the letdown still sinking in, way too aware now that if he didn't get off this goddamned island soon it was only a matter of time before he started vandalizing these mansions instead of playing pranks, or finally caved and started to cop a serious drug habit, or pounded ten-too-many beers some night and had a head-on collision. If he didn't escape this place for real, for good, in another year or two he'd fall into the trap of seasonal work, the same cycle of poverty in the winter and endless hours of work all summer that his mom, Gina, went through each year with her bosses, the Sheffields. Maybe only a matter of months or weeks before he slid down into the same slippery pit most of the Hamptons locals never managed to crawl out from.

Feeling gut-punched, Corey exhaled and moped down the front steps between two giant flowerpots that were meant to mimic Grecian urns, tempted to tip them over and smash them, but then noticed a black Ferrari and white Mercedes convertible sitting side by side in the crescent-shaped driveway. The cars meant people were likely inside. The dark windows meant they were likely asleep. The conversations he'd overheard the past two weekends and the overall look of the house meant they were the exact Wall Street types he liked to mess with.

Headlights appeared in the distance on Dune

Road just before he slipped between the bushes along the west side of the house and ninja-climbed onto an oversize air-conditioning unit, not hesitating or doubting the wisdom of this at all as he hoisted himself up to a flat section of the roof and scurried over to a shadowy section of the wall. As soon as the headlights passed, he quickly checked the second-story windows. *They always leave at least one unlocked,* he thought, a rule that once again held true. Buzzing from adrenaline, he used his putty knife to pluck out the screen and jimmied open the unlatched window, then angled his body in over the sill and stepped down into a dim space with a coffee table centered on a cheetah-print rug, a wraparound couch and a wide-screen TV. From there, he tiptoed into the hall. A few doors down, he arrived at a bedroom doorway and immediately stepped back. With his hood still raised and half his head concealed, he peered past the jamb at a couple sleeping on a king-size bed.

Even with the ocean roiling on the other side of the glass wall, it was quiet enough in the room to hear them breathing when he dropped to his knees and edged his way toward them, trying to ignore the stabs of pain in the cartilage of his kneecaps with each movement across the hardwood. Slowly, he rose to his feet and leaned beside the bed until he was within a few inches of the couple—a pretty blonde woman in her thirties and a much older man with ghost-white hair—their features softened by the bluish light from the moon hovering outside the balcony door. Corey lingered there, still as ice, so close that he could smell the woman's white-wine-and-cheese breath. This had always been the ultimate high, daring them to catch him.

Compelled to push the limits, he leaned even closer, ready to run when he whispered next to the woman's ear, "You are . . . ugly."

A moment passed as he listened to the faint rumble of the ocean waves mingled with their soft snores, and watched them, the bodies of both sleepers in the exact same chalk-outline positions in their silk sheets as when he'd arrived, their eyelids still closed, their dreams as peaceful as ever.

Corey sighed and rubbed his sore knees, staring at their dead-calm expressions before he turned and went out. Much less cautiously than he'd entered the house, he walked with heavy steps along the hall and down a wide spiral staircase. In the kitchen he broke one of his rules by flipping on the light, then opened the stainless-steel refrigerator and found it well stocked with imported beer, so he opened one and chugged half of it before returning the open bottle to the shelf. The milk—yep, that's how he'd prank them. A quick search of the cupboards and he located the bulk container of Morton salt, which he emptied into the open milk carton and swished together before quickly returning everything where he'd found it. He cracked a smile, thinking of their expressions in the morning when they munched a spoonful of cereal or slugged the first sip of coffee with horribly salty milk mixed in. But still, this didn't seem enough; so just after he tiptoed from the kitchen through the vast living room and eyed the deck through the sliding glass doors, he stopped, turned toward the staircase and whispered, "What if I woke them up on purpose?"

This violated one of the most fundamental rules of his ninja code—don't do anything stupid to increase the risk of getting caught. But the decision had been made even before he'd finished asking the question, and with his next step the door latch turned in his gloved fingers and he exited the house onto the deck, intentionally setting off the alarm, a siren blaring as he backpedaled toward the oceanfront railing. No more than a few seconds passed before lights flashed on in the window above the balcony and two shadowy figures entered the frame. Corey ducked down like a gargoyle at the corner of the deck, not sure yet what he wanted to do.

Then the thought struck like a lightning bolt—*not all of us are on vacation*—and he shot to his feet with his hands cupped to his mouth and shouted, "Go back to the city!"

He heard the woman shriek and the man call out, "Holy shit!" from the other side of the glass, and then in a blink their silhouettes vanished from view.

They'd be calling the cops, of course, so now he really did need to haul ass out of there, and with Bruce's words flowing through his head, *Be water, my friend, be water,* he launched his body sideways over the deck rail and became a river rushing down a cliff face, long-jumping and sprinting over the dunes, his legs pumping as if he were running in free fall all the way down the beach to his truck. Key turned, e-brake released, he pulled onto Dune Road and shifted gears about as quickly as he ever had. After the first sharp turn onto a sleepy side street, block after block his tires squealed past stop signs as if they were nothing more than pylons marking off racetrack curves.

A few blocks later, he slowed to cruising speed and pushed the hood from his head. Now that he'd made it a mile or so from the beach house, the high had already mostly faded. He downshifted to first gear and rolled to a stop sign. Though it was still early, the entire neighborhood had an air of sleep, even the ranch house to his right with the blue light of a TV flashing through a space between the drapes. He wasn't ready to head home, wasn't ready to go catatonic like the working-class people in these small houses.

Not yet. There was still one more spot to hit up in Southampton before calling it a night, the mansion he'd debated burglarizing for so long. The idea seemed too crazy the last time he'd considered it, for one because he'd never robbed any of these rich people, only pranked them, but tonight breaking into the Sheffields' summer estate might be the only way to stave off the sense of suffocation he'd felt all day long. With the holiday weekend closing in like walls of a massive vise, he had to do this tonight—or wait until the fall.

A few miles later, with Iggy Pop and The Stooges blaring from his door panel, it made perfect sense to take the night to a whole new level and rob his mother's bosses before they came out from the city; before Gina came home crying after one of the longer, more grueling workdays; before he joined her for the summer as the Sheffields' servant boy. Iggy reinforced the necessity of the much higher risk mission— the need to do it now—as he belted out one of his early-seventies punk anthems, the lyrics to "Search and Destroy" entering Corey's brain and seeping much deeper inside his chest as a truth he'd never been able to articulate for himself. His fingers tapped steadily on the wheel when he turned off Main.

He drove slowly for another block or two, his pulse beating in his neck as he turned left at the pyramid of cannonballs and the antique cannon on the edge of town. A couple blocks later, he downshifted around the bend, rolled to a stop and parked beside a wooded section of Gin Lane. From there he didn't hesitate at all. He hustled along the grass bordering the roadside, past hedgerows and closed gates and dark driveways, until the Sheffields' driveway came into view. A life-size pair of stone lions sat atop wide stone bases and bookended the entrance, two males with full manes and the house number chiseled onto their chests. Corey knew the lions held a double meaning. His mom's boss put these statues out here partly because they looked imposing, the type of decorations kings used to choose, but also because they stood as symbols of August birthdays, the same astrological sign as Mr. Sheffield's first name—Leo.

He stood still for a moment, looking between the bars of the tall iron gates crowned with spikes. Beginning tomorrow morning, and then all throughout Memorial Day weekend—just as he had the past few summers—he'd spend long days working there. Gina would be so pissed if she could see him now. She'd at least threaten to disown him if she ever found out he'd broken in, but that would be a hollow threat anyway, and he'd already convinced himself that she'd never know. The Sheffields should have paid her more to begin with, even if she didn't have a deadbeat husband like Ray pissing her meager savings away on his court fees and gambling debts. But the memory that sealed Corey's decision tonight had been replaying in his mind for almost a year—the dinner party last summer, when Sheila Sheffield yelled at his mom right in front of him and about ten guests, berating her for accidentally dropping a crystal chalice that she said cost more than Gina's yearly salary. While Leo and the grown Sheffield kids looked on dumbly and didn't bother to make a peep, Corey had followed Gina into the kitchen and stood a few feet away from her, unable to think of what to say to console her while she cried. Ever since then, he'd wanted to get back at them all.

*Fuck these people,* he thought.

He would rob them, and smash some windows on his way out so they wouldn't suspect anyone who worked there. All he had to do was make sure not to leave any evidence behind, definitely no fingerprints, and he'd take the extra precaution of scaling the gates rather than punching in the code.

He wriggled his fingers into his gloves. Crickets chirped away in the shadows, his only witnesses as he looked over each shoulder and back through the bars. He let out a long breath. Then he gripped the wrought iron and started to climb.

Moonlight splintered between the old oak

branches and cut across his body like blades. It took only a few seconds to grapple up the bars, though a bit longer to ease over the spear-like tips while he tried to shut out a nightmare image of one of them skewering his crotch. Relieved when his legs reached the other side unharmed, he shimmied down the bars like a monkey and dropped, suddenly hidden from the outside world by the thick hedge wall. Poised on one knee, he turned to his left and scanned the distant mansion's dark windows, the eaves and gables. The perfectly manicured lawn stretched for acres in all directions, a few giant oaks with thick limbs and gnarled trunks the only natural features between the faraway pines along the property line and a constellation of sculptures. A scattered squad of bronze chess pieces stood as tall as real-life soldiers, with two much larger pieces towering behind them—a three-ton slab of quartz sitting atop a steel column and a bright yellow Keith Haring dog in midstomp on its hind legs, each the size of an upended school bus or the wing of a 747, all the sculptures throwing sharp shadows across the lawn when Corey rose to his feet, leapt forward and ran toward the Sheffields' sprawling vacation home.

His sneakers crunched along the pebble driveway, his steps way too loud against the quiet until he made it across the deeper bed of beach stones in the wide parking area and passed through an ivy-covered archway, still at top speed while he followed the curved path of slate down a gentle slope, and then pulled up at the corner of the porch. Breathing heavily, he grappled up the post and high-stepped onto the railing, wiping sweat from his forehead when he turned to face Agawam Lake. The moon's light came ladling down onto the water like milk and trailed into the darkness of the far shore, while in the reeds beside the nearest willow tree a pair of swans sat still as porcelain, sleeping with their bills tucked at their breasts.

*No one will know,* he thought. The crickets kept making a soft racket in the shadows. The swans seemed like another good omen. But then a light went on inside one of the mansions directly across the water, and Corey pulled his body up from the railing, thinking he should get inside before someone saw him. He quickly scaled the corner porch beam and trellis while trying to avoid the roses' thorns, even as they snagged his sleeves and pant legs. Then, like a practiced rock climber, in one fluid motion he hoisted himself from the second-story roof up to the third-floor gable. He crouched there, looking, listening. The house across the water with the light on was too far away to know for sure, but he didn't see any obvious signs of anyone watching from the picture windows. Probably just some insomniac millionaire sipping whiskey and checking the numbers of a stock exchange on the other side of the world.

Confident that he should press on, Corey half stood from his crouch and took the putty knife from his back pocket to pry open the third-story bathroom window, the one he'd left unlatched the previous day when he'd come there with his mother. The old window sash fought him with a friction of wood on wood, but after straining for a few seconds he managed to shove the bottom section flush with the top, and was struck immediately by the smells of Gina's recent cleaning—ammonia, lemon and jasmine, the chemical blend of a freshly scoured hospital room. Balanced at the angle of the roof, he stared down at the neighboring properties once more. Still no sounds, no lights, no signs that anyone had called the cops, so he turned and stretched his arms through the window and shimmied down until he felt the toilet lid with both gloved hands and his sneakers left the shingles, all his weight sliding against the sill as he wriggled in.

Although he hadn't been sure whether he'd ever go through with it, he'd plotted this burglary for weeks, the original iteration coming to him during Labor Day weekend last year. The first step had been to ask Gina if he could clean the Sheffield house with her for a few extra bucks before the summer season began. She'd raised an eyebrow but agreed, approving at least of

27

her teenager's out-of-character desire to work, and throughout the past week, whenever she'd left him to dust and vacuum the third floor, he'd had his chance to run recon and plan the point of entry. He knew she wouldn't bother to check the latch on a closed window three stories off the ground, not after she'd scrubbed and ironed and Pledged all day. And more important, by then he knew those upper-floor windows had no seal-break sensors. He knew this because a few days earlier he'd left this very same window open before Gina armed the alarm, and afterward nothing happened—no blaring sounds before they pulled away, no call or drive-by from a security officer. So tonight, again, the security company wouldn't see any flashing red lights on their computer screens. Not yet anyway, not until he smashed a window downstairs and staged a sloppy burglary scene on his way out.

Despite knowing that nobody would be out till Friday, his footsteps were all toe as he crept from the dark bathroom and into the hazy bluish hall, and yet, even with all this effort to tread lightly, the old floorboards still strained and creaked each time his sneakers pressed down. Trailing away from him, a black-and-white series of Ansel Adams photos hung in perfect rows, one on either side of the hall, hundreds of birch trees encased in glass coverings that Corey had just recently Windexed and wiped. Every table surface and light fixture and the entire length of the floor gleamed, immaculate, too clean to imagine the Sheffields had ever even set foot in here, let alone lived here for part of the year. He'd always felt the house had a certain coldness to it, and thought so again now, even though it had to be damn near eighty degrees inside with all the windows closed.

After slowly stepping down one set of stairs, Corey skulked along the second-floor hall, past the doorway to Mr. and Mrs. Sheffields' master bedroom and then past Andy's and Clay's rooms, deciding to browse Tiffany's bedroom first, his favorite room in the house. The Sheffields' only daughter had a floor-to-ceiling bookshelf full of hardcover novels, stage plays and poetry collections, a Super 8 projector, stacked film reels and three antique cameras. He'd spent as much time as possible in this room during his previous workdays, mainly staring at the paintings mounted on three of the walls, and now lingered once more looking at each textured image, surprised all over again that a rich girl had painted these shades of pain, these somber expressions on the faces of dirty figures in shabby clothes, compositions of suffering he'd have expected from a city artist teetering between a rat-hole apartment and a cardboard box in an alley. They all had something, that's for sure, but one portrait had always spoken to him much more than any of the others. He stood before it and freed it from its hook.

At the window he noticed the light had gone off at the mansion across the lake and figured the insomniac must have drunk enough for sleep. Although he knew he shouldn't, he flicked on Tiffany's bedside table light to get a better look at the girl in the painting, her brown eyes, full lips, caramel skin, her black hair flowing down to divots between her collarbone and chest. He knew Tiffany had painted it, but also that it wasn't a self-portrait. She looked nothing like the girl she'd painted. Anorexically skinny, Tiffany had dyed-blond hair and usually wore too much makeup. In one photo with her parents and two older brothers, while the rest of the family had dressed in country club attire, she had on a tank top and frayed jean shorts, dark sunglasses, the only one of them with any tattoos, the only one barefoot on the grass.

Corey searched her shelves until he found the photo of Tiffany's best friend, the girl from the painting, Angelique. He'd seen her at the estate plenty during the previous summers, and last Labor Day weekend they'd talked many times, their conversations lasting longer and seeming to have more depth until finally he summoned the courage to ask her out. Her long pause had made him wish he could disappear, and then those four awful words, *I have a boyfriend,* had knocked the wind out of him just before he nodded with his eyes to the ground and walked away. Reliving the disappointment, he killed the lamplight and lay on the bed with her photo on his chest, and then, stupidly, closed his eyes.

Sometime later he snapped awake with his head turned toward the window, disoriented for a moment by the depthless darkness pinpointed by stars. His eyes opened wider as he realized he'd not only been asleep on Tiffany's bed but had been awakened by the sounds of voices. He sat bolt upright and left the bedsprings creaking, stumbling to replace the painting on its hook and then tiptoeing out into the hall, listening attentively to the ambient noise coming from downstairs—a thud, maybe from the heavy refrigerator door, a few muffled words, drinking glasses clinking against the marble counter. One step toward the stairs and he stopped. The floorboards seemed softer in certain spots. He had to keep moving, so he leaned forward and took the next step as if attempting to navigate a minefield purely by feel. Another creak in the wood followed, but not quite as loud as the last, while the voices, both of them female, sounded closer than they had a minute ago.

He sensed them at the base of the stairs, heading up. If he didn't slip out of sight in the next few seconds, they'd see him. He'd never been caught before. He'd always been a ghost, a ninja in the shadows—one who would never hurt anybody in the houses he visited. But of course, they would assume otherwise. If they saw him half crouched like this in the dim hallway with his hood up, he'd have no chance to explain that he meant them no harm. Without a doubt, he would scare them in a way he could never apologize for. He could already imagine their screams.

By some miracle he managed to slip under Tiffany Sheffield's bed just before the girls reached the top of the stairs. He lay there, his gloved hands clenched around the framed photo of Angelique that he hadn't thought to put back on the shelf, staring wide-eyed at the base of the doorway. Footsteps and Tiffany's shrill voice filled the hall with echoes. They stepped closer toward the bedroom, about to catch him, about to run off screaming before calling 911. Corey made his promises with his chin against the floor. *God,* he thought, *please get me out of this. Just get me out of this and no more breaking in, I swear.* But the voices had already descended upon him, the light flicked on, and the first girl to walk in went clomping past in three-inch wedges. He recognized the swirly pattern tattooed on her ankle from Tiffany's photos.

At the bookcase she burped and said loudly, "I should really alphabetize these fuckers."

"Wait on the projects till tomorrow," the

other girl said as she walked in. "Just grab *Casablanca*."

"Angel, you beautiful bitch," Tiffany said. "I love you more than anything."

"Love you, too, lil' missy."

"Yeah, but I love you more. More than fat little beavers love to nibble on branches, or woodpeckers love to peck on a pole, more than Trump loves wearing fucking *dryer lint* on his head. And another thing, my Portuguese sister— Brad doesn't deserve you. What he deserves is a raging case of crabs from one of those strippers he likes so much."

"Jeez, Tiff," the other girl said, laughing. "You're a graphic one tonight."

"You know what you need now? I'll tell you what you need—you need a real man. Holy shit, yes! You need a Bogie, kid! Like Rick, from the movie!"

"Yeah, well, too bad that's a fictional guy from an old movie."

"If I were a man, I'd buy me a white suit and get on my knees and marry you."

Her friend kept laughing as she answered, "Too bad you're not my type. That probably would be easier."

"Where in the— You see that movie anywhere, Angel-face?"

"Seriously, Tiff, why'd you drink so much in the car? That driver thought you were nuts."

Silence followed and Corey scratched his nose, fearing he might sneeze. If he did, he was dead. No way around it. Totally dead.

"Tiff, you okay? You need to—"

The feet belonging to the Sheffields' only daughter stumbled out the door, followed by the sound of her puking in the bathroom across the hall. Tiffany's friend stayed put and sighed, her black sandals no more than a few inches from Corey's nose. When she stepped away from the bed, Corey couldn't help himself. He edged closer to the ruffled skirt at the base of the box spring and gazed up from the shadow . . . There she stood, facing the bookshelf. Angelique. Her black hair streaming down her back, a thin white sweater half off one shoulder, dark blue formfitting jeans, just enough of her profile in view for the strangest sense of peace to envelop him as he slipped silently back under the center of the bed and settled with his chin between his hands, hands against the floor. She lifted one sandal heel and removed something from the shelf, then left the room, calling out, "Tiff, I found *Casablanca*. You okay?"

The next few minutes passed amid a wash of bustling and moans and stressed floorboards before the overall shrink and fade of sound when the girls descended the stairs. Corey stayed put below Tiffany's bed awhile longer, listening with his ear cocked toward the door. As soon as he felt convinced that they weren't on their way back up, he crawled out and tiptoed up the stairs, then climbed out the bathroom window like the survivor of a bad car wreck, once again standing at a steep angle, doing his best not to make any noise while he muscled the window closed.

The moon cast its metallic blue haze over the lake side of the house as he inched his way down the roof and dropped from the third floor to the second and scrabbled down the trellis. His sneakers touched down on the ground with a soft thud. No reason yet to make a beeline for the gate, just stay low and move like a jungle cat along the layer of bark mulch between the flowerpots and shrubs for the entire length of the porch.

Outside the corner window of the billiard room, where he knew the Sheffields kept their projection screen TV, he rose from a squat until his eyes peeked an inch above the sill and both girls came into view. Safely concealed by reflections from the antique table lamps and images from the movie flashing against the glass, he looked at Angelique sitting sideways on the couch with her hand in a bag of gourmet cookies and Tiffany with her head on her friend's thigh. His breath began fogging the lower corner of the window, and rather than drawing attention by wiping it away, he sank to his heels to let the evidence of his presence disappear.

With his arms wrapped tightly around his knees, he debated leaving. This felt different from the other break-ins, the pranks, the little rearrangements and refrigerator sabotage. With Angelique, since he didn't consider her a stranger at all, this felt suddenly more like an invasion, like an accidental violation. For Corey to stick around and watch her through the window struck him as shameful, too close to the kind of pathetic shit that Peeping Toms or stalkers might do when they liked a girl. And besides, he could talk to her again tomorrow, during his first work shift of the weekend, after she and Tiffany and the rest of the Sheffields and their guests settled in to celebrate Memorial Day—but only if neither of them caught him outside the window now. In that case, not only would his chances with Angelique be torpedoed forever, but within the hour a cop would be writing Corey's physical description on a little pad, and soon after that the Southampton Town Police would be cruising the neighborhood on the lookout for him.

He squinted through the rhododendron branches. The sleeping pair of swans beside the glimmering lake water was still a good omen. As long as he stuck to his usual code of invisibility and silence on his way out, he'd be all right. He couldn't bring himself to leave yet, though, because Tiffany was talking about Angelique's ex-boyfriend again. Raising his head closer to the windowpanes, he heard Tiffany repeat what she'd said upstairs, that she and Angelique both needed to find a *Humphrey Bogie* of their own. And then between yawns she added, "Angelic one, could you pretty-please-with-sugar-on-top open up one of those windows? It's hotter than a monkey's butt in here."

Corey felt a twinge in his chest and pressed his back against the rows of cedar shingles, sliding down to sit on his heels. He crouched more tightly against the house just before the seal broke above his head. The handle kept cranking for the tall window to swivel open. Despite all the heavy scents from the mulch at his feet and the new buds on the branches all around, as soon as the window opened wide, he smelled the fabric softener on her clothes, the flowery trace of conditioner in her hair. Being this close to her surpassed any high he'd ever felt before, but he had to be smart. Invisibility and silence.

Not wanting to risk blowing his cover but still not able to go, he stayed there with his arms around his knees for the next two hours, and without needing to look inside again he knew Tiffany had passed out right away, while Angelique stayed awake watching the entire movie. Corey listened along, imagining what she might be feeling, mentally watching scene after scene and taking in each of the main characters' lines of dialogue. He knew without looking that

Angelique loved the movie, every moment of it. And yet, since he'd never seen *Casablanca* before, after the end credits finished and he heard her trying to convince Tiffany to go to bed, he climbed back up to the roof, believing that he'd watched the classic black-and-white story with her in color.

# TWO

Hours earlier, Leo Sheffield sat alone in the back of his limousine, stuck in Midtown gridlock, snorting a line of cocaine. He pinched his nose and poured another drink, growing more impatient as he rested his chin on his fist and gazed out the tinted window at the lights of Times Square. Electronic billboards glowed and flashed advertisements for movies and TV shows and a slew of services and products, while mammoth talking heads and anchorpeople mouthed brief summaries of the news highlights, closed-captioned transcripts stamped out below a giant video clip of a protest, and another screen showed the president boarding Air Force One. Leo wanted to lower the divider and climb up front and honk the horn himself, bored to death and also feeling boxed in by all the stimuli and information flashing and streaming by; instead, he cut a new line of coke on his pocket mirror and filled his nose, and with wildly blinking eyes then did his best to focus on the demon-red numbers of the Dow Jones scrolling around the corner.

If the traffic ever finally moved, he would be on his way to pick up Henry, the plan being to spend the whole night with him out at the estate in Southampton, his last possible window to see him before the first big weekend of the summer began. Also the last night before he would once again need to don his trusty old mask and summon his thespian skills to play the role of good husband until sometime Monday. He daydreamed about the hours ahead with Henry— who'd sounded stable enough on the phone that afternoon, despite having spent the better part of the week under observation in Brooklyn Mount Sinai after a suicide attempt.

Traffic still hadn't moved, only the sea of people flooding the sidewalks and weaving between bumpers amid honking horns. Leo drifted back to two nights earlier, when he'd received a text from Henry saying he'd been all right since his release from the hospital on Monday. He'd excused himself from Sheila's cocktail party in their Manhattan penthouse and locked the door to his home office to ensure the privacy he needed to make a call, carrying his drink out to the balcony as he dialed, feeling as though he'd forgotten to exhale all night when he sighed stale air from his lungs.

On the third ring, Henry answered sounding drugged. "Hey, I was hoping you'd call."

Leo looked back through the balcony doors at the locked office door and spoke low. "I may not be able to talk long, but I wanted to check in."

"Thanks."

"How you feeling?"

"All things considered," Henry said, "I'm all right. I miss you, though."

"Me, too," Leo said. He rested an elbow on the balcony railing and sipped his Scotch. In the distance the red lights of an airplane blinked. The faint city noises, car horns and screeching brakes, drifted up. He gazed down at the streetlamps and treetops of Central Park. The first and only walk he and Henry had taken together in public began right there on the walking path a block or so from his building, that night around Christmastime, after Sheila had fallen asleep with Prince Valium and Leo snuck out. He'd planned to end the affair during that walk, but the snowflakes settling on Henry's shoulders and the crown of his knit hat, and his smile, had caught Leo off guard, effectively melting his worries away. Although the feelings on his end had never grown strong enough to consider divorcing Sheila and scrapping the life they'd shared for so long, the parting hug with Henry that night had lasted long enough for him to sink into watery visions of fantasy, to imagine a parallel universe where they could be together in public during daylight as well.

Leo turned as a knock sounded against his office door, whispering into the phone, "Sorry to cut this short but I can't really talk now. Sheila's summoning me back to her goddamn party. We're still on for Thursday, right?"

41

"I'm counting down the minutes."

"So am I."

This silence, when each man waited for the other to say goodbye first, had often filled Leo's face with warmth over the past six months, though now Henry's recent drama had become the elephant that took up all the space in whichever room Leo inhabited. He needed to make sure Henry wouldn't do anything so stupid or impulsive again—and so, after going back and forth about it, he'd invited him to Southampton for both their sakes. The prospect of seeing Henry's stitched-up wrists, and a night of crying and consoling, didn't appeal at all, but Leo did care for him, and despite the fact that he'd grown ambivalent about their future, even before the events of this week, a part of him did want to see him.

Back in the Square, Leo bent forward and snorted another line of coke from his pocket mirror, smudged up the excess with his finger and rubbed the powder along his bottom gum. He pinched his nose and inspected it in the mirror until he'd wiped the nostril clean. The car crawled ahead while he stared at the bright advertisements for three more stoplight cycles, and then his driver finally managed to bully the limo through the dense crowds crossing against the green light.

What felt like ages later, they pulled to the curb

and Leo swung open his door. Henry entered, dressed in the charcoal-gray pinstripe Leo had purchased for him some months back, looking weary as he settled onto the leather seat across from him, honoring Leo's rule that they never touch in public, and not in front of Pete, not even with the dark divider up. Leo swung the door closed thinking it felt wrong not to hug him, but regardless, as the limo pulled away from the curb, he set his drink in the side console and leaned back.

After an awkward silence, he asked, "You all right?"

Henry nodded with his head turned toward the window but didn't say anything.

"Sorry I couldn't come see you," Leo said. "I did try, but they don't allow any visitors in the behavioral unit."

"I'm not blaming you," Henry said, and Leo knew he wasn't talking about seeing him at the hospital. "I know how busy you are," Henry went on. "I just wish we could see each other more often."

Leo chopped a mound of cocaine with a razor blade and raked out three new lines.

"Well, we're together now."

"Yeah," Henry said, "for one night."

Leo handed over the coke straw and pocket mirror, and during the exchange their fingers touched and he pulled his hand back as if from a sudden flame. Grinning, hoping the mood would lighten soon, he mixed a vodka tonic for Henry and poured another single-malt for himself. Henry's stoic expression didn't change, though, and when he leaned down and snorted his first two lines, the white gauze of his bandages peeked from the jacket's cuffs. Pinching at his nose, Henry held the mirror out like a waiter, but Leo waved him off and prompted him to have another.

Henry's eyes focused on his own arm. "You saw this."

Leo slugged his drink, his eyes starting to water, imagining what Henry's arms looked like under the gauze and padding. "How bad is it?"

"The stitches itch, but otherwise . . ." He leaned back and kicked off his shoes. "I might not get to see you again for most of the summer, right? That's what you said?"

"I'm really sorry about that."

"No, no, it's fine. I tried to kill myself, but I'm still here, so let's just have a good night."

"I'd like that," Leo said, yet the atmosphere in the car had grown dismal. He'd never seen someone look so deflated, especially not Henry, who'd usually been a fountain of energy. He sipped more of his drink and tried to feign a smile. No matter what Henry said tonight to let him off the hook, it was obvious—he'd done this to him. He'd pulled the rug out, crushed him.

Last week, exactly six months after their first

full night together, Henry had said "I love you" at precisely the wrong time, a mere moment before Leo had planned to tell him he'd be spending the summer with Sheila and the kids out in Southampton, working from there as well, and that he might not get too many opportunities to call, either. Something broke in Henry then; Leo had seen it and then bungled along, babbling nervously about how he cared about him, cared a great deal in fact. But the truth was, he hadn't considered whether he loved him. Now he worried that Henry did blame him, and might even have a grudge. And what a nightmare if he decided to tell someone at the company, or Sheila—or much worse, what if he tried to off himself again?

Leo needed another minute to shrug off the paranoia that always set up like icicles in his veins during the early moments of their rides together, but which now had been compounded by Henry's wrists and forearms. Behind the blackout glass, Pete sat up front and focused on the road, playing his role in the charade. He must have known Henry wasn't just some ordinary business associate. Only a dunce wouldn't have put two and two together by then, and even before all the drama this week, Leo still felt a hell of a lot more than uneasy at the thought of anyone knowing about this affair. But that didn't matter as much anymore.

As he looked at Henry now, it killed him to see such a dull glint in his eyes where there had always been so much light. Leo nearly leaned across to kiss him but felt an internal brake engage before he'd moved an inch. If anyone ever found out he'd been cheating on his wife with a man, a much younger man no less . . . The fallout still terrified him too much to risk it. *No, he thought, I'll wait.*

An hour into the drive up the Long Island Expressway, Frank Sinatra crooned about a woman with loose morals from the limo speakers, and Leo couldn't help but croon along now that Henry's mood had dramatically improved by the third or fourth drink. Soon after Frank finished singing smack about the woman in the song, Henry suddenly curled in on himself, his drink sloshing over the rim of the glass as he fell into a fit of laughter.

"What's so funny?" Leo asked.

Henry snorted two lines in quick succession, laughed more even before he raised his face from the coke and pinched his nose. He took a moment to pull himself together, and Leo leaned closer. Henry wiped away tears, cleared his throat and finally shouted over the music, "I was thinking about the night when Sheila tracked you down at the hotel and almost caught us, and then accused you of having an affair—with a woman." He

46

paused, laughing hard again. " 'Tell me her name, Leo! Tell me the bitch's *name!*' I couldn't get enough of that story when you told me the next day, and I still can't believe she thought your housekeeper might be the other woman. What's her name again—Jada?"

"Gina."

"Seriously, your wife is a piece of work. I mean, come on—your housekeeper? You two have been married longer than I've been alive, but does she fucking know you at all?"

Leo had laughed along with Henry about his wife's mistaken assumption that he'd been having an affair with a woman in the past, and though she'd been especially off-base in suspecting Gina, she hadn't been wrong about the affair part. So now, the fact that Leo was riding to Sheila's home-away-from-home with Henry, with the man he *had* been with at the hotel that night in February, the guilt welled up; as difficult as Sheila could be at times, he couldn't bring himself to laugh, not at her expense, not now.

"Let's get back to what you were saying earlier," Leo said, eager to change the subject. "That ridiculous idea that Americans are tired of the mega-marts, and that we should dump those stocks and any mutual funds that rely on them. Where do you come up with this stuff?"

"It makes perfect sense! More and more people, myself included, have too much information

47

about the worker exploitation, and are willing to drive out of the way to shop at a mom-and-pop instead of one of the Goliaths like Walmart." Henry took a hefty gulp of his drink and pointed at Leo's nose. "You missed a little something there, Pablo Escobar. And in case you haven't noticed, capitalism is killing the planet."

"I knew it, I've been seduced by a goddamned commie."

"Well, you know what they say."

"What do they say, *dimples?*"

"Commies do it till they're red in the face. Get it? *Red* in the face!"

Sinatra kept on crooning while the two men laughed to the point of coughing and mixed new drinks. Henry's laughter finally trailed off while Leo was in the midst of snorting one more line. The moment he looked up from the pocket mirror he found Henry staring at him, deadpan, with an eyebrow raised.

"They probably shouldn't have let me out of the psych ward," he said.

"No, why is that?"

"Because I must be crazy to be in this limousine of yours with this misogynist's anthem playing. Didn't the whole Rat Pack scene end way back when you were my age?"

"Good stuff never gets old."

"Everything and everyone gets old, Papa Bear, and eventually it all dies. Now that I'm thinking

48

of it, can we please kill this crusty, dusty, grab-her-by-the-crotch old-man music?" Henry paused and held his glass at his bottom lip. "Quit smiling at me like that, Leonard."

"Don't call me Leonard."

"Fine, but one more song from Old Blue Eyes and I'm gonna start looking over my shoulder for someone to bring me a fucking gold watch for my retirement."

Leo set his drink in the side console, removed the gold Rolex from his wrist and handed it over. "Here," he said. "For your retirement."

Henry drained his drink in a few gulps and poured a new one, tonic water still foaming over and dripping off the side when he accepted the watch. He let it dangle from his fingers and slung it around in circles. "Joke or not, I'm keeping this, mister."

"Goddamn it," Leo said, mouthing his words so he wouldn't be heard above the music, "I want to kiss you right now."

Henry shifted to the edge of his seat. "I'm not the one stopping you."

Leo smiled, suddenly aware of an over-whelming need to answer nature's call. Through the intercom he asked Pete to pull over for a pit stop, and a couple minutes later, somewhere around the crossover from Nassau to Suffolk County, the limousine parked at a gas station and Leo stumbled out.

Wobbly and disoriented, he crossed the parking lot toward the unisex bathroom, even more off-balance when he entered the weird light from a twitching fluorescent bulb against the dirty floor-to-ceiling tiles. One eye closed at the sight of flies buzzing around chicken bones and a black banana peel in the trash can. Then he glanced over at the filthy toilet, missing both a lid and a seat. After relieving himself, he looked into the cracked, graffiti-scrawled mirror, where his face split into jagged shards, and stood there thinking about Sheila, about how formal they'd been with one another for as far back as he could recall.

Through no fault of hers, a few uninterrupted hours with his wife in any scenario had felt for years like a chore, like something to endure. Maybe now that the kids were all grown it might not be so selfish, but rather an act of kindness, to finally separate. Especially now that another summer was set to begin tomorrow, which meant three straight months maintaining a calm facade while Sheila went fussing about over germaphobic missions to clean everything, though not cleaning anything herself, of course, but rather, directing Gina and the other employees from room to room with lists of anal tasks and a battle-pack of disinfectants.

One of the long light bulbs over his shoulder ceased its twitching as it shut off, and in the half-light his broken reflection stared back. "Just get through the weekend," he said. "Then do the right thing, and finally end it."

A knock on the bathroom door resonated inside the dim tiled room, which prompted him to look away from the mirror and pump the grimy liquid soap container above the sink. He rinsed quickly and reached out with a wet wad of paper towel as a barrier between his hand and whatever microbes might be thriving along the thin dead bolt on the door, slid it across and opened up, and then found Henry standing there with a maniacal grin. "Mind if I cut in?" he said, purposely grazing Leo's pant leg with his hand as the two passed through the doorway in opposite directions.

A few feet from the car, Pete stood facing Leo while talking quietly into his cell phone, but promptly finished his call and slipped the phone into his jacket pocket. "You could have kept talking," Leo said. His jaw trembled from all the cocaine. His left nostril begged him to scratch it but he'd promised himself not to pinch at his nose. The drinks had long since kicked in, too, which made it a challenge to focus on his driver's face.

"Oh, it's fine," Pete said. "Just checking in with my wife."

Leo would have preferred to slide onto the leather seat in the back of the limo than engage in conversation, but felt obliged to make the gesture and fill the unnervingly calm space with noise.

"Remind me, how long have you been married?"

"Eight years," Pete said.

"And you have kids."

"Yep, a boy and a girl. He's—"

"That's wonderful."

His driver grinned and Leo made a mental note not to steamroll him again.

"And how old are they, Pete?"

"He's seven and she's four."

"That's excellent."

"Can't believe my little girl will be in kindergarten next year. Time definitely flies."

Leo laid a hand on Pete's shoulder and sifted through actuary tables of phrases in his overstimulated brain, straining for something to say. He wanted to ask Pete what he thought of him traveling from the city to the Hamptons with a man thirty years his junior—damn, closer to thirty-five years younger—but instead, Leo reached out to lean against the car and heard himself say through a mild slur, "Well, you know what they say. We're all working for someone."

Pete's silence compelled him to add, "You know, with kids—when you have kids, you're really working for them." Pete nodded while still wearing the obligatory company smile, and Leo cringed as words continued seeping from his mouth, slur-heavy and uncensored. "Kids, Pete, wives—they all want this or that, or it's what families do, and then they're all grown up and you realize you didn't do something you wish you had, or you spent all that time with your head down, trying to provide. Then one day, one day—you just don't know—"

He stopped, embarrassed by the look on Pete's face, detecting a hint of pity, a hint of judgment. Then, mercifully, they both turned their heads as the metal bathroom door squealed at the hinges, strained open and swung closed with a heavy clang. Henry made his way over, fidgeting with his belt, his eyes wide as quarters. Pete held the door for the two intoxicated men, and Henry ducked and entered while Leo scraped together an excuse for not making much sense.

"Sorry. Working too hard," he said. "Haven't slept much the past few days."

"Nothing to apologize for, Mr. Sheffield."

"You're a good man, Pete."

Roughly an hour later, just after midnight, they finally turned off Gin Lane and passed through the electronic gate. As the car crept up the driveway Henry zipped down his side window, marveling at the lawn sculptures. "I've never seen anything quite like those," he said, pointing at the giant bronze chess pieces. "So where's the pool, out past the house?"

Leo answered yes, but added that it might be a little chilly until he got the heater cranking for a while. "Give it about a half hour to heat up and it'll be perfect," he said, leaning closer to Henry beside the open window. "In the meantime, I have some ideas for how to keep you entertained."

Upon exiting the car, Leo handed his driver half the bills from his money clip, clapped him on the shoulder and double-checked the time when he would be returning in the morning to pick up Henry. "My employees are expected to arrive at roughly eight thirty," he said.

"Not to worry, sir," Pete said, looking down at the almost comically huge tip in his hand, and nodded to Leo as he pocketed the wad of bills. "I'll be here at seven thirty, eight at the latest."

"Good man, Pete."

Leo stood on the first square of the slate path on the edge of the lawn and watched the limousine slowly snake its way back to the gates, before leading Henry to the kitchen door and fumbling with his keys. When he found the right one and turned it inside the lock, he paused, confused by the lack of resistance. The alarm panel didn't beep as he pushed the door open, the light beside the keypad a steady green. Gina must have been the last one there, since no one else had any reason to be. Okay, no need for Sheila to know. She would flip if she knew the alarm hadn't been set and the house had been unlocked with nobody home, but people made mistakes. Gina had worked for them and done her job well for so many years now, she deserved a pass.

The two men entered the kitchen and Leo opened the refrigerator, quickly unsheathing a bottle of Dom Pérignon from the chiller, where a sea of identical bottles stood in tight rows. After handing Henry the champagne, he opened a glass-fronted cabinet and pulled out two long-stemmed flutes. They carried the bottle and glasses upstairs to the second floor, and as soon as they entered the master bedroom, Leo pressed a button on a wall-mounted panel. "The thermostat for the pool heater," he said before repeating what he'd said in the car. "Give it about half an hour and it'll be perfect."

The two silver handles turned in his hands and he pushed open the balcony's French doors, letting the night air breeze in. He and Henry stood on opposite sides of the bed for a moment, the thin white drapes waving and rippling dreamily between them. It occurred to Leo that they shouldn't use this bedroom. Sheila would be sleeping here tomorrow, and Gina wouldn't think to replace the linens beforehand since no one was supposed to be out until morning. No tragedy, though; they had seven other bedrooms.

"Come out here," he said, already stepping onto the balcony. His breathing felt labored, his heartbeat a bit too fast. With Henry beside him and cricket noises as a calm background, he spoke softer. "Magnificent night, isn't it? I wish you could stay the whole weekend."

"I'm just glad I'm here with you now." Henry touched Leo's cheek, and they kissed, which could have been the most perfect moment if Leo's mind hadn't begun to race, the worry ramping up even before he opened his eyes. Henry had those bandages on his arms beneath his jacket sleeves and had looked so incredibly sad when he slid into the limo. And now they were alone. And Sheila would arrive tomorrow afternoon. And Henry was holding him so tightly, as though he'd begun worrying as well, but for a different reason, clutching him like a life raft.

The kiss had lasted only a few seconds, yet for Leo everything had taken on an odd aura. As he watched Henry unwrap the foil and unwind the wire from the champagne bottle, he wondered if he'd made a big mistake bringing him out here. Leo's thoughts registered as screams while Henry filled their glasses to the point of overflowing, and they spent the next minute sipping in silence, looking out at the lake and the trough of bluish light cradled on its surface.

"I want you to forget about everything for tonight," Leo said, hoping to supplant his own negative thoughts with words Henry would like to hear. "Forget that I'm married, and that this has to be a secret, and that we won't get to spend much time till September. We're together now."

Henry stared for quite a while before he leaned in and kissed him again, then eased away and rested his head on Leo's shoulder. "What I'd really like," he said, "is to imagine that, for tonight, we're the only two people on earth."

"Alright, that sounds—" Leo's thought cut short. He lowered his glass and turned toward the bedroom. "Did you just hear something?"

Henry kept his head pressed to Leo's suit jacket. "I don't think so. What did it sound like?"

"A creak? A scrape? I don't know exactly."

"After all that coke you might be a little paranoid, you know."

"You're probably right," Leo said, still focused on the doorway across the room. "Speaking of which, there's plenty more. Are you game if I set us up with a few more lines?"

"I'll do a couple more if you're going to, but I have to warn you, with all the meds in my system— Wait, I think I just heard something, too."

Leo leaned down to the pocket mirror and cut more coke with the razor blade, thinking for the first time since meeting up with him that handing a razor to Henry had been incredibly dumb, callous even. Trying to shrug off the thought, he set the mirror aside and stepped toward the bedroom doorway, calling out, "Hello? Is anybody there?" though he realized the pointlessness of such a question even before he'd finished speaking. But someone *could* be there. The alarm had been disarmed and the door unlocked, so someone else might have come out early for the holiday weekend. A relative would answer; a burglar wouldn't. The silence set his imagination in motion—men with knives, men with guns, ransom demands. He squatted down and stuck his head into the hall, but after seeing nothing out of the ordinary he inhaled deeply, stood once again and slunk back into the room. Only then did it occur to him that he didn't have a weapon, so what could he realistically hope to do if he did come across some crackhead thief with a knife or a gun? *I could get my pistol from the wall safe,* he thought. *Should I? No, I'm too high and too drunk to be handling a gun. And what was it that Henry said about being on lots of meds?*

"It's an old house," Leo said, feeling thoroughly frazzled as he dumped a larger pile of powder onto the mirror and chopped at it and raked a series of fat cables along the surface. "It's the wood settling, that's all, the crossbeams and such. Like you said before, we're the only two people on earth. And also like you said, I'm just being paranoid."

Henry wrapped his arms around Leo's mid-section and hugged him from behind. "You might be happier in this life here, if not for me."

"You make me happy." The truth of Leo's words mired him for a moment in the paradoxical state he'd felt during other secret moments with

58

Henry, a simultaneous flood of gratitude, worry and frustration. Though he wasn't *in* love with him, Henry had brought Leo some much needed light into his life. They each proceeded to snort the monstrous lines and chase them with glass after glass of champagne. Soon the bottle was nearly empty, and by then Leo's head seemed to have filled with helium. His veins and inner ear buzzed. He'd begun levitating.

Henry peered over the balcony railing. "I'm going in now," he said.

"What about your bandages? You're not supposed to get those wet, right?"

"Fuck it." Henry snatched up the bag of coke, already racing out of the room as he called back, "See you in the pool!"

Leo stayed on the balcony for a couple more minutes, slugging the last of the champagne. When Henry entered his view down below, he leaned over the railing, smiled and waved, but Henry hadn't looked his way before an acute pain entered Leo's chest. Henry didn't see Leo drop the empty champagne bottle, either, and had no way of knowing that he was staggering into the bedroom, shouldering his way past the dresser and flopping backward onto the bed, his heart hammering away like pistons in a Lamborghini going a hundred miles an hour.

Plenty of the men in Leo's circle had broken their coronary cherries years ago, but he hadn't yet. *Goddamn it,* he pleaded with the ceiling, *please don't let this be a fucking heart attack . . . not now . . .* The bedspread may as well have been the surface of a gurney while he breathed through the pain, groping for equilibrium. He needed this sharp pressure to pass and some semblance of balance to return. Those last few lines may have been a few too many. Who was he kidding? Of course it'd been too much. Men his age couldn't do more than a dozen lines of coke, down a bottle of Scotch and chase it all with champagne in the span of an hour or two, and expect to survive. His nostrils burned all the way to the base of his brain. Too hot on the bed. Too many layers of clothes.

*This isn't a heart attack,* he thought. *Just calm the hell down.*

He blinked and gasped, staring at the ceiling until the constriction began loosening, the crown molding in the corner slowing its spin, and slowing more . . . slowing down . . . until finally it stopped swirling altogether. He wanted to join Henry and swim with him under the moonlight; he wanted to make the most of the night. Not knowing if this would be their last chance to swim together, or possibly even their final private night, he would make it downstairs and join Henry in the water. He would. But first Leo needed a minute alone, to breathe.

# THREE

Earlier that afternoon, Corey's mother, Gina, sat swathed in her old pink bathrobe, rocking in her grandmother's creaky hand-me-down rocking chair, peering out through a slit at the edge of her drapes. She'd positioned herself beside the slim opening between the fabric and the window frame so she could remain hidden and still have a view of the driveway and the walkway leading to her front door. If Ray actually followed through with his promise to pick up more of his boxes, she'd want to see him coming.

For hours now, she'd been listening to a classic rock station and dulling her anxiety with Klonopin and cheap red wine, popping another pill when a good Zeppelin song came on, another when Freddie Mercury and Bowie sang together, washing down two or maybe three more in one go when the DJ announced Pink Floyd would start off the next set. Somewhere along the way she'd lost track of how many pills she'd swallowed and how many times she'd refilled her glass, but it must have been plenty since closing one eye helped her see much better and the gallon jug had been full at noon but now was at least a third of the way gone. This would be the last Thursday she'd have off from work before the Sheffields arrived tomorrow and the first long weekend of the season started, the last day she'd have to herself for the next hundred days.

Another full set of songs blurred past without her paying much attention, but then "Honky Tonk Woman" penetrated her pill haze and she smiled while muttering along with the refrain. The song ended sooner than it was supposed to, though, and Gina cringed as a loud commercial for a fish market cut in—a man and his wife yelled excitedly about their rock-bottom prices, jabbering like meth-heads about clams and flounder and fluke. *Jesus,* she thought, *no sane person should ever get so excited about crab cakes.*

She stood from the rocker, barefoot and off-balance, steadying herself with her free hand on the arm of the couch, all the while thinking she might have to smash the stereo. Sure, Ray would yell when he saw it, probably follow suit and break something himself, but screw him, it was her stereo after all, even if he considered it his. She'd told him to get out months ago, but now it really was time for him to pick up the rest of his stuff. Time for him to finally stop using these "appointments" to take some, but not all, of his clothes and boxes. No more excuses to see her. Time for him to finally leave her the hell alone. He'd dragged his ass and mooched off her for too long. Three years together, and only the first year or so with any moments worthy of a photo album, with the past two years amounting to nothing more than a volatile trudge toward separation. Factor in the infidelities, the drunken arguments, the money he stole, the night two months back when she told him to get out and stay out—after he'd hit her again . . . Another glass of wine or two and she might just haul the rest of his shit to the curb and post a FREE sign on the pile.

More wine gurgled into her glass as a car insurance commercial fizzled off and bled into an obnoxious ad for a pizza parlor. Gina pushed herself from the couch arm, wobbling for a moment. She couldn't listen to one more goddamned commercial.

The terry cloth robe felt softer against her skin than it had an hour ago, and her vision had a syrupy quality, as though she were looking at the living room furniture through a mason jar when she baby-stepped over to the coat rack by the door and grabbed her sons' old baseball bat. Swinging it with one hand while sipping wine, she felt the urge to assault the stereo growing, if only to kill the commercial block. But then the liquid running along her fingers and dripping on her toe caused her to gaze down. She laughed at the dark splash on the floor, until she thought of how the wine pooling and stretching along the wood grain of the scuffed old boards looked like blood.

Her glass was almost empty but she managed

to spill some more the second she recognized the opening measure of "Free Fallin'," its simple chord progression, clean and uncluttered—and here came the first line—Tom Petty's charcoal voice singing about a good girl. Gina swayed along with the music with her eyelids closed, but they fluttered open almost immediately in reaction to the glass slipping from her hand—and then the slow-motion fall, her awkward attempt to catch it, then the explosive sound from the glass smashing against the hardwood. She staggered back, the walls now set on a spin cycle, flinching with her entire body as the bat also slammed down and clattered. She closed one eye and watched it roll over the wine and slowly come to rest.

The knock on the door entered her chest like thunder, pitching her even farther off-kilter and sending her lunging for the couch arm, but not in time to keep from stepping on broken glass. Cursing under her breath, she clutched her wounded foot and plucked a long sliver of glass from her big toe and two smaller shards from her arch. A series of fierce knuckle raps rattled the door and she squinted in that direction, mumbling, "Hold your goddamned horses, I'm coming." Her first step hurt like hell but she managed to hobble away from the puddle and glass, her footprints splotching behind her a dark blend of blood and wine.

More annoyed than anything, she cracked the

door open. Ray nudged it wider and greeted her in his usual smooth-talking way. "Hey, sexy. Happy to see me?"

"Took you long enough," she said, yanking him in by the arm, already disappointed to see a gold chain and crucifix displayed outside his tight red T-shirt. She closed the door and watched him rub his jawline, her face flushing with heat when she saw him looking at the broken glass and finger lakes of cabernet.

He rolled the bat with his shoe. "Whoa," he said with a grin. "You have a little accident, Gina, or what?"

Watching him take off his Yankees cap and smooth down his hair a few times, Gina couldn't for the life of her recall why she'd wanted him here. He owed her thousands of dollars. His contracting business had been in the toilet even before the cops picked him up for his second DUI. *He had hurt her.* And worse, *he'd threatened her sons.* He'd belittled them, hovering a hair away from fistfights with Corey for a year or more. And now he had a lawyer to pay and a pile of fines. He'd always had a blinding compulsion with sports betting and scratch-offs, and the increasing debt provided an excuse to gamble even more. In his mind, he needed one big win to fix it all, but in the meantime he'd had to supplement Gina's "loans" by selling pills to regulars at the bar, or else fall short of the fees for his case and pay for it in an entirely different way—thirty days in jail.

"Goddamn, what a mess," he said, and flung his hat onto the couch like a Frisbee.

Her first thoughts: *I don't love you. I don't even like you.* But she needed him to cooperate and at least take some of his boxes, maybe even the rest of his clothes along with them, so she batted her lashes and met his puzzled look with a smile, only then realizing that her teeth and tongue had probably been stained purple. She brought her lips back together and her hand to her mouth, surprised at how badly she'd just slurred when she asked if he wanted some wine.

The room blurred like a scene through a rain-coated windowpane and she closed her eyes, feeling hollow, dizzy, then settled into a familiar space, faintly aware that her arms had wrapped around Ray's back and her head now rested on his shoulder.

"Yeah," he said, "I'll have some of that rotgut you drink. But first—"

"You're gonna take your stuff, right?" she mumbled, and heard him answer, "For once, just do me a favor and stop fucking talking, G."

His hand settled on the loose knot of her bathrobe belt, and with one deft movement he whipped the fuzzy cord through the loops. Gina's skin prickled as the robe fell open. She forgot all about his faults and bit his lip, curling her body back as he bit hers. Her eyes closed once more, and then somewhere along the way she fell into thinking about how she'd typically go to any lengths to avoid emotional discomfort, but in moments like this how much she craved physical pain. It seemed the only way to escape anymore. Alcohol hadn't been working, not as it had for so many years, no matter how much she drank. She hadn't wanted to think about the significance of this. She'd kept herself together most days but had also made promises to her sons after a handful of the rougher nights, when they'd seen her bleary-eyed or hunched over the toilet or staggering in and out of a blackout. She'd even considered sitting in the back of an AA meeting and seeing what that was all about, though she hadn't made it to one yet. Each time she'd promised to stop drinking or at least cut way back, she'd meant to commit to changing for Corey and Dylan. Truly, she had. But whenever she did manage to string together a week or two of sobriety, in the same way other people might mourn the death of their best friend, she missed the relief she'd been so accustomed to finding in a bottle of wine or a pitcher of beer. And worse, each time she'd tried to quit, she snapped at the boys more often; she snapped at other drivers on the road. And although he usually deserved it, she didn't feel good about snapping more at Ray, either. The word kept coming to mind—*snap. Snap, snap, snap, like a mousetrap . . .*

Ray kissed her neck and twisted her arm behind her, his calloused hand raking the small of her back while his other hand held her head arched backward by the hair—which hurt a little, though the shiny streaks of pain reminded her why she'd married him. He pulled harder and she heard herself squeal, suddenly removed from the room, the accompanying flood of endorphins like hundreds of tiny flashbulbs bursting inside her veins, a flurry of bright pulses, an opiate effect flooding her abdomen and chest while the air ensconced her in the steamy heat and humidity of a jungle. Here again the pleasure and pain Ray had provided on the better days during their marriage had begun working its magic, dulling her anxiety about the upcoming crazy work weekend at the Sheffield estate, erasing all the mundane details of the day . . .

But then he ruined it, squeezing her face too hard in his rough hand as he shouted, "Hey! You're not fuckin' passing out on me, are you?"

She opened her eyes to find that he'd dragged her down the hall and onto the bed they used to share, crimson smears and spots already decorating the cream-colored down comforter like a Jackson Pollock–inspired crime scene, her foot or toe or both cut deep enough for a few stitches.

Ray peeled off his T-shirt while Gina searched for the neon red numbers on her alarm clock, panicked now, realizing that he'd arrived late and she had no idea what time it was or what time it should have been to be safe. Although the boys had said they wouldn't be back till late, she had no reasonable guess as to when they might come stomping through the front door, and no good thoughts as to what they'd do if they discovered blood and broken glass in the living room and Ray in the bedroom on top of her. Dylan would probably throw something that would leave a crater in the drywall before storming out, maybe wouldn't speak to her for a few days, but Corey had a lot more of an edge to him. After seeing him come home with a black eye last week, she'd been worrying. And he had exactly zero love for Ray. If he walked in on this, who knows, he might come charging back in with the bat, and swing.

"We shouldn't do this," she muttered, but Ray just kept chewing on her ear. "Really, we shouldn't." She'd tried to sound serious but the words came out garbled, as if she'd spoken underwater. Her worry faded, though, as he distracted her, kissing her inner thigh and then hovering there, tying tiny bows with his tongue all around her softest skin.

She inhaled deeply and stuttered, "Promise me you'll take your stuff when you go." But Ray wasn't listening. He wanted sex, nothing more. And so did she, though she hated herself for this need. It only took a second to worry again, to snap back to the reality of their past—the beating he'd doled out two months ago, the reason he didn't live there anymore.

This. This shouldn't be happening—

"Stop," she said, barely able to hear her own words with all the blood thrumming in her eardrums. She'd come to hate him. His violent temper. His complaints like drips in the soundtrack of her days and her dreams, his knack for holding a mirror up to all her flaws. But then things had gotten worse, so much worse. Dangerous. She shoved him, managing to create a little space between them, then summoned all her remaining strength to push him farther away.

"Get off me, Ray. This is a mistake. We're done."

"You hear something?" he whispered, still panting, his body rigid and his eyes focused on the bedroom door.

She mumbled, "I said to get off me," and as he did, she rolled to her side. "I feel sick."

Not looking at her, he whispered again, "You hear that? Sounded like a car door."

She didn't answer. The wine and pills had reduced the room to a hazy splinter of light. Her limbs each lay heavy as an ocean liner, while her head and torso had begun levitating, disintegrating to mist, the parts that mattered most all insubstantial as a hologram.

70

"Fuck is wrong with you?" He crawled off the bed and listened at the door. Gina's eyelids fluttered open just enough for her to fix on his naked body, to linger on the dark hair on his shoulders and the way it spread away from his spine. His hand turned the knob so as not to make a sound, but he couldn't keep the hinges from straining when the door cracked open.

She watched him turn and creep over to the bed, and just then a sensation like a trio of slithering eels entered her stomach and a sour taste burned the back of her tongue. She barely had time to swivel her head to the side before the afternoon's wine came spewing out over his arms and hands and splashed over the comforter. Barely conscious of Ray's cursing or of him backing away, she wretched more of the red liquid as though purging a demon, unable to calm the spasms.

"Jesus," he said, "you're a fucking disaster . . . Hey, can you even hear me? Just nod if you can hear me." She strained to answer, and at the same time tried to discern his face from the smudges of movement and shades of color. "Someone just parked," he said, followed by the faraway words, "Fuck this, I'm so fuckin' outta here."

*Take your stuff first,* she mouthed, faintly aware that the words had likely never left the shelter of her mind. In the haze, she sensed him snatching up his clothes and flinging the bedroom door open. Ray, her soon-to-be ex-husband, the townie piece of shit, he'd shown his true colors. How in the hell had she allowed herself to even come this close to having sex with him? Well, she'd damn sure never meet with him like this again. She'd be sober next time, and he'd take his goddamned boxes, and that would be the last she'd see of him. She faded closer to surrender and let her eyelids fall, a deeper sense of defeat sinking in with each soft echo of his shrinking footsteps, followed by the opening and closing of the door.

The silence may have spanned an hour, or may have lasted no more than a few seconds. Her eyes had been closed long enough for her to doubt that Ray had ever even been there. Then a door opened and closed. It seemed someone had entered the house through the front, not the back door, which Ray had slammed shut either on his way out or possibly in her dream.

Footsteps pounded down the hall and then her younger son called from the bedroom doorway. "Ma! Open your eyes!" Dylan pushed up one of her eyelids and covered her body with something soft, her robe maybe.

She mumbled an apology as he shook her. "Ma! Wake up!"

Her neck refused to hold up her head, the blur dimming more and more, until finally she lay overwhelmed by darkness. Her eyelashes clasped shut. Fading in the direction of the deepest sleep, she wished she could do as her son had asked. Find the strength to wake up.

For him. She wished she could.

# FOUR

Nearly half an hour had passed since *Casablanca* ended, and Corey was still sitting on the Sheffields' roof beside the third-story gable, gazing at the moon and its light glimmering on the lake water. He took one last toke of his joint, tapped the roach against the asphalt shingle and placed it in his cigarette pack, only then noticing the insect sounds swirling up from the landscape. After all those months not seeing her, the sight of Angelique had rattled him. He'd never been in love. Not that he'd had a hard time getting with girls, but he'd never felt anything like this, his blood thrumming at the thought of her, a drowsy calm during this unexpected period of proximity.

The depths of his thoughts deepened so much more when he was high, or so he thought as he lay back on the warm roof shingles and stared out at the lake. A minute or two passed and he drifted, wondering if everyone he knew spent their lives finding ways to cover up their fear. The tough-guy acts of his friends had gone stale a long time ago, and Mick's idea of settling down in their hometown and starting a landscaping business with Corey fueled a recurring nightmare. Nothing scared him more than the vision of spending his entire life right here. Most of the adult locals drank a lot but still didn't seem happy. And *no one* liked their job. Everyone Corey knew worked as a servant to some degree. He'd grown up knowing his family was poor, or working-class at best, but ever since he began working with Gina at the Sheffield estate he'd seen his family's status in stark contrast. They had to work their asses off to afford the bare necessities, while the Sheffields could loaf around, all day every day, doing nothing and still have everything.

His string of trespasses in wealthy homes the previous summer may have begun out of curiosity and for the thrill, maybe also as a sort of benign fuck-you to the One-Percenters, but now he realized he'd been driven to it as an escape from the visceral awareness of his lowly station in life. If only for a few minutes, he could pretend to live where they lived, imagine being someone who had so much more than the minimum. The disparity between the wealthy and the working-class locals out East was just too extreme. He'd seen too many vacationers driving collectible cars worth more than his mother could make in ten years, sociopaths with perfect teeth and Botoxed faces driving to or from a summerhouse worth more than Gina could ever dream of making in her lifetime. He knew of too many private beaches where millionaires or billionaires had bought the right to keep the lowly locals away. He'd heard of too many places that he and the other locals would never see—the über-exclusive places—the world-class golf courses, the country clubs with valets, the nightclubs with bouncers in tuxedos and VIP areas where the bottles cost a thousand bucks apiece.

He couldn't pinpoint exactly when, but sometime during the past few years he'd begun to both hate his life for all it lacked, and to hate the rich for all they had. If not for the feeling that he needed to stay here, to watch over Dylan and to make sure his mom didn't fall any deeper into the bottle, he'd have been counting down the seconds before he could finally get off the Island in the fall. If only he could bring himself to leave, he'd start his freshman year at one of the upstate schools that had accepted him this spring, and then never live here again. He exhaled long and slow as the daydream of freedom began fading, prefaced as it always was by the clause: *If only*. The schools needed his enrollment letter within the next couple weeks. If he failed to mail it in by the deadline, he'd be stuck for at least another year, killing time, wishing he were anywhere but here. Maybe he could go. Maybe Dylan would start showing up for school more and stop hanging with the burnouts who were destined to live forever in their parents' basements. Maybe Gina would sober up and get rid of Ray for good. Or maybe all these thoughts of escaping this place amounted to nothing more than a far-off, pointless dream.

He'd been staring out at the lake for a while by the time a light went on in one of the windows below him. He uncrossed his legs and stood with his sneakers angled along the roof's steep pitch and scaled down from the third floor to the second, creeping over the shingles quiet as a mouse on cotton. Beside the dormer, he peered at the edge of the glass pane and saw Angelique helping Tiffany into her bed, Tiffany drunk and stumbly again. In all the moments he'd watched them, he'd never seen Angelique take a sip of alcohol, which seemed strange considering that Tiffany always had a drink in hand or within reach. For a stick-thin girl she could really put them away, but now the Sheffields' daughter appeared to have passed out the instant Angelique brought the covers to her chin.

Angelique turned off the lamp and exited the bedroom, and Corey followed in the same direction across the roof to the next dormer, one bedroom over, where she flipped on the light and sat on the end of the bed, leaning forward with her hands covering her face. Although the double-paned window dampened the sound, Corey guessed she was crying, and wished he could figure out a way to suavely walk in and sit on the bed beside her and comfort her—nothing more, just offer comfort. He raised his fingertips to the glass, but his hand shot down as Angelique's head jerked toward the bedroom door. Corey's body also tensed up at the sound of crunching pebbles coming from the other side of the house. Soft light skimmed the peak of the roof and grew brighter while the sound intensified, the source of both he knew without yet seeing—tires rolling over the driveway stones, headlights.

He climbed back up to the third-story roof, looked over the peak and saw the limousine approaching, the gates behind it creaking closed. Then a burst of red from the brake lights splashed across the driveway and the long black car parked beside the slate path at the corner.

The driver emerged and opened a side door for a man with a paunch and salt-and-pepper hair to step out first. It was Mr. Sheffield, followed by a thin, much younger man, both dressed in suits. The headlights beamed against the hedges and the side entrance to the kitchen while Mr. Sheffield handed something to the driver and then beckoned the young man to follow him inside. The limousine swung around and crunched back down the long driveway, paused for the gates to swing open, and pulled out onto the pavement of Gin Lane. Meanwhile, keys had been jingling below and the kitchen door opened and closed.

Corey inched down to the second-story and sidestepped over to Angelique's room, but she'd already left, so he scurried over to Tiffany's window and peeked in and found her trying to wake her friend. No movement from Tiffany, only Angelique's quick head turns toward the doorway and her inaudible but obvious pleading. Then her body halted. Corey knew she heard the men inside the house. She'd been thrust into the exact same position he'd been in when the girls had arrived unexpectedly, and now she had to slip out of sight right away or face the consequences.

Watching her, he empathized so intensely that her paralysis became his paralysis, even as the panic jitters traveled like an army of spiders racing into his fingers and toes. He imagined whipping the window open and swooping in and saving her, but his body remained locked. He couldn't help. She was all on her own, with only a few seconds to hide.

She chose the closet.

# FIVE

Soon after the two men entered the house, lights winked on in the master bedroom and Corey shifted over to the dormer closest to the poolside edge of the house. With the lake glimmering behind him, he peeked through the window, only to find that Leo Sheffield and his friend had already stepped through the double doors and out to the balcony. He heard their voices drifting in the open air around the corner of the house, heard the young stranger mention swimming in the pool, and weirdly enough—something about bandages. He psyched himself up to climb, and their words dropped away as he grappled up to the third-floor roof. From there he concentrated on pressing his sneakers with the utmost care along the shingles, and at the peak he spread his legs and forearms out on either side like a frog.

He leaned just far enough over the roof lip to see the balcony railing and the well-dressed young man pouring champagne. Both he and Mr. Sheffield licked their lips and pinched at their noses, all fidgety while the bubbly wine filled the flutes and overflowed sparkling foam, neither of them seeming to relax until they clinked glasses and tilted their heads back for a long sip. They stared at one another and then out at the lake, slurping some more from the flutes, and Corey looked on, feeling as if he'd been absorbed as part of the background, while only soft nighttime sounds could be heard—the crickets, slight rustles in the oak and pine branches, a bird flapping in a low flight path across the water. And still no words spoken when the younger man leaned in, and Mr. Sheffield leaned as well, closing the distance until their lips touched.

The moment they kissed, Corey immediately covered his mouth with his hand. *Holy fucking shit!* Instantly, simultaneously, this qualified as both the most amazing moment of any of the break-ins, and by far, the biggest, most unexpected secret he'd ever stumbled upon. Shaking his head and wearing a huge smile, he crept back, just as Mr. Sheffield said, "We're together now," and the young man followed with something about being the only two people on earth. Determined not to let out a laugh, he must have lost focus, because as he crouched to drop down to the next level, he slipped. One sneaker skidded like a quick scuff of sandpaper, and to keep from tumbling off the roof, he clutched the shingles so tightly that he scraped each one of his fingertips raw just above the nails.

With his right leg dangling and his head cocked to listen for any signs that they'd heard him, Corey didn't move for at least a minute, hanging stone-still, breathing as inaudibly as possible, concentrating on shrinking his breath. He stayed like this until it seemed he no longer needed to breathe, until it seemed he'd become part of the roof.

Another minute or two passed and he still hung there motionless, though the men's voices had grown faint and eventually faded completely. Using extra caution, he dropped from the roofline and made his way over to Tiffany's bedroom, where Angelique had been hiding. The open closet door told him she'd already left, so he sidestepped back over to the master bedroom window, looked in and saw Mr. Sheffield laid out on the bed with his eyes closed and both hands balled into fists, talking to himself. Five or ten seconds passed, and then suddenly, as though he'd been shocked with jumper cables, Mr. Sheffield leapt to his feet and began peeling off his suit, his tie, his shirt and socks, every stitch except for his blue-and-white-striped boxer shorts whipped from his sweaty body in a frenzy. And just as quickly as he'd undressed, he went heel-stomping out the door and into the hall.

Corey leaned against the edge of the second-story wall and angled his head to the side, looking past the balcony toward the pool, expecting to see Mr. Sheffield barreling across the lawn to join the young man for a swim any second. And yet minutes passed and he saw nothing but the thin guest with the bandaged arms sitting with his legs in the pool water, all his clothes except for his underwear piled beside him, along with something in a small plastic bag that he kept bringing up to his nose. The empty acres seemed to embrace the quiet, so when Corey heard the man's loud snorting and hacking echoing up each time he pressed the bag to his face, he knew the situation exactly. *No wonder they were so jittery out on the balcony,* he thought. *But damn, this guy must be a serious junkie to jam that much coke up his nose in such a short time.* And unbelievably, the man kept at it, snorting as if in a solo competition for the most fiendish dope fiend of all time, snorting without pausing to take a breath, reminding Corey of Tony Montana fatalistically shoving his face into a mountain of white powder toward the end of *Scarface.*

He couldn't believe how strange the night had become.

Then, finally, the man stopped and released a terrible sound. As if Corey's thought about the violent demise of the most iconic cokehead in film history had been a prophecy, the thin man must have suffered some sort of a rupture, because he started shrieking with his head pitched forward, and then dropped the bag in the pool, where it floated for a second and then sank. With both hands pressed to his face, he let out another sound of pure agony. Then a few fainter shrieks while he kept one hand clamped over his nose and held out the other, as if inspecting his fingers in the moonlight. Even from that distance, Corey could tell that blood now covered the lower half of the man's face, as well as both his hands and a good portion of the bandages on his forearms. Corey ground his teeth and gripped the roof tighter, staring, anticipating the outcome of the awful sequence that had already begun unfolding in slow-motion.

Mr. Sheffield's friend placed both hands on one of the stone slabs bordering the pool and tried to stand. He stumbled sideways, and then his head jerked back suddenly, violently, as if he'd been struck by lightning or shot between the eyes. His knees buckled, and rather than falling into the water, his entire body pitched sharply to his right. Corey felt the grit from the roof shingles gouging his fingertips. The fall seemed to take a full minute while he held his breath and didn't blink at all, but finally the worst moment arrived—the side of the man's head smacked the stone edge, hard, with a sound like a coconut being cracked open. His limbs went limp. He twitched once, and then flopped headfirst into the water.

A sheet of darkness slid past Corey's shoulders. He tried to swallow, turning for a moment to face the wide swath of clouds creeping overhead, and then looked back down, blinking until he could focus again on the pool. The man's mouth and nose lay fully submerged, and the whole area, from the lake to the house and beyond . . . quiet. Eerily quiet. Corey pressed his palms to the roof peak and pushed himself up to crouch, then inched backward a few feet but stopped there, positioned sideways on his thigh. He had no idea what to do. Knowing the man down there might die, but incapable of climbing down, he briefly considered jumping from three stories up. He'd heard about what happens to a person when they're in shock. This frozen feeling, this must be it. Wishing he could move, he could only watch.

Even the insects and other nocturnal creatures seemed to cease all movement, as if they too had begun holding their collective breath, waiting to see if either Corey or Mr. Sheffield might reach the man in time to save him—that is, if the man had any time left at all. He'd lost a good amount of blood from the hemorrhage alone, even before he cracked his skull, and had been losing more each second. He'd been underwater for a minute, maybe two, maybe even three by now, knocked unconscious at the very least, though possibly even killed the moment he'd fallen in.

The clouds passed. The pool water must have been heating up the entire time, because now it whispered a faint layer of steam all around the man's outstretched, bandaged limbs. He lay still. Floating. Much too still, and for much too long by the time Mr. Sheffield finally entered the frame, crossing the lawn dressed only in boxer shorts, carrying a bottle in one hand and a silver tray propped above the other that flashed like a mirror in the moonlight.

About ten yards from the pool he called the man's name, "Henry . . ." then called out again, "Henry, I brought treats!" but the floating man remained silent and still. It took a few more steps for Mr. Sheffield to see him floating facedown. Corey watched his mother's boss stop short and drop the bottle and the tray, which crashed like a gong on the lawn. He ran full stride the rest of the way to the water and came plunging down the stairs, dived forward and swam frantically to the midpoint of the giant pool.

Arms flailing, he wrestled with Henry's limp body, spitting water as he struggled to keep both their heads above the surface of the deep end. As soon as he could stand, Mr. Sheffield hauled his friend across the shallow end and up the pool stairs, dropped his torso just above the water line at the top step and began pressing on his chest. After five or six compressions, he leaned down to breathe into his mouth, then repeated the series again, shouting, "Breathe!" over and over, like a mantra, before he finally resorted to sledging down on Henry's chest with the side of his fist.

Corey couldn't get any air himself. He sank down and lay on his stomach with his nose pressed to the roofline. His raw fingertips hurt as he clawed at the grit of the shingles, but he couldn't let go. Instead, he pressed even harder, tearing his own skin as though someone had hypnotized him and ordered him to do so. No more than twenty minutes ago he'd seen his mother's boss kissing the man on the balcony, who now wasn't answering or moving or showing any indication that he was still alive. He'd never seen a dead body before, but once Mr. Sheffield finally gave up on beating him back to life, not only was Corey sure Henry was dead, he realized that he alone had watched him die.

A subtle movement entered the low end of his vision and he crept back as Angelique stepped out onto the balcony. He pressed himself flatter to the roof and kept his eyes fixed on the men in the pool, imagining that Angelique had momentarily been turned to stone, unable to comprehend the scene on the pool stairs. Then he nearly choked, as Mr. Sheffield raised his head mid-sob and looked right at the balcony. Right at her. In that moment of recognition, she must have understood. She'd just become a witness—a witness staring down at him with a dead man in his arms.

Corey heard her bump into one of the French doors on her way inside and her bare feet slapping against the bedroom floorboards as she raced deeper into the house. Mr. Sheffield stepped back a few feet into the shallow end but didn't look away from the balcony, not even when his arms went slack and Henry slipped from his hands, the body sliding into the middle of the pool and drifting. He stood waist-deep in the film of steam, his chest and arms pale in the moonlight, staring at the vacant balcony for what felt to Corey like a very long time; until a sudden lunge, and then, with mechanical movements, he returned to the top of the wide staircase and rose up out of the water with his boxers clinging to his thick legs. He took a few awkward steps onto the lawn, grunting, whimpering, stumbling a bit while he got some momentum, and then went loping off like a wounded animal toward the house.

Corey skittered down the shingles and dropped to the second story, sweat trickling down his back. Mr. Sheffield must have assumed exactly what Corey had, that Angelique had viewed him as a killer. Not only that, he was obviously fucked up in more than one way, drunk, high on coke, traumatized—and now charging around the corner of the house like a man possessed. What was he about to do? Would he hurt his daughter's friend? Corey edged over to the gutter, planning to jump from the second story and run inside. He couldn't remain hidden much longer, but also couldn't pull the trigger yet to blow his cover. Hoping she might get away without his help, his pulse pounded along the side of his neck. Loud noises emanated from the house and the windowpanes rattled. Then a heavy slam sent vibrations into his thigh and knee. He leaned out a foot or two from the gutter at the sound of strained hinges, saw the screen door swing wide and Angelique running out barefoot and leaping from the porch steps. He watched her sprint across the lawn with the breeze off the lake blowing her hair out behind her in a dark funnel, and a few seconds later the screen door flung back open with immense force and smacked the wall. Mr. Sheffield hauled his heavy body off the porch, chasing her across the lawn while he shouted, "Stop running so I can explain! I just want to talk to you!" and then even louder, "Stop, goddamn it!" calling out with such desperation that Corey knew this rich guy had completely snapped.

Angelique obviously knew this as well, as she screamed back, "Get the fuck away from me!"

Corey steeled himself for the fall, counted down from three and then leapt from the roof. He landed beside the bushes lining the porch with a shunt of pain in each ankle and tumbled next to a squat statue of a cherub, which he grabbed and cradled, thinking a heavy chunk of stone might come in handy. Staggering to his feet, wincing, he started to run, his pulse thrumming in his ears while his legs pumped hard toward Mr. Sheffield, who was roughly twenty yards ahead of him, charging forward with his arm outstretched toward Angelique. The gap between them had shrunk, already slim enough now for Mr. Sheffield's finger to graze her shoulder blade and for her to slap at him. She zigzagged and dodged his hand and kept shouting for him to get away from her, then took a sharp turn at the lake's edge and kept running along the last strip of grass before the bulkhead.

Insect noises swelled up from the bushes and reeds while Corey trailed them with the stone cherub in his arms, aware that neither had seen him yet, and also that within the next few seconds the three of them would converge in a violent collision. Angelique appeared to be tiring, falling back once again to within a mere inch of Mr. Sheffield's reach. Then his hand snagged her shirt and he yanked her toward him. She flailed, no longer running, her arms swinging wildly to slap at his face. Corey closed in on them, though too late to keep his mom's boss from tackling her. She landed on the lawn with a thud that sent a small bird in the nearest willow tree flying from its nest, and Mr. Sheffield pinned her to the grass with her arms out to the sides. She screamed with his hand clapped over her mouth, squirming, punching and slapping his jaw and neck, while he struggled to hold her down, shouting, "What are you doing here? No one's supposed to be out yet! Stop fucking hitting me, and just let me—"

Corey cut him off by lowering his shoulder and plowing into his back hard enough to flatten

90

him, and then, as soon as Mr. Sheffield began struggling to his knees, Corey whacked his skull with the cherub. The blow instantly sent him falling forward in a heap, like a lion shot with a tranquilizer dart, and all two-hundred-plus pounds of him flopped lengthwise on top of Angelique, who let out a sound that was a cross between a gasp and a scream.

Corey tossed the bloody cherub into the bushes and leaned with all his strength to push Mr. Sheffield to the side, then grabbed Angelique by the wrists and pulled her the rest of the way free. They stayed on their knees with a foot of space between them, breathing like asthmatics, until suddenly she fell against him and clutched him in a hug.

# SIX

His first thought was to run away—don't say a word, just run away. Instead, after she'd held him tightly for about thirty seconds, Corey gently removed her arms from his shoulders and knee-walked over to check Mr. Sheffield.

The wound had drenched the hair on the back of his head in blood, some of the blood had already painted the grass blades beside him, some of it now slick on Corey's hand. Angelique began wheezing, possibly hyperventilating as she scooted over to the railroad tie atop the bulkhead that separated the lawn from the drop down to the lake. She and Corey stared at each other until her eyes lowered, and she crept back a bit more, as if in reaction to the blood on his hand. His chest pounded. Sweat coated his forehead and rolled along his stomach and spine. He wiped his hand on the grass and then held both palms out, rising from his knees, hoping she would see that he only meant to help.

Still breathing hard, he heard his voice crack as he asked, "Are you okay?"

She looked up at him with wide eyes, but sounded drowsy as she answered, "I know you . . ." A breeze swept the willow branches beside them with a gentle rustling sound while she stood up and stepped toward him, slowly, as though she'd just awoken from a deep sleep. "Corey? Why were you— Why are you *here?*"

He didn't know how to answer, but before he even had a chance she brought her hands to her face and muffled sounds escaped through the spaces between her fingers. He reached out and gently placed a hand on her arm, and the moment he touched her she flung her arms around his shoulder blades again, her hug cinching him in place, snug as a straitjacket. His thoughts immediately split down two tracks: On the one hand, the long-running fantasy of holding her was now no longer a dream. On the other hand, Mr. Sheffield could be dying at their feet—from a wound he'd inflicted.

He held her until the sounds of her wheezing and sniffling began tapering off, and then looked over her shoulder, swallowing hard when he saw that a light had come on in one of the picture windows in the mansion across the lake, the same window he'd seen illuminated when he'd broken in here. That glow now appeared to him as a giant eye staring from across the water. He felt exposed out there in the moonlight, and the hug-induced spell abruptly broke.

"If you're okay now," he said, with his mouth still beside her neck, "we should probably leave. Before he wakes up."

Releasing her hold, she raised her head from

his shoulder just as the breeze strengthened to a gust, the lake water rippling and the willow branches sweeping the ground when she tilted her head slightly to the side. "Wait," she said, "why were you—" She looked away and swiped at her eyes, sighing before she went on, "I guess it doesn't matter why you were here. I don't even want to imagine what might have happened if you weren't. I really don't want to think about that."

Corey mopped the sweat from his forehead with his shirtsleeve while a feathery sensation rose beneath his ribs like the flapping of a wing. He needed a cover story, and couldn't believe that during all the time sitting on the roof he hadn't prepared one.

"You're sure you're okay?"

"Honestly? I have no idea. That was so beyond fucked up." She pointed at Mr. Sheffield. "And what about him? What do we do about him now?"

They both looked down in silence for a long beat.

Corey knelt next to him and pressed two fingertips to the side of his neck until he found a pulse, and then cocked his ear to his nose.

"He's just knocked out," he said. "And the spot where I hit him looks bad but it isn't bleeding much anymore, so I think he'll be all right. We should really go, though, before he wakes up."

Angelique nodded while looking past him. The distant voice over his shoulder that held her attention also prompted him to turn his head. Tiffany had called out from inside the house, and although the sound had been muted from that far away, Corey imagined her approaching the porch, his worry confirmed when the lights popped on in one of the lakefront rooms on the first floor. He cringed while counting down—*three, two, one*—and then right on cue, the screen door screeched open and Tiffany shouted with hands cupped at her mouth. "Angel? You out here?"

Angelique pulled Corey over to the bushes at the corner of the lawn and they crouched there, a few feet from the retaining wall and the gently lapping water.

He squinted through the leaves and whispered, "What should we do?"

"You're asking me? How the fuck should I know?" She squeezed his arm hard enough to leave a bruise. "This is all so crazy!"

"We should just get out of here," he said, prying her fingers off while holding eye contact. "We can figure out what to do after that."

"Alright," she said through shallow breaths, "you're probably right, but first just stay here while I get her into bed. Right after she's asleep, we can go." She raised her head over the bushes and immediately slunk back down, whisper-shouting, "What was up with her father chasing me like that? Or that guy with him in the pool!"

Tiffany called her friend's name again from the porch, sounding strung out now, singing her words. "Angel . . . Where in the fucking *fuck* are . . . you . . ."

"Shit!" Angelique grabbed him again, squeezing harder with each word. "She's not going to stop calling my name until she finds me. And if she starts wandering outside she might see him out here and think we attacked him or something." She squinted toward the porch, still whispering but sounding even more worried. "Tiff didn't see any of it—the pool, the three of us running . . ."

"No, she didn't see anything," Corey blurted.

*Goddamn it,* he thought. *Now she knows I was watching them. How else would I know Tiffany didn't see?*

"Just don't move till I'm back, okay? Please, promise me you'll stay here." She faced him, her eyes desperately wide.

"I promise."

Angelique started toward the house, whispering over her shoulder, "Stay there, and stay hidden," and he did as she told him, crouching behind a holly bush and beneath the wispy purple leaves of a Japanese maple. He hoped she'd missed the point of what he'd just said. But whether she had or not, he'd wait there for her. Come to think of it, he'd risk prison to make sure she was all

96

right—and thinking back on the chase, knocking a man out was one thing, but he wondered now if he might have been willing to kill if that's what it would have taken to save her.

About ten feet away, Leo Sheffield still lay on his side in the same awkward position—one arm extended above his head, half his face pressed to the grass, his chest perceptibly rising and falling with each sleeping breath. Corey watched him through the crosshatched spaces between layers of spiky leaves. He and Angelique needed to be long gone as soon as possible, otherwise they'd be in a cop shop answering questions all night, maybe in a cell after that. But if Mr. Sheffield didn't regain consciousness soon, somewhere along the way to wherever the hell they were headed, they would have to call an ambulance.

He crept out onto the lawn and reexamined Mr. Sheffield's head wound, thinking back to that night when he'd done the same for Gina after she passed out at the kitchen table and fell, smacking her head hard enough to bleed. *Good,* he thought, Leo had a nasty wound but it wasn't seeping. And he hadn't stopped breathing. He'd wake up at some point with a horrible headache, but he wouldn't die.

Corey stood, exhaled, and then for some reason felt an overwhelming need to take one last look at the dead man in the pool. Thinking back to the chase and Angelique screaming, he ran up the sloped lawn, worried now that a neighbor had heard her, or that someone at the house across the lake had looked through a telescope and seen, believing that at any moment he would hear the sirens. Without a plan in mind, he aimed his cell phone camera and took a series of photos of the dead man's face, wider shots of his body with his bandaged arms out wide, each of the photos framed with the Sheffield house situated clearly in the background—then he stopped, disturbed by his impulse to document this stranger's death.

*Why am I taking photos?*

The thought nagged at him. He still couldn't believe that any of the crazy shit he'd seen or been a part of over the past hour had really happened. Henry, the man floating a few feet away from where he now stood, had died right over there on the ledge beside the pool, a man who'd been brought to the estate in secret by his mom's billionaire boss, who'd kissed him and drunk champagne with him and done coke with him, and then Henry had done so much coke he'd basically exploded his own head.

As far as Corey knew, he'd been the only one to see any of the true events, the only one to hear Mr. Sheffield call out to Henry by name. Regardless, Leo definitely wouldn't want either the true story or Angelique's version of what she'd witnessed to get out, and now that Corey had seen him so crazed when he'd chased her, there was no telling what he might do to save himself.

He snapped one more photo before hurrying back down the slope and returning to his hiding place in the bushes. Once there, he crouched, chewing his fingernails, waiting. Wishing he could go, but waiting. No idea yet where they should go. Hoping the girl in there who'd hugged him would come back outside soon, hoping she hadn't changed her mind.

He kept on watching, waiting to run. Waiting. Watching no discernable changes in the windows for so long that at a certain point he wasn't thinking much of anything, other than the promise he'd made to himself when he jumped from the roof—that he would do whatever it took to keep her safe.

# SEVEN

She crossed the lawn, running most of the way. Tiffany had yelled her name twice before reentering the house, and now Angelique crept up the porch steps, calling to her through the screen door with a forceful whisper, "Tiff, I'm out here."

The door swung open, the springs and hinges creaking more than usual after they'd been overstressed and warped when Mr. Sheffield had come barreling out less than ten minutes ago. Tiffany crossed the threshold looking annoyed, her eyes puffy, pillow lines like pink lightning bolts imprinted along one of her cheeks. She appeared even more disoriented than when she'd passed out, wobbling in the doorway, slurring, "Angel, what're you doing outside? What time is it? I don't remember getting into bed."

Angelique couldn't allow her to linger on the porch any longer. She needed to guide her friend upstairs and return her to bed before she discovered the unexplainable body on the far corner of the lawn. How could she explain to Tiffany why her lunatic father, who Angelique had once considered a good man, was knocked out and sprawled on the grass, with a blood-covered stone cherub lying nearby? And craziest of all, what about the body still floating in the

100

pool? Had Mr. Sheffield killed him? *One thing at a time,* she thought. *Just get Tiff into bed first. Then get the hell out of the house and back to Corey. Like he said, we'll get far away and then figure out what's next.*

"It's late, Tiff," she said, taking her friend by the arm. They entered the house and she led Tiffany across the wide living room, talking as they walked. "I came down to the lake after I couldn't sleep. It was so nice out, I thought I might as well sit by the water for a while. Come on, let's just go back to bed."

On the way up the stairs, Tiffany yawned and paused against the banister. "Hey, did you hear something outside before I came out?"

"Like what?"

"I think something woke me up, like screams or something."

"You were dreaming."

Angelique guided her into her bedroom and kept the light off while she helped her under the covers and pulled the patchwork Amish quilt up to her chin.

"Everything's fine," she said, kissing her on the cheek. "Sleep now."

"Stay the night in here with me, Angel-fish, like when we were still in elementary."

"No thanks, slutty-pie, you kick in your sleep."

Tiffany shifted into her cutesy voice. "Don't you love me, though?"

101

"I do love you." A sudden queasiness filled her stomach as she recalled Mr. Sheffield pinning her wrists to the grass. As much as Tiffany played the rebel of the family, she adored her father. She would believe whatever lie he told if it ever came down to Angelique's word against his. "Sweet dreams, Tiff," she said softly, and then had to look away. She stared out the window and the moon stared back at her. Nothing to do for now but wait for Tiffany to cease shifting around for a more comfortable position and to pass out.

As she assumed, it didn't take long, and once she felt reasonably sure that it was safe to leave, Angelique tiptoed out into the hall and down the stairs. She eased the creaky screen door closed behind her and looked out across the moonlit lawn, aware now that during the brief walk through the house she'd begun sweating. Her thoughts began kaleidoscoping—the insane chase and the helplessness she'd felt when she'd been pinned down spliced with flashes of his face during his crazy-eyed breakdown or the attempted assault or whatever the fuck that was. Then the miraculous appearance of a guy she'd flirted with the past two summers and almost kissed last September, who had to have been on the property before the chase in order to save her like that. But why? Why had Corey been there? And her best friend, now passed out in her bed . . . she loved her psycho dad because she'd never seen his psycho side. Or did Tiff know something more about him than she let on? She hadn't seen that poor dead man in the pool, that was for sure, and hadn't seen her dad standing over him, and definitely hadn't seen his hands on Angelique's wrists while he yelled in her face, looking like he wanted to kill her. Also, where could she and Corey go now, and how long could they stay away? By her leaving, would the police think she had something to do with any of this? Would she end up a suspect instead of a totally freaked out witness? The questions kept on spiraling, the complications too overwhelming, the need to get away—*I need to get away*—the thought that finally rang out loudest, supplanting all the rest.

She looked toward the lake but couldn't see. Her chest tightened. She tipped to the side, light-headed, way off-balance. The landscape returned to her like a funhouse mirror and then began flattening, two-dimensional, pixelating, everything solid turning to dust and swirling over the surface of a depthless movie screen, the lawn, the lake, the porch rail, the willow trees all squeezing together. She bent over and wheezed, whispering to herself, "This feeling will pass. I'm okay . . . I'm okay."

With each new breath her lungs sucked more oxygen. Her vision adjusted, blurred again, cleared a bit more. Slowly, the vertigo relented. The outlines of the low-hanging tangle of branches from the willow at the far corner of the lawn sharpened against the bright surface of the lake, and she could see Mr. Sheffield still splayed out as he'd been when she left. She inhaled deeply and exhaled the dizziness and sickness until gravity reattached the soles of her bare feet to the porch boards. Her balance returned, and she stepped onto the grass. She began jogging down the slope, initially feeling completely alone in the world, then picked up her pace as she was suddenly overtaken by the sense that dozens of unseen neighbors across the lake were watching her through high-powered binoculars.

Slowing only slightly as she passed Mr. Sheffield, she reached the bushes and whispered to Corey, "She's asleep. Let's go."

He motioned for her to follow him, and together they hurried over to the bulkhead, where he hopped down first and extended his arms to help her down. "Careful where you step," he said, just as her feet sank an inch or two into the layer of muck along the dark water's edge. It smelled of algae and some sort of marine decay. She hadn't remembered to put on shoes, and for some reason that thought, the reality of not being properly prepared, triggered her to look back over the bulkhead wall at Mr. Sheffield.

"Wait," she said, "what if he's dying?"

"I've been thinking about that while you were inside," Corey said. "We should call an ambulance once we're off the property. Not from one of our cell phones, though. A pay phone if we can find one. Come on."

"Wait, but—don't you think—" She stopped short and they both squatted down, their eyes even with the lawn.

Mr. Sheffield coughed. Then he groaned. A second later he groaned again while sliding his right arm up and reaching to touch the back of his head. He lay there for a while, then pushed himself up to sit and stared at the blood on his fingers. The insect noises rose in volume and became a blanket rising and falling all around while Mr. Sheffield struggled to prop himself on a knee, facing the house. Angelique looked at Corey and saw her own panic reflected in his unblinking stare. Gripping his arm, she turned again to watch Mr. Sheffield, who'd attempted to stand but lost his balance and had to place both hands on the ground. He made an awkward movement and managed to get to his feet, swaying a bit before taking the first step away from the lake.

Corey whispered directly into Angelique's ear, so softly he barely made any sound. "He's okay. Let's go. We have to go. *Now.*"

# EIGHT

Leo kicked to the surface, choking, desperate to cough water from his lungs. But then the dry hacking burned his throat, and though he still couldn't see, he felt the cut grass under his palms, the soil against his fingertips. Dressed in nothing but damp boxer shorts, he'd just come back to life, balled up in a fetal position on his lawn in the middle of the night.

He hadn't been drowning. No, he hadn't been submerged at all. But he'd seen Henry floating facedown in the pool with his bandaged arms outstretched. He'd tried to save him, but he'd failed. And so he'd simply held Henry in his arms, gazing down at his wide pupils, his eyelids pulled all the way back, as though he'd been entranced by the night sky.

A breath of wind came sweeping in from the lake, tussling Leo's thinning hair, feathering his bare midsection. Hazy light airbrushed his limbs the blue-gray skin tone of an alien. Grass blades stuck to his tongue and lips, which he spat and plucked away, and as he pushed himself up to sit, a high-pitched frequency entered his skull, swelling with each movement.

He reached up and pressed lightly against the wound on the back of his head. His blood pressure worried him more than the streaks of pain. It seemed his heart had swollen, and was now strobing three times too fast. He needed to calm his pulse. One more beat-per-minute and he'd surely go into cardiac arrest. He sat straighter, groping for one of his personal trainer's mantras, flashing back to their most recent yoga session. Balance and harmony, life—it all resided within the breath, pranayama, the slow in-breath, the slow out-breath. *Breathe, Leo. Remember to breathe.*

The blood on his hand had come from touching his head. He stared at his wet fingers for a moment, confused as to how he'd been knocked unconscious, the opaque liquid looking more like ink than blood.

Groaning and muttering to himself, he propped himself on a knee and swiveled to face the lakeside porch and unlit windows of his summerhouse. With his fingertips he examined the back of his head again, still clueless as to how he'd been so seriously injured, hazy as to how he'd even ended up here on the lawn. He strained to sit up but gravity pulled him toward the earth, and so he lay down with his face pressed to the grass, thinking of Henry, his shock of black hair, his smile, the flecks of amber in his corneas that Leo had once told him in certain lighting looked like embers.

He recalled lingering in the house while Henry

had been outside at the pool, how he'd collected the bottle of Glenlivet and bulled his way around the kitchen, fixing them a plate of finger foods while making a terrible mess between swigs of Scotch straight from the bottle. At some point during that time, Henry had had an accident. It couldn't have been more than ten minutes or so. That's all it had taken. Leo hadn't heard him call out, hadn't seen him slip and smack his head on the granite coping by the swimming pool stairs. He could only guess that this had been the story of how Henry died.

He pushed his body upright from the lawn, his right hand returning to the throbbing head wound, his short breaths escaping like spurts from a shriveling balloon. He kept his hand on his head as he forced his legs to steady, and stood there for a minute, the earth swaying like the ocean beneath a rowboat. His boxers clung to his thighs, still damp from when he'd been in the pool. Images from earlier in the night flashed behind his closed eyelids. He'd been chasing his daughter's friend before he lost consciousness. That's how he'd ended up here, so far across the lawn.

He took his first baby step up the slope toward the pool. With one arm hugged to his ribs and the other slack at his side, step by slow step he closed in on the waking nightmare: Henry's soaked bandages and his body floating there far beyond the two gurgling jets in the shallow end, the darkness of the water without the pool light ever having been switched on making it impossible to tell the extent of the bleeding before Henry had died. *He's really dead,* Leo thought. *Dead* . . .

His head throbbing, he waded into the lukewarm water and dragged Henry back to the shallow end, cradling him in his arms. Staring down at his eyes, he saw that the embers in his corneas had been extinguished, less life to them now than the surface of a mirror. Henry's spark replaced by a pale glaze. *I did this to him,* Leo thought. *I did this.*

# NINE

"Look at him," Corey whispered. "He's walking. He'll be fine. Please, can we just leave?"

She let go of his arm. "Maybe he just seems like he's all right, but he's not. We should watch him for a while to make sure."

Corey turned and looked across the lake at the mansion with its picture windows radiating light. "We should already be gone," he said, realizing he sounded more worried than he had up till then. "I just bashed my mom's boss over the head. Hanging out here is crazy."

"I'm staying," she said. "I have to." She pushed her hair back behind her ears and crouched in the muck with her forearms on her knees. "Wait with me, please? I promise I'll go with you once we know he's not going to end up dying overnight."

Corey closed his eyes and brought his hands to his face, then silently answered with a nod. She rose to stand and he stood up beside her, and together they watched Mr. Sheffield stagger away from them, until finally he reached the pool stairs, his legs and then part of his torso steadily disappearing as he stepped into the water, less and less of him visible until he was nothing more than a tiny disembodied head in the distance.

Angelique pulled herself up and over the low

bulkhead wall, sank down on one knee and looked to Corey for confirmation that spying on the injured Mr. Sheffield was indeed the most responsible plan. Rather than saying anything, he simply hopped up from the muck to join her, and then the two of them hurried along the bushes and the tall hedgerow at the property line, then cut over to the porch, where they crept past the steps and cherub statues and tulip beds until they reached the corner post. There they knelt behind a cluster of rhododendrons covered in magenta blooms, perfectly hidden and yet with a good view of the pool.

Corey felt Angelique fumble for his hand while they watched Mr. Sheffield and his young friend in the shallow end, wisps of steam hovering and swirling along the surface of the water, the lunar light saturating both the living and the dead man's skin with an ethereal shade of white. Corey held her hand tighter, thinking of Gina for the first time since all the craziness had begun, worried now that if Mr. Sheffield could snap like that on Angelique, he could just as easily snap on his mom.

Nothing made sense anymore. Angelique had known Leo Sheffield since before she and Tiffany had even started grade school, and for years had considered him a second father, a surrogate anyway, the only father figure who'd stuck around. But now that she'd seen him in those awful primal moments when he'd chased her and slammed her to the ground, she doubted she'd ever truly known him at all. For all she knew, he'd murdered a man tonight. *Holy shit, she thought, what if he really is a killer?* She hadn't let herself follow that line of thinking since he tackled her—that he'd actually killed the guy out there with the soggy bandages draped from his arms. She knew she should get away, but this bizarre water funeral or whatever the hell this was with Mr. Sheffield leaning over the dead man held her in place, too curious to leave.

After staring through the bushes for another minute or two, she glanced over at Corey crouched beside her. He lived in the Hamptons, she knew that much, but undoubtedly somewhere altogether different than this multimillion-dollar estate beside Agawam Lake. His mother would be working here tomorrow, and he probably would be, too. She'd talked with him often enough during the past couple summers that she looked forward to seeing him, and around Labor Day last year had even considered answering yes when he asked her out. He liked her; that much had always been obvious. But why was he next to her now? Why had he been here in the middle of the night, right when she needed him? She couldn't imagine why, but whatever his reasons, he'd saved her, and without question his presence was the only thing keeping her from losing her mind.

Leaning closer to him while they both kept their eyes on Mr. Sheffield and the dead man in the pool, Angelique thought back to her view from the balcony and the fact that she hadn't seen how the man had died. As messed up as the view had been when she looked down at them, she'd made a quick assumption that Tiff's father had killed him, but what if he hadn't?

*He must have,* she decided. *If he didn't kill him, then why chase me? And would he have killed me, too, if Corey hadn't hit him? But if he did kill the guy, why is he so distraught now, like he's in mourning?*

Just then Corey tapped her arm, which made her flinch so intensely she had to plant her palms on the ground to keep from pitching forward into the bushes.

He didn't make a sound as he mouthed the words *Can we go now?*

She turned and looked through the branches at Mr. Sheffield leaning over the floating body, his head lowering even more, those small noises either muttered words that she couldn't quite hear or the sound of him sobbing. Mesmerized all over again, she shook her head and whispered, "No, we should wait a little longer. I need to be sure."

Corey continued looking at Mr. Sheffield with his head lowered over the dead man in the pool. He had leaned closer to Henry's face while pulling the body just above the steaming water, and Corey was suddenly riveted by the weirdness of it all, now just as interested as Angelique was to see what the drunk billionaire would do next.

Mr. Sheffield said something to his friend, as if whispering a secret to him. Then he eased closer and pressed his lips to the dead man's mouth. Angelique clutched Corey's sweatshirt in her fist, and without looking at him exclaimed in the quietest whisper, "What—in the—fuck?"

# TEN

Leo cradled Henry in his arms, half expecting him to magically awaken when he leaned down and kissed his lips. It felt so wrong not to feel a response, wrong as well to taste chlorine and something more metallic, which he realized a moment later had been blood.

After dragging Henry by the wrists from the pool stairs to the lawn, Leo stared at the peaceful face of his lover for some time, silent, his mind blank until he finally registered that the sun would be rising in a few hours. He drank a long pull from the bottle of Glenlivet that lay beside the silver serving tray on the ground, and knelt next to Henry, whispering, "I'm sorry, I'm so sorry," over and over, until he nearly choked. He tried to rise from his knees, but fell, and then fell again. On the third try, he did manage to stand, though he teetered like a toddler as he took half steps, continuously slugging from the bottle. He headed toward the house with his belly sloshing like the sea in a storm, but also feeling as though he'd been hollowed out, his legs barely functioning. Seeing double, he gulped down more Scotch and nearly fell to the ground several times.

Ten or twenty feet from the kitchen door, he

paused to bend over at the waist with sour saliva stretching from his open mouth and a river of poison threatening to rush out, while the mob of chanting crickets quickly morphed into a chorus of whispers, rising in force like a series of storm-swept waves, echoing toward him from every direction. With everything spinning, Leo dropped the bottle and pressed his palms to the sides of his head, but to no avail. The white noise swelled louder and louder inside his ear canals until finally it closed in on him and coalesced into one deeply personal command, spoken with the same baritone voice he still heard in his most unsettling dreams—the voice of his dead father, Leonard Sr., bellowing: *Don't be such a fucking girl . . . Be a man . . .*

In his drunken sway, he held his arms out like an agitated ape and considered shouting back, "Go fuck yourself!" though he knew shouting at a voice in his head made no sense. It had to be in his head. Right? The dead don't speak. And Leonard Sr. had been dead for more than forty years. No god would ever send that voice to him, especially not now, a voice meant only to crucify him with the words his father had uttered so many times with his belt in hand. And yet the words repeated as though lodged in his head, with a sick, throaty resonance: *Don't be such a fucking girl . . . Be a man . . .* Leo took a couple hesitant steps toward the kitchen entrance and

116

closed his eyes. He swayed some more, and then suddenly the old man's phantom voice instructed him to snap to it and dispose of Henry's body.

Staggering inside the house, Leo found the mess he'd made, though he had almost no memory of making it. The refrigerator door hung open, pieces of a broken dinner plate lay in the sink, a jar of blue-cheese-stuffed olives had spilled out over an array of cold cuts and soggy scraps of baguette and marble rye. Through blinding flashes of pain from his head wound, he began scooping the ruined food into the trash can with both hands, making note to take the bag out when he'd finished cleaning. Then he ran through all the other details he'd need to address—the champagne glasses and the empty bottle upstairs, Henry's clothing beside the pool, the possibility of blood to clean from the pool's granite coping.

*Fuck me,* he thought. *The blood. What can I clean it with? Where does Gina even keep the cleaning supplies?* He gripped the top edges of the trash can and doubled over. An invisible fist hammered his stomach and it emptied like a levee during a breach, a flood entering the trash bag, grotesque sounds eking from his throat.

Angelique's face appeared in his mind, looking down at him from the balcony. He swiped the water from his eyes and the spittle from his mouth with the back of his hand and steadied himself against the marble countertop. Should he search the house for her? After the way he'd scared her, surely she was gone by now. But someone else had knocked him over the head, someone he'd never seen. Another awful thought set in. His head turned and tilted toward the ceiling, in the direction of his only daughter's bedroom. Angelique had been there, which meant she must have come out early with Tiffany . . . Where had she been when her friend mistook him for a killer from the balcony? What if she'd heard Angelique screaming? What if she'd seen? Where was she now?

The silence began suffocating him. He pressed his palms to his temples, fearing he was going mad. Even if his little girl had witnessed it all and fled the estate believing that he was a monster, what mattered most now was the much more pressing problem, the much more urgent thought: *They'll all think you killed him.*

With a new surge of energy, he dropped the plate shards into the trash bag and wiped down the countertop in wild patterns, imagining the headline and the photo of him being perp-walked down courthouse steps in cuffs, his company's stock plummeting even before a prison guard led him to his cell. The champagne glasses and the bottle—he had to get those before he forgot. He couldn't forget anything. He had to eliminate every trace of Henry's presence in the house and on the property, and as much as possible, erase him from his life.

Gnat-like spots flitted all around him as he hustled up the stairs and thought about the text messages to and from Henry on his phone, the call history, Pete driving them around the city—and tonight, the extra-loud final hour during the drive out here to the estate. He could talk to Tiffany at some point and coax her back to her daddy's side, convince her that everything about tonight had been the result of an awful accident, nothing sinister, nothing malicious; but the rapidly growing list of complications plagued him even as a new voice broke through and spurred him on, speaking either from a great distance or from deep within: *Get it together, Leo. Or you're going to burn.*

He stomped into the bedroom, collected the glasses and bottle and his scattered clothes, and stepped through the balcony doors, pausing there to look out at the pool, and then the trees, and then over at the lake. None of the homeowners surrounding the lake had boats, at least not motorized ones, not since an ordinance passed in the eighties outlawing them for their noise and disruption to wildlife. Goddammit, if he only had a fucking rowboat. All the details mattered, but most of all he had to find a safe place to hide Henry. He looked once more from side to side, scanning the blurred property. His eyes lingered on the pine trees. He squinted, gripping the balcony rail, contemplating whether he could actually do it—whether he could dig a deep enough hole.

Sometime later, with one eye closed to keep his balance, he exited the house and staggered over to Henry's body beside the pool. Once there, he unfolded an afghan from the master bedroom trunk and laid it out flat, turned Henry by the wrists and wrapped him like a mummy. He kept going back and forth, one moment thinking, *I should call the police, tell them it was an accident,* only to clench up, deciding once more, *No, no one can know.*

This inner conversation played on a loop as he took his first step and began dragging the body away from the pool and across the north lawn. Henry only weighed a hundred and forty, maybe a hundred and fifty pounds, max; but it seemed now that his weight had doubled since he'd died, or that the wrapped body actively resisted Leo's efforts, dragging like an old-fashioned plow tilling the lawn behind. Foot by foot, grunt by grunt, eventually Leo pulled him past the garden, then past the bronze chess piece sculptures, then past the tennis court fence, locked in a mechanical rhythm—step, heave, step, heave . . .

Though his legs shook and his back had begun to spasm, he finally arrived at a secluded spot in the shadows of thick pines. The same moment he dropped Henry's body, he fell to his hands and knees. He couldn't stand for a while, no matter how hard he tried, and in that helpless physical state the argument in his mind broke down. He abandoned the idea of calling the police.

Still dangerously dizzy from the head wound and all the substances in his system, he assessed the time he'd just spent cleaning the house, the entire process in hindsight now seeming so programmed, as if his father's voice or some other quasi-fascist force had moved his arms and legs like a puppeteer. He knelt beside Henry's wrapped body and apologized, slurring the same words so many times that his rambling resembled the recitation of a prayer. No matter how temporary the disposal, he had to do it. *You know you won't survive prison, not even the white-collar kind. One mistake now and it's all over.* He continued on like this while bulling around inside the landscaping shed and searching for tools, and while he carried the shovel over his shoulder, still under the belief that the safest course of action would be to bury Henry—bury him along with the suit he'd had on when they arrived from the city. *Oh Jesus,* Leo thought, *what happened to my gold watch?* Henry may have taken it off beside the pool, but he may have still had it on when Leo wrapped him in the blanket.

Leo crept back under the boughs beside the lawn and quickly unwound the afghan from Henry's body, only to find both his thin wrists bare. He emptied the garbage bag and sifted through the pieces of clothing, scrounging until he found the gold Rolex in a jacket pocket. He stared at it, a slight gleam from the moon striking the clock hands where they split across the diamond at the three o'clock line. He sighed, slid the band around his own wrist and clasped it in place. The watch felt foreign against his skin. As soon as he returned to the master bedroom, he'd put it in his safe. He never wanted to see this damned watch again.

The spaded shovel plunged into the layer of pine needles and topsoil next to the body, but immediately hit something hard, and when Leo tried again his hands seized up, filled with vibrations. He dropped the shovel and ran his fingers over the ground. He'd hit a series of thick roots from the neighboring pines. After a few attempts in other spots and the shovel hitting only roots, he was sweating and out of breath, and suddenly the facts of the moment struck him as absurd. What the hell was he thinking? Why had he thought burying him made any sense? Wishing he could lie down next to Henry and sleep before figuring out what to do, he gazed back across his acres of property toward the lake. Even at such a great distance he could see that on the other side of the water the dot-size picture windows of the Millman estate glowed with honey-colored light. Someone may have been looking out in the middle of the night when Angelique screamed. Someone may have seen him dragging a body from the pool.

But then the possibility of a faraway witness gave way to the hazy recollection of chasing his daughter's friend, and then the lack of memory where it had been cut short—someone had hit him from behind, someone he hadn't seen. He let the shovel rest and stood up straight to look around. So many places where a person could be hiding, watching him from the shadows. A sound like the snap of a twig jerked his head to the side.

He squinted at the darkness beyond the pines bordering the lawn, and whispered, "Is someone there?" so softly that he barely heard his own words. The pine boughs swayed in response to the breeze, but otherwise he heard no sound, saw no movement. He kept staring, though his thoughts drifted back to when he'd discovered Henry in the pool. What if his accident hadn't been an accident? Was it possible that the man who'd knocked Leo over the head had first attacked Henry? Was some maniac crouched over there in the woods? He stared awhile longer, squinting harder at the general section of darkness where he'd heard the snap. Nothing moved aside from the breeze-blown branches and the pine needles softly swirling along the ground.

*I'm losing it,* Leo thought. *No one's out there. But the police are probably already on their way.*

It would be light soon, and while he still needed to check the house to see if Tiffany had somehow slept through it all and was still in her bed, Sheila and the boys would be on their way within a matter of hours. Their friends and his yes-men and business associates would also be stopping by randomly throughout the weekend. He would have to act normal, put on a happy face while suffering through lightning bolts of pain from his head wound and the mother of all hangovers that awaited him—and all the while, somehow suppress the urge to scream.

He leaned with all his weight and pulled Henry into the pines, thinking back to some of the cold words his father had shouted more than half a century ago after catching Leo playing with his sister's dolls. In tandem with the emotional beatings, as a sort of daily ritual, his giant palm smacked five-year-old Leo's naked backside, while the little boy, between shrieks and sobs, promised to be a good boy, and on some days promised never to act like a girl again. The miserable old bastard's words and all those spankings and belt lashings had set down roots deep within him all those years ago, and now he sensed his father hovering in the boughs just above his shoulders, judging him, his eyes set upon him like blazing orbs, his ghost-hand controlling the breeze.

From his deathbed, when Leo was seventeen

124

years old, Leonard Sr. had instilled in him the formula for success—marry well, work hard, invest, reinvest, never show weakness, always put family first. Leo had failed to live up to most of those expectations. He'd failed to keep his promises, or so he thought as he forged ahead, dragging Henry's body over gnarls and knuckles of surface-level roots and rocks and a bed of pine needles, disappearing a bit himself as he did, drifting back decades into the memory of his father picking him up at Penn Station, after the headmaster had informed Leonard that his one and only son had been disciplined at his boarding school for indulging his desires with another teenaged boy. Then their arrival home, Leo cornered in his bedroom, the old man's razor strop dangling like a boa constrictor, the cracks across Leo's bare legs, Leo staring at the family photo on his bureau while his dying father hauled off on him and shouted . . . *No son of mine . . . No son of mine . . . No son of mine . . .*

The flap of a bird's wings snapped Leo out of his trance. He kept pulling Henry deeper into the darkness provided by the pine boughs until he'd entered a moonless, cave-like space between the tallest pines at the property line. There, he blindly gathered a pile of dry needles from the ground, felt along the length of Henry's wrapped body and dropped them overtop, covering him as best he could in the dark. He would come back sometime tomorrow to check on him, hopefully to move him, but sunrise wouldn't wait much longer. For now, this would have to do.

He stumbled back over the same thick roots and trudged with arms out to keep from walking head-on into a tree, all the while his lips muttering along with his thoughts.

*No one can know. I'm so sorry, Henry. But no one can ever know.*

# ELEVEN

Angelique had just watched Mr. Sheffield drag the rolled-up body away from the pool a few lumbering steps at a time. She'd trailed him from the shadows with Corey at her side, until finally he set the body down on the edge of the lawn, turned and began backtracking toward the pine trees where they'd paused to hide.

A few seconds later, she peered out just far enough to see him slogging past, limping the way Jack Nicholson had while wielding an ax in the snowy maze at the end of *The Shining*. After her friend's father passed the tennis courts and entered the toolshed, Angelique took a step away from the tree trunk, baffled by the sounds of metal clanging and a series of thuds against the shed's wooden floor and walls. When he emerged with a shovel over his shoulder, she gasped much louder than she should have, folded her ankle, and Corey held her close as they ducked back behind the trunk.

She crouched stone-still until Mr. Sheffield passed by with the shovel. A man she'd known for most of her life, this man she'd respected and at another time would have said she loved: Was he really about to bury that poor guy from the pool? Would he try to kill her and Corey if he discovered them here? Would Corey be able to fight him off? She should have been sick with fear even acknowledging these questions as very real possibilities, but for some reason she felt strangely calm, almost numb. Despite her new hatred for him and the base insanity of the whole situation, the notion of fleeing before seeing how this horror show would end made no sense at all. Fascination had replaced the fear, and if she did feel anything at all, it was a sense that she'd detached from all the emotions that had triggered the panic attack on the porch. To a certain extent she and Corey no longer existed on the Sheffield property, but instead now hovered one dimension removed from his actions, experiencing this less as participants and more like moviegoers in theater seats. She and Corey hid behind the fourth wall, as the audience, while Mr. Sheffield forged ahead, the real-life performer. The star of the most warped reality show of all time.

When Mr. Sheffield stepped to the side and slammed the shovel down, Angelique leaned out a bit more, realizing he'd given up on digging. She watched as he leaned over the wrapped body, and with a grunt began dragging it into the woods between two giant pines, the darkness swallowing him.

She waited a minute, and then she and Corey left the shelter of the trees. He touched her arm, and the moment she faced him he asked the

128

same question he'd been asking ever since this craziness started, though this time simply by raising his eyebrows.

She nodded, and whispered, "Okay, let's go."

The fact that she was still barefoot hadn't occurred to her as they ran across all that soft grass of the lawn, but once they hopped down from the bulkhead and forged ahead into the reeds it made their escape more complicated. Corey held her arm over his shoulder and acted as a crutch while they traversed sharp twigs and other barbed things in the lake mud. In the shadows from the neighboring trees, they hiked side by side through a tangle of dried branches and vines along the bank, creeping farther away from the Sheffield estate as they passed an upturned, decrepit old rowboat with sun-split oars, and then the brown husk of a Christmas tree.

After a few more steps in the rough terrain it became too awkward to rest her weight on him, so she held Corey's hand as they pushed on toward the fence line of the Sheffields' next-door neighbor, whispering about the plan to make a run for Corey's truck as soon as they made it through the brambles and weeds along the uppermost edge of the bank.

The moment she noticed the pair of swans in the tall grass, she held Corey back and raised a finger to her lips. The sight of the two sleeping birds had startled her, but then felt like the strangest of gifts, such an unexpected peaceful sight after so much fear and stress. She gripped Corey's hand tighter and kept her finger at her lips, wondering if the female was nesting, and if the baby swans, the cygnets, might be due to hatch. They stood still while she stared at the birds with their long necks bent forward, recalling a much simpler time when she'd skimmed an illustrated book about swans that had been on the living room table in the Sheffields' house, back when she and Tiff had just entered their teens and used to sit by the lake and talk about boys, daydreaming together about who they would marry.

Swans mate for life, a fact that had always made these birds that much more beautiful in her mind. And the female did appear to be nesting. The male's neck bent to his breast like a question mark, just as hers did, and yet he also held his body angled slightly toward her, as if to shield her from danger. These two majestic birds, this couple, they would mate for life . . .

She took a step, wondering how many humans could say the same. Then she whispered to Corey, urging him to be careful not to disturb the reeds or the dead branches bordering the nest.

"Try not to wake them," she said, and he nodded, seeming to understand that everything depended on their stillness.

# TWELVE

At the neighbor's wooden driveway gate, Corey
bent down with his fingers interlaced, cupped
Angelique's foot and gave her a boost up. She
gripped the top and swung one leg over, and
as soon as she dropped on the other side, he
backed up a few paces, ran and launched himself
upward. The same ankle that had turned when
he'd jumped from the roof filled with fire, but
he shrugged off the pain and grabbed Angelique
by the hand, holding on tightly as they sped two
blocks up Gin Lane, each looking over their
shoulders along the way. "That's my truck," he
said, slowing when his rear bumper came into
view. He noticed her limping a little when she
approached his passenger-side door, and once
they both hopped inside the cab and he'd turned
the key, he watched her bend her leg to inspect
the sole of her right foot.

"Oh man," she said. "Can you help me with
this?"

He flicked on the dome light. The short hike
along the lake's edge had ravaged her feet, and
now, in better lighting, he could see the extent of
the damage, the most prominent detail being the
thick splinter in her heel.

He nodded, taking her foot in his hands. "But

we shouldn't be here too long, in case a cop comes pulling up."

Angelique sniffed and squeezed his arm, still looking at her heel. "You think they might?"

"Maybe," he said, peering up at the windshield. "One of the neighbors might have heard you screaming." The pickup's engine puttered while he worked the buried end of the splinter forward with his thumb and eased it out through a bead of blood.

"Thanks," she said, leaning back, and he gripped the gearshift knob, about to put it into first. But then he turned his head as she placed her hand on top of his. "Really, thank you," she said, and quickly kissed his cheek. He stared, knowing the kiss had nothing to do with the splinter, though his mind was blank as to what he should say.

After a pause, she cradled her foot and said, "We should probably start driving, huh?" He agreed and shifted into first, but before they pulled away from the bushes she added, "If you want to tell me why you were here tonight at some point, that's cool, but I'm not going to ask. Not tonight, anyway."

"It's—" he began, but she cut him off.

"I'm just glad you were."

His Adam's apple rose and fell and sweat filled the pores on his forehead. Her lack of inquiry was a mercy. She spotted his pack of cigarettes on the seat and took one out, and he flicked his lighter while the truck cruised in first gear along the shoulder of the road, cupping the flame in his hand even though the windows were closed and no wind could disturb it. She inhaled until the fire kissed the tobacco with a mild sizzling sound, then let the smoke out slowly through her nose, while Corey lit one for himself.

"I don't usually smoke," he said over the sound of the engine. "Just once in a while."

"Same for me, usually only when I'm with Tiff and she's been drinking a lot. I don't drink, so I figure I should feel okay about the occasional bad habit."

After the curve along the lakefront houses' hedges, they approached downtown Southampton, greeted by a glowing red stoplight beside the pyramid of cannonballs and the antique cannon at the intersection. Corey wanted to say something that didn't have to do with the thin man's body or the chase or how he'd hit his mom's boss so hard they'd spied on him to make sure he didn't die of a brain hemorrhage, but nothing else came to him.

He'd been thinking about Angelique for so long, wondering if he'd only imagined her flirting with him last summer, hoping all those smiles when they'd spoken in the house or by the pool had been her way of sending signals that he should ask her out. Although he'd reached a point where he'd been much more relaxed around her by Labor Day, after looking through windows and lingering on the roof so he could be close to her tonight, he now felt he was sitting on a giant eggshell, one stupid line away from fucking everything up. He'd imagined plenty of scenarios with her, but never one remotely like this—thrust together after a sudden whirlwind of violence, fleeing the scene of more than one crime. He couldn't slip up now, and yet the silence continued eating the oxygen in the truck cab. Feeling the pressure to say something, anything, he ended up rambling, "So then, uh—why don't you? You know, why don't you drink?"

"Long story," she said, exhaling a drag out her window.

"Sorry," he said. "Maybe I shouldn't have asked that."

"No, it's okay. It's not that I wouldn't want to talk about it, it's just literally a long story." She faced him and he flashed another quick glance away from the road, thankful to be in the low light of the truck cab. Otherwise she'd have seen his face had turned beet red.

"All I can think about now is seeing Tiff's dad when he leaned down and kissed that dead man," she said. "I mean, how fucked up was that?"

Corey downshifted for the upcoming curve, figuring the best way to avoid saying something stupid would be to not say anything at all.

"Did you see Tiff's dad with that guy when they were in the pool, before he died?"

*Fuck,* he thought, *how do I answer without giving myself away?* He inhaled smoke to delay, hyperconscious that he still had to walk a tightrope.

"He didn't kill him," he said. "Not sure if you knew that already."

"He didn't? What happened, then?"

"That other guy hit his head, I think. Then maybe he drowned, or else hitting his head might have done it. Or maybe he OD'd first. I don't know for sure about that part, but I think they were both pretty wasted."

Hoping he hadn't already given away too much, Corey gripped the steering wheel tighter, noting distractedly that the ash from his cigarette was beginning to curl. He braced for her next question, sifting through a handful of flimsy reasons why he might have been at the estate in the middle of the night. The best excuse he could come up with was that he'd left something there when he'd been working with his mother, his wallet maybe—and since he needed it and couldn't wait until morning, he'd thought he'd sneak in when nobody was home and pick it up. Innocent enough, right? No harm done, nothing creepy there. Would she believe that? What bullshit. Of course she wouldn't.

A set of headlights from a car in the other lane

began expanding and brightening, and Corey squinted as Angelique said, "So, do you know who that guy was?"

"Not really."

He made a show of shielding his eyes with his hand until the car in the other lane passed, hoping to appear distracted long enough by the bright headlights for a lull in the conversation, which worked—she didn't ask another follow-up question, and for the next few minutes they sat in silence while Corey drove outside of Southampton along a farm road that would take them through North Sea, Noyack and Sag Harbor, all the way to East Hampton if they decided to go that far. He let out a breath, his knuckles finally relaxed enough to take his left hand off the steering wheel and to flick his cigarette butt out the window. She did the same before settling in on her side with the posture and sharply focused gaze of someone who'd just awoken from night terrors—her knees bent at her chest, one arm hugging them tightly, the other shoulder braced against the door, one of her fingernails between her teeth.

Corey drove them down long stretches of country roads, resisting the temptation to sound smart by telling her that most of the farms out there were owned by CEOs like Leo Sheffield, or by famous actors, or by other multimillionaires who didn't have a drop of ancestral blood connecting them to this rich soil or the rugged family-farm way of life. They passed rows of lettuce and cabbage, railings with grape vines, fenced-off fields where horses roamed during the daylight. He thought more about the land, how it would have been converted by then to businesses or perfect green lawns for perfectly ugly condos or McMansions if the wealthy landowners who'd purchased so much of it years ago hadn't wanted the area to feel like an escape from the city. They'd encapsulated their sliver of the country life, preserved their own quaint idea of the countryside by renewing the black-and-white images of eastern Long Island from back when the locals and a small population of visitors lived in simpler times, the period when life revolved around the harvest. The landowners out here had invested in the narratives they'd read about in coffee table books and seen in films and television shows based in the bucolic setting of the old Hamptons. For a fraction of their extravagant wealth, they could own their own wide vistas with rows of vegetables that would be sold at roadside stands, or horse corrals and hay fields, or rolling acres of wine grapes growing fatter on the vines, plumping in the sun.

But Corey also knew the main reason many of these farms, at least those with a summer home on the property, had been resurrected or kept alive. They made for an interesting conversation piece at cocktail parties in Manhattan or other Hamptons summer homes. Hosts like the Sheffields could say things like, "Oh, meet the so-and-sos, they have five acres in Sagaponack, and the lettuce in our salads came straight from their farm!" His thoughts drifted further and he fell into imagining what farmers in the Midwest or down South, or especially the peasants who worked the land in third world countries would think of these "farms" of the Hamptons.

Angelique rolled up her window, which cut the sound of rushing air and disentangled him from the sweeping thoughts about these towns out on the East End, where some of the richest people in the world owned these views on either side of the road, where they arrived from the city after driving past the exit for the less desirable area where he'd grown up in a tiny house raised by a single mom. This girl next to him . . . what did she know about how he and his family lived? Could he blame someone who came from tons of money for not understanding his life? For the first time in all the hours of daydreaming about seeing her again, he felt a quiver of doubt, and began squirming in his seat at the thought that he may have built her up too much to see her as a real person, flaws and all, and that maybe his pot-laced daydreams over the past year had turned her into a fantasy.

"That look in his eyes," Angelique said absently.

"I'll never forget that look when he was on top of me."

Corey kept his focus on the road and leaned into the curve, his blood pressure rising now as he envisioned Mr. Sheffield slamming her to the ground. He started to answer, "Maybe we should still call—" but she cut in.

"That look," she said, "that was so—just so fucking *crazy* . . . But the guy in the pool, I don't even know what to think of that. You're sure he didn't kill him?"

"Pretty sure."

"Then why didn't he call someone? And why drag him into the woods? And before that, why did he fucking *kiss* him?"

"I think he loved him," Corey said, flashing back to the two men on the balcony. "But I don't know why he dragged him all the way out there, either. I think he was drunk, maybe coked-up, too. He could've just panicked, I guess."

"Love?" Angelique sounded appalled.

He shrugged with both hands still on the wheel. "It's not like he's happily married or anything. You probably know better than I do that Leo and Sheila don't exactly like each other that much. But maybe he always just wanted to be with a guy." Angelique turned her head toward him, expressionless when he glanced over. The engine noise and sound of the tires against the road filled the space before he added, "It surprised me, too, though."

"Why haven't we called the police yet?"

"And tell them what? I don't mean we shouldn't—just saying."

She fidgeted and pulled her knees back up to her chest. "I have no idea what to do now. Or what to say to Tiff. No fucking clue."

"Want me to drive you to the city? I will if you want."

"I can't go back there."

"The Sheffield house or the city?"

"Both, I guess. But definitely not the city."

"What? Why not?"

She stared out her side window and didn't answer right away. When she did, she sounded much more tired than she had since they'd begun driving. "I was supposed to stay with Tiff and her family for the whole summer before I go back to school. I don't really have a place to live otherwise." She tapped a cigarette from the pack and took Corey's lighter but didn't strike it. "But that's another story. An even longer one."

"You can tell me," he said. "I mean, if you feel like it." He pressed in the clutch and let the truck roll in neutral as they came to a Stop sign where the farm road had looped back south and ended at Montauk Highway.

"Thanks," she said. "Maybe later. I'm pretty fried right now." She tucked her legs on the seat and sat cross-legged. With his foot on the brake, Corey angled his head toward the driver's-side window and gazed up at the stars. A strange new feeling overtook him when his view returned to the windshield and he looked both ways, a sense that he and Angelique had survived some sort of apocalyptic event, that they were now the last two people on earth. Then he realized the root of that thought, as he recalled hearing the young man mention something like that on the balcony just before Corey had begun climbing up the roof.

He turned and faced her while she stared through the windshield at the empty highway. Almost no traffic at all this late, this early, during this purgatory time between days. 4:30 a.m. The sun would be rising sometime in the next hour or so. He had to decide which way to turn but wasn't sure why one direction would be better than the other. They could go anywhere. The school year was over aside from his graduation ceremony, and he didn't really need to be there for that. He didn't have to be anywhere all summer other than at the Sheffield estate to work with his mother, and he could probably wriggle out of that as well, except then he'd need to scrape together some money somehow. If he decided to enroll in one of the state colleges that had offered scholarships, he still wouldn't need to be anywhere near the Hamptons until he moved up to the campus in August. And if he called Gina from some other state, or even from across the Canadian border, what could she really say? He wasn't a kid anymore. Thanks to her and Ray and their drinking and fighting, and also for having to look out for Dylan and most of his fuck-up friends these past few years, he'd already been way too grown-up for way too long. The panicky feeling returned. He still couldn't imagine leaving them, but with all that had happened tonight, he also couldn't imagine staying.

He flicked the right blinker on, then switched to the left, then flicked that off and stared at the Stop sign. Life on the Island, especially once you were out on one of the forks, meant you always had only two paths to choose from. East or west. Getting far away seemed the only smart move, but still, he couldn't decide which way to go.

"Hey," she said, with a hand on his arm, "can we drive to the ocean?"

Thankful to have a destination, he nodded and shifted gears while making a right turn. They drove west and passed through two or three towns along Montauk Highway without talking and without seeing another car on the road, then crossed the Southampton town line and approached a red stoplight and a cluster of shops off to the right. The light switched to green before Corey even had to downshift. Still no other cars, only the blazing fluorescence from the gas station mini-mart, with a hunched older man at the counter and an eighteen-wheeler parked diagonally in the lot while a worker refilled the underground tanks.

"You know what's really crazy?" Corey said. "I'm supposed to meet my mom at the Sheffield house in about four hours. I'm supposed to work there all weekend."

Angelique's head turned sharply. "Are you gonna go?"

The fantasy of driving to Canada or somewhere way out west had never taken hold, since he knew all along that he barely had enough gas money to make it halfway up the island, and didn't have a passport, either. He sighed as he answered, "Yeah, I kind of have to show up. But Leo never saw me. I really don't think he did, anyway."

"Good thing for you he didn't."

"I wonder what would happen if I dropped you off there in the morning, a little while before I start work."

She shook her head. "No, I don't think that would be a good idea."

"You didn't do anything wrong, though. And where else can you go for now?"

"Anywhere." She shuddered. "Anywhere but there."

"Wait, but think about it. He definitely won't want anything about tonight to come out, so you have all the power. Maybe you say something when you first see him, like you figure there'd been some kind of accident with the guy in the

143

pool, and as long as he doesn't do anything crazy again like he did when he went after you last night, you won't tell. I bet he kisses your ass all summer."

The idea sounded crazy even as it came from his mouth, but when he glanced over at her with her knees up to her chin she seemed to be considering what he'd said.

During the fifteen or twenty minutes that followed, he continued driving west through Southampton and into Hampton Bays, and then headed south, steering through quiet residential neighborhoods of his hometown en route to the ocean. They crossed the Ponquogue Bridge surrounded by bay water and with the first hints of morning blue tinting the horizon, the moon hanging low, stars still dotting most of the black above them but now with a thin strip of indigo hovering at the horizon.

At the base of the bridge, he turned right and drove down to L Road, a bumpy sand-covered patch that dead-ended at the dunes. They stepped out of the truck and walked past the guardrail accompanied by the sound of white water rolling in and crashing rhythmically on the shore. Angelique's hair whipped and whirled in the wind. She paused once the breaking waves came into view, and held her arms to her chest.

"You cold?" he asked, already wriggling an arm from his sweatshirt. She shrugged and grinned, and within a second he'd slipped the heavy shirt over his head and handed it to her. "Here," he said, and when she half-heartedly waved him off, he repeated, "Really, here."

"Are you actually for-real this nice, or are you just on your best behavior because I had such a shitty night?"

"Just being myself, I hope."

"I guess we'll see about that," she said, and slipped the sweatshirt on.

"Want to sit for a while?"

She answered by taking him by the hand and dropping down onto the sand next to him. As crazy as the night had been, in one way anyway, things couldn't have turned out better. Until then he usually hadn't had the opportunity to talk with her for more than a few minutes at a time, not with Tiffany around, not while on the clock at the estate, where Sheila Sheffield kept him in perpetual motion rearranging lawn furniture or staking down tiki torches or carrying something from one floor of the house to another. But here they were, sitting together at the ocean, and Angelique was wearing his shirt.

"So, I guess I'll start," she said, and only then did he realize she'd been staring, waiting for him to speak. "You asked why I don't drink, right?"

Shivering, he answered, "Only if you want to say."

"It's fine. I want to tell you. It's not because I'm

an alcoholic or anything. My sister is six years older, and she— Oh shit, you're cold, aren't you? I feel bad you gave me this. You can sit closer if that'll help."

Corey's face filled with heat and for a moment he didn't feel cold at all.

"Okay," he said, nervous about how close *closer* meant. Then he scooched over a few inches but left almost a foot of space between them.

"I mean you can actually have your arm against my arm, so I'll block the wind for you."

"I just didn't want to . . . It's just that I—" He moved over more until their arms pressed together at the shoulder, and mumbled, "Sorry, I feel like an idiot."

"It's all right." She placed a hand on his forearm, quickly rubbing it to warm his skin.

He gulped, and immediately cursed himself for being so awkward that he actually gulped.

"So, you were saying something about your sister?"

"Oh yeah," she said. "It could take a while to get into details, but the short version is that Carrie—that's her name—she went to about five rehabs by the time she was twenty-one, for drinking and for a lot of drugs. She took off with a guy to live in some kind of commune somewhere upstate about six months ago, and I haven't heard from her except for one letter right after she left.

I'm not sure if she's still clean, but the guy she hooked up with was a fucking whacko, so who knows what the place they're living in is like, or if they're even still there. I only met him once and he was weird, like religious-zealot weird. I'm pretty worried but I don't know what I can do to convince her to come back. Anyway, because of her, my mom made me promise when I was still a kid that I wouldn't go down the same path Carrie did, so one of the things I told her before she passed away was that I'd never have even a sip of alcohol, and it's still true."

"Sorry, when did she—when did your mom pass away?"

"A few months ago."

Corey watched her cradle a handful of sand and let it sift through her fingers, the grains flying off sideways in the wind.

"I was eight," he said. "My dad, though."

Angelique turned and faced him. "How? Or, I mean, what happened to him?"

"Motorcycle accident. He moved out of our house way before, when I was little, and my brother and I didn't see him after that. I guess I never really knew him, but it was still hard when he died. My mom got remarried a few years ago, but that's already pretty much over now."

"My dad's married, too."

"You like your stepmom?"

"I haven't met her."

147

A gust of wind snapped Corey's shirt like a flag in a nor'easter and stirred her hair like soft tentacles, sending much of it swirling over his face as he leaned sideways to speak directly into her ear. "I hope it's okay to ask this, too, but what did you mean when you said you don't have anywhere you can go?"

She pressed her palms to the sand and faced the ocean, leaning forward as a succession of waves broke and swept foamy layers of water up the shoreline slope, the pause lasting long enough that Corey wished he'd let her steer the conversation. But then she surprised him by edging closer and answering with her mouth only a few inches from his.

"Before my mom passed away we had a one-bedroom apartment in Brooklyn. Then the rent didn't get paid for a few months while she was in the hospital, so we got an eviction notice right after the funeral and I had to put all our stuff in storage during spring break. Since it's summer break from classes now, Tiff said I should stay with her in Southampton till next semester starts. But now that her father pulled that crazy shit, looks like I'm stuck for the next few months with no place to go."

Corey shivered so intensely he had trouble seeing straight. "What about staying with your dad?"

"He's been in prison since I was twelve." She

picked up a small shell from the sand and turned it in her fingers. "That's the thing," she said. "Tiff's the closest thing I have to family, and since there's no way I'm staying with her now . . . I guess I don't really live anywhere."

"What did your dad do to go to prison?"

"Basically, he's just a shitty person. Always has been from what I've heard."

"Sorry, I'm kind of confused. I thought your family had a lot of money."

She leaned back on her elbows as she laughed for a second, and then held the blowing hair from her face. "Nope, we never had much. I haven't talked to my dad since before he went away. My mom worked for Sheila Sheffield at her nonprofit, and when Tiff and I were little we met at their work and became super-close. I guess Tiff hadn't made friends with other kids at that point, so Sheila wanted her to get to see me more and decided to pay for me to go to the same private schools. She must have spent a few hundred thousand dollars—maybe even more—to send me there from the time I was five until I graduated last year, which is a big reason why my mom worked for her so long. I know she can be kind of bitchy sometimes, but Sheila's got her good side, too."

"Wow, I had no idea," Corey said. He placed his hand over hers and gently calmed her fidgeting as he balled her fingers over the shell. "I always thought you were rich like the Sheffields."

"Sorry to disappoint." Angelique shook her head and grinned. "But what you don't know about me could fill a dump truck."

"Alright, I'm starting to get that now." Still absorbing the new knowledge that she was just as working-class as him, he grinned back at her, nudging her with his shoulder. "So you're homeless in the Hamptons, and I spent all the money I have on that piece-of-shit truck we drove here in."

"Ain't we a pair," she said with a full smile. A sign, he hoped, that he should lean closer. And he did, to within a couple inches of her face, barely able to see with her hair blowing over his eyes.

He wanted to kiss her more than he'd wanted anything in his entire life, but wasn't sure if it would catch her off guard or freak her out, so he lingered there with his eyes perfectly aligned with hers for what felt like a long time. Then he finally heard her say, "Guess it's up to me, then, huh?" and her hair engulfed him, flowing all the way across the back of his head as her lips pressed against his.

He collapsed backward onto the sand, no longer aware of the cold or the slapping wind, no longer aware of the waves. He forgot all about knocking out and nearly killing Mr. Sheffield, and the dead body at the estate, and about how his mother expected him to show up for work there in a few hours. He forgot about her drinking her way into the hospital, and how much he hated Ray. He couldn't have cared less about any of the guys around town he'd thrown down with in recent months, or any of the other townies he didn't want to become. This . . . this erased it all.

He could have died right then and there and felt he'd lived a full life, because for the first time ever he didn't feel the need to escape this place. He wanted to be there—with her, and her alone. Nothing else mattered anymore, nothing other than her, nothing outside this lightly crushed feeling of her weight on top of him and their arms wrapped around one another—and the fact that, when he'd leaned in, she'd been the one to lean the rest of the way.

# FRIDAY

# THIRTEEN

Through her windshield Gina watched a small group of people congregated in the early-morning half-light beside the church wall, exchanging hugs, smoking and talking, a few of them laughing. Since she'd already committed to giving this a shot, she breathed out the anxiety and shut the engine off, thinking that if she didn't get the cult vibe and actually felt these meetings might help her stay sober, then all the better. But either way, she'd do her best to start the day with a dose of self-care before the Sheffields and the early guests arrived from the city.

The sun had just come up, ribbons of color still dissolving into a backlit mist of acrylic beyond the sandbox and swing set on the other side of the lot, where she imagined well-mannered children played while their parents held Bible studies inside one of the rooms with stained glass windows. The online meeting schedule had listed two choices for such an early hour, and this one was supposed to start in ten minutes. Today would be her test run. If these people by the wall and the others inside all turned out to be a bunch of Jesus freaks, so be it, she'd head to work after at least trying something new.

She closed her car door and rummaged through

her purse for a piece of gum, hobbling slightly thanks to the cuts on her foot from the broken glass yesterday afternoon. On her way to the entrance she glanced up and noticed a gray-haired woman by the church's side door, smiling at her. She'd hoped she could blend in and not have to make small talk with anyone, imagined she would sit in the back of the meeting and absorb whatever tips for staying sober those who spoke had to offer before leaving five minutes early, but now she'd already been roped into shaking hands with a stranger simply by making eye contact.

"Welcome," the woman said. "I'm Maryanne." One by one, three men of various ages and a woman much younger than Gina also shook her hand and introduced themselves, and when they finished Maryanne looked on warmly and asked, "Is this your first time here?"

"Is it that obvious?" Gina blushed, unsure why the mellow laughter from the small group comforted her.

"Oh no, honey," Maryanne said, "I'm here just about every morning, so I tend to notice new faces. Have you been to any other meetings?"

"This is my first meeting ever." Gina's own voice sounded foreign, meeker, as though a shy teenager had spoken for her.

"Welcome," the oldest of the men said. "You're in the right place." He had long gray hair pulled into a ponytail, janky teeth and faded, indecipherable tattoos on the backs of his hands. His clothes were pure biker—the worn leather jacket and chaps over his jeans, the heavyweight boots, the whole bit.

A pang in her chest, and out of nowhere Gina thought of Anthony, her first husband and the boys' biological father. They'd been no more than kids when they started dating, still kids when her plans for college a few years after high school derailed and Corey came along. Anthony had loved his old Valkyrie more than anything, and two years into their marriage, while Dylan was still a baby and Corey a toddler, he'd left a note on the kitchen table, an apology for taking off for the big summer rally out in Sturgis. The sentiment had tapered off with a promise to call from South Dakota and an estimate that he'd be back in a week or two, but he never called, and never came home. He'd left Gina to care for their two young sons on her own, and she'd known nothing of his whereabouts until that death notification from the police six years later. Having to tell the boys their father had passed away after that phone call . . . Irrational as she knew it was, she resented him for dying—for dying after living as he'd wanted to live, for disappearing from their lives, and then speeding down the California coast on Highway 1 and taking one of those cliff-fronted curves a few feet too wide.

The biker and the young woman stubbed out

their cigarettes in a five-gallon bucket filled with sand, and everyone aside from Gina began moving toward the door. She couldn't take the first step yet. Although she felt a degree of gratitude for their kindness, her driver's seat tugged at her like a high-powered magnet. If she went inside with them and committed to this, wouldn't she have to keep coming to church basements like this one—and bare her soul or listen to sob stories or whatever these people did—for the rest of her life? That's how it worked, wasn't it? Her neck tensed as though it had been clapped in irons. She couldn't do it. She should think of an excuse to turn around and hurry to her car and leave, maybe say something about her kids, or rattle off an abbreviated story about how she forgot something at home that needed to be taken care of before work. But the thought of lying made her even more anxious. These smiling people, especially Maryanne, seemed to have some deep insight into Gina's story after knowing her for only thirty seconds, and they would all know her excuse was exactly that—bullshit—and for some reason she already cared about what they thought of her.

"Well," Maryanne said, "looks like it's about that time." She placed her hand on Gina's back as a gentle directive after the rest of the group filed in ahead of them. They stepped through the doorway and down a set of echoing stairs, through another doorway and into a starkly decorated room with beige cinder block walls and rows of metal folding chairs.

An elderly man with an old fedora sitting cockeyed on his head noodled around on the keys of a very old upright piano in the corner. Roughly twenty other people stood or sat, scattered about the basement, many of them a decade or so older than Gina, but also some closer to her age, as well as a few with baby faces, and one or two who looked so old it may not have been a stretch to say they'd been alive during prohibition. A group of four stood by a large coffee urn with disposable cups in hand while most others began choosing their chairs, and a bald man with a red-and-gray beard sat behind a battered old desk talking to a few men and women in the front row. Gina scanned the two boards hanging on the wall just above the bald man's head, each with sentences spelled out in Old English font, the lines numbered one through twelve. She noticed the word *God* came up from time to time, and again had a moment of panic when excuses to flee rushed through her mind like white water.

Then Maryanne tapped her shoulder and handed her a small piece of paper. "That's my number," she said. "You don't have a sponsor yet, do you?"

"No," Gina said, nearly swallowing her gum. "Honestly, I'm not sure I'm looking for one."

Maryanne smiled. "Trust me, you want one. Think of me as your temporary sponsor for now. I don't usually do this, but something about you makes me want to offer this time."

"Really?" Gina's posture softened, her thoughts suddenly freed from the critical filter. Although she hadn't vocally accepted, the absence of a refusal seemed to suffice for each of them. The bearded man in the front of the room knocked twice on the surface of the desk and everybody not already seated found a chair, the metal legs creaking and scuffing against the cement floor as they settled in. Gina had seen a few movies and TV shows with people in AA meetings, but couldn't believe she was actually sitting in one herself. The idea of introducing herself as an alcoholic in a room full of strangers set her heart beating way too fast. She glanced at Maryanne, thinking she had a maternal air about her and yet also some obvious experience in the trenches. A mama bear, equal parts caregiver and badass. Now that Gina had a moment for it to set in that Maryanne had offered to be her sponsor, even though she had no clear understanding of what that meant, she felt as if she'd just won the lottery.

*Maybe I can do this,* she thought. *Maybe being sober won't be so bad.*

The man at the desk handed out three laminated sheets and asked a few people to read, and then the chairperson spoke about how he'd felt like an outsider as a kid, went into his drinking as a teen, and at some point skipped ahead to his troubled first marriage. Although Gina intended to listen, she drifted back and forth from the room to her own recent memories, finally subsumed by the aftermath of her awful make-out session with Ray yesterday afternoon, and the hazy space that followed, when she'd regained consciousness in the ambulance.

The last thing she'd heard before the slam of the ambulance doors had been the voice of her best friend, Cindy, calling Gina's youngest son by name and telling him he could ride with her. Thank God for Cindy, but Dylan had seen her like this—his mother, a drugged and drunken disaster. Broken glass and a puddle of wine on the living room floor, blood and vomit on the comforter and God knows where else. The ambulance siren cut through her thoughts. Fingers pried an eyelid wide and a bright light blinded her. Something cold pressed against her chest. Machines beeped and rippled. The whole vehicle shuffled and rocked while the driver gunned the engine and weaved through traffic. Gina strained to say, "Please," but her tongue fought against the back of her throat and refused to finish the sentence. Her hands clenched but still no sound escaped. A paramedic with a deep voice said she shouldn't try to speak.

And later that night, after having her stomach pumped, she'd spent what felt like hours speaking to two different doctors for the psych evaluation, her frustration growing the longer she pleaded for them to believe that she hadn't intended to go so far overboard with the pills and wine, until finally she convinced them she hadn't attempted suicide, and the nurses allowed her to see Dylan and Cindy. Her youngest son entered the room and stood beside her hospital bed picking at his thumbnail, his hair hanging past his chin when he leaned down.

"You okay, Ma?"

Gina nodded and met his eyes with hers. "You shouldn't have to worry about me."

"It's all right."

"No, it's not."

Laughter in the meeting room crept in, dissolving the memory of those first steps of her walk of shame down that immaculate hospital hall with her hand on Dylan's shoulder and her best friend's arm around her. She opened her eyes and focused on the gray chair backs and heads directly in front of her, only then realizing she'd had them closed. Maryanne listened intently to the woman sharing, with her head turned toward her and a wide smile. Gina did her best to listen but seemed to have missed a key portion of the story, the funny part, and eventually drifted once more, caught up in a flurry of looping thoughts about Ray, and the boys, and the weekend ahead at the Sheffield estate, all of it finally blending into a ball of noise fueled by worry. She heard fragments of a few more shares but somehow the rest of the hour whisked by, and suddenly the chairperson announced that the meeting had come to an end.

Unsure what had just happened or why sitting in a room with these people held a slight appeal, she promised herself she would come back tomorrow. If she were on her own, she might not bother with any of this weird self-help shit, but she was desperate to be a good mother more than ever before, more than she'd ever wanted anything for herself. And because of that, she would come back.

On their way out, about halfway up the stairs, Maryanne took her by the elbow. "So let's just start off by you calling me at least once a day, and also anytime you feel triggered to drink."

Gina agreed and thanked her, and when they stepped outside into the daylight, Maryanne gave her a firm hug, and after a few beats still didn't let go. "All you have to do is get through today, and then we'll start over tomorrow," she said, releasing her grip. "Take care, hon. You can do this."

Gina crossed the parking lot in a daze, closed her car door and buckled her seat belt, but waited to turn the key. She fell into a different sort of trance than she had in the basement, staring through her windshield in a dream state, analyzing the small crowd beside the church wall one by one. The biker handing a cigarette to a short man with a potbelly and a mustache; a woman in a business suit who'd shared something about dating in sobriety, leaning in to hug the bald man who'd led the meeting . . . *Who were these people?*

Gina's stomach turned. The peace she'd felt moments ago had already vanished and the marathon of work at the Sheffield estate awaited like a hangman's noose. Memorial Day weekend, the billionaire family and their spoiled grown children and a troupe of entitled guests—for the twelfth consecutive summer Gina needed to suck it up and do what she had to do in order to hold on to a job that had whittled her down a bit more each year.

She turned the key and the CD in her stereo began playing the same Beatles song she'd been listening to when she arrived—"Yesterday." She let the music swallow her, letting go as she let Paul McCartney do that thing with his voice and his words where pure warmth seeped into her bloodstream through her skin. She closed her eyes and let her hands rest at her sides. If only things could be that way . . . all her troubles, so far away . . .

All ten fingers curled around the wheel, all

squeezing tightly. She opened her eyes as the song faded down to its end, thinking she might still have enough time for a twenty- or thirty-minute nap before having to head to the Sheffield estate, a nap she desperately needed now that she'd awoken to the fact that, after returning from the hospital, she really hadn't slept at all last night.

Her car rolled slowly to the parking lot's edge and she shut off the stereo. She paused there with her right-hand blinker flashing and her new sponsor centered in the rearview mirror. The sun had just finished rising. She had to get to work soon. If not for Leo Sheffield intervening on her behalf last summer, first when she showed up horribly hungover, and later when she broke Sheila's precious fucking chalice, his wife would have fired her. She needed to show up this morning in good form.

Suddenly, a powerful vision of her sitting alone in a bar and ordering straight whiskey popped into her brain. It made no sense at all; she didn't even like whiskey. Plus, it was seven in the morning, and she hadn't even left the property where the AA meeting had taken place. But now that she'd thought about whiskey, she could taste it—that first sip.

And that's when Gina knew she was truly fucked. No two ways about it, she *needed* a drink. Goddamn it, did she ever.

# FOURTEEN

Angelique opened her eyes to threads of Easter egg colors bleeding away from the lava-red dome of the rising sun. She watched the birds spiraling and calling out in the soft orange light that bathed their feathers and blanketed the beach, hoping this sense of safety with Corey wouldn't end once the sun rose higher above them and the day began for the rest of the world. His arms around her supplied some key element she'd been missing, something substantial and warm in the base of her stomach, along with a hum radiating along her spine. Something with weight as well, like an anchor. He kept her from floating away.

Even so, Mr. Sheffield's face continued creeping in, poisoning her peace with worry—his bloodshot eyes and the spit flying from his mouth when he'd shouted. The lack of air when his entire body had pressed her down. She couldn't fathom crossing paths with him ever again. How could she explain that to Tiffany?

With her mouth next to Corey's ear, she whispered, "You awake?"

"Sort of," he said, shifting his shoulder on the sand.

"How long now until you have to be back there?"

He held her tighter as he answered, "A couple hours or so," his voice trailing off into a yawn.

Her eyelids sank for a moment, but then her throat tightened and she sat up straight, Mr. Sheffield's crazed face returning in a close-up. "I can't go there," she said, her voice flittering. "Seriously, you have to help me figure this out. What am I going to do?"

As if he'd just snapped out of a much calmer dream than her snapshot nightmares, he propped himself on an elbow and faced her, the sunrise light enhancing his cheekbones and jawline and setting an orange spark in each eye. "I just had an idea."

"Okay, what?"

He sat up straighter. "You don't want to stay there, and I don't really want you to go back, either. But you'd need money if you didn't, right?"

"Yeah, so?"

"Well, Leo Sheffield has plenty."

"What are you saying—ask him for some?"

"No, more like *tell* him an amount to give you—so you'll stay quiet."

"You're saying I should blackmail him?"

He looked at her without blinking. A long pause crept by.

"Yeah," he finally said, "but let's not call it that."

Angelique plunged her fingers into the chilled

sand and stared out at the cords of white water rolling in to the shore. After all those conversations that she'd prompted last summer and the summer before, it had always been obvious that Corey was a good guy, a puppy dog with muscles, and she loved the way he looked at her, especially since they arrived here at the beach, as though he'd never imagined a girl could be so beautiful. Add to that, he'd saved her from harm, and may have in fact saved her life. Trust had never come easily, but when it came down to who she trusted to help her through the next phase of this insane situation, at this point the list of names began and ended with Corey. And yet his suggestion struck her as crazy. *Tell the father of my oldest friend to give me a bag of money, or else threaten that I'll go to the cops?*

"I'm not sure I can," she said. "I just can't imagine saying the words."

He didn't push, instead he sat beside her and held her close, both of them facing the water. A few minutes passed, and the longer she stared out at the sunrise over the ocean and contemplated his loose plan, the less scary and more plausible it became. Maybe she could do it. She hadn't been an angel all her life, not by any means, so who knows, blackmail might come easier than she'd first imagined. She watched the waves breaking on the shore, thinking about her less-than-proudest moments over the years, like the first time she stuck something under her coat and walked out of a high-end clothing store without paying, back when she was twelve, and then how she'd shoplifted dozens more times throughout her early teens. And much worse, that period a bit later when she and Tiff teamed up and enacted a bullying campaign against Jane Nelson, after Jane "stole" the guy Tiff had been crushing on, Jane finally defeated when her mom checked her into a rehab for eating disorders. And just a month ago, when she called Brad and said she took a pregnancy test and it came back positive, then didn't return his calls or texts, and instead let him stew on the prospect of being a nineteen-year-old dad for a couple days, just to get some payback after he'd cheated on her. Even though Brad *had* acted like a creep and deserved some stress in his cushy Upper East Side life, this had been a new low. Brad may have deserved it, but Jane hadn't. Remorse couldn't erase the damage done, no matter how much Angelique wished it could have.

No, she hadn't been a saint, far from it. But she'd never threatened to take someone away from his family by sending him to prison, something she knew a bit about thanks to her convict father. Yeah, Tiff's dad had done a horrible thing when he chased her down, and maybe another *really* horrible thing if Corey had been wrong about him not killing the guy in the pool, but what exactly should she say to get the money?

*Don't overthink it,* she thought. Leo Sheffield must have been on the verge of cracking by then, probably way more scared than she and Corey. He'd do what she asked, because she could end him with a phone call or a short statement in person at the nearest precinct. He'd pay, and as long as she convinced him she would keep his secrets safe, he'd be glad enough to do it.

Corey's arm around her shoulders and his calm energy allowed her to play the tape all the way to the end. At least he had an idea. And what other option did she have? If she decided against returning to the Sheffield house, she realized she had no plan B for the day whatsoever, not even a seed of an idea aside from running off without a destination, penniless and without even a spare change of clothes—without even a pair of shoes. She couldn't take off without money, obviously, and Tiffany couldn't help because she never saved any of the money that Leo put on her debit card. She had no doubt that Corey would have given her whatever money he could scrape together, but it seemed safe to assume he was dead broke, just like her.

"Okay," she finally said. "If I do this, though, how much should I ask for? Or I guess I should say, how much do I tell him he has to give me?"

"Not sure," Corey said, shivering as the wind

picked up. "How much do you guess he could come up with in cash over the weekend?"

She bit her bottom lip and ran through a series of figures before answering. "Ten, maybe twenty thousand?"

"More than that," he said, hunched forward with his arms tight against his ribs, clenching his jaw when a gust blew his T-shirt halfway up his back. "The guy's worth over a billion. I'm betting he has a lot more than ten or twenty grand already in the house. And I bet if you scare him bad enough it won't take him long to come up with a lot more."

"Okay, yeah, that's all fine and good, but it's a holiday weekend, so how's he going to get huge stacks of cash when all the banks are closed?"

"To start, he has a wall safe in the master bedroom. I'd say there's a good chance he has at least a hundred grand in there, maybe more, maybe way more. Really, what the hell else would he have a safe in his summerhouse for? If you tell him a number, whatever he says, he can at least give you what's in there first. Why wouldn't he? Anything less than a million is like pocket change to a guy like him, anyway."

"So how about I tell him a million?"

She'd said it without really thinking, more as a joke than anything. But then she watched Corey consider the amount, the sunrise colors like bonfire flames overlaid upon his pupils. He sat up straight. His jaw relaxed. He grinned, and then she did as well. No need for another word now that he'd begun easing his face over, each of their grins much wider just before he kissed her.

She kept her eyes open at first, watching the bottom edge of the sun break free from the horizon. Then she closed them, and kissed him back.

# FIFTEEN

After leaving Henry hidden in the woods and trudging a slow zigzag back to the house, Leo labored from step to step upstairs, the pain in his head unbearable by the time he walked the second-floor hall and reached Tiffany's bedroom doorway. He peered in, his eyes immediately watering over at the sight of her sleeping face. Born six weeks premature, so impossibly tiny during those early hours in the pediatric unit, Tiffany had grown to have the strongest personality, or at least the most brutally honest one, of anyone in the family. Though for reasons beyond his comprehension, while she was so quick to criticize her mother and brothers for their decadence and self-centeredness and their opulently wealthy circles of friends, she still allowed Leo an undeserved pass; even at this contentious age, he remained on a pedestal in her mind, the same one where she'd placed him as a child. *She'd slept through it all tonight,* he thought. *Thank God she hadn't seen.*

Back in the master bedroom, while gathering his clothes from the bedspread and floor, he found his cell phone and discovered a missed call from Sheila that had come right around when he and Henry had arrived at the estate. Her voice-mail message awaited him. No way in hell did he have the capacity to listen to it now. She would be here soon enough, too soon. Too many people would be here, and far too soon.

Feeling as though he'd gained a thousand pounds overnight, Leo walked slowly back downstairs and into the kitchen, where he flung open the freezer door, dropped handfuls of ice into a large plastic bag and wrapped it in a dish towel. On his way out of the house, he pressed the cold compress to his head while scrolling through his texts with Gina from last summer. The final one had been his apology for not speaking up when Sheila tore into Gina for breaking the crystal chalice. The rest of the text thread from earlier in the summer consisted mainly of his panicky requests for her to cover for him with Sheila in a variety of ways, and her responding with comforting assurances, more than once stating: I'll take care of it. She'd been the one to buy his wife an appropriately glittery necklace with his platinum card after he'd forgotten their anniversary, the one who so often had appeased her on his behalf, and yet Sheila consistently treated her like shit. This poor woman—with a white-trash husband and two teenaged boys to raise on her own—she'd been the one Leo had trusted over the years to bail him out or to keep his secrets or to hold her tongue when he spun some fiction in regard to his whereabouts, when

174

the truth had been that he'd come out to the estate midweek to escape Sheila. For years now, Gina had been the only person he could rely on to lie for him. If ever he needed her help, he needed it now.

As he made his way over to the pool, though he had no clear idea what he even could say to her, he called her. By the third or fourth ring he realized that she wasn't going to answer. Her voice-mail greeting played. Leo cleared his throat and muttered something about needing help, his words hanging in the air while he squinted at the screen and fumbled with the phone to end the call. Gina would be here to start her workday within the hour, but she couldn't help. No one could. No help was on the way. He would receive no quarter, no shelter from this unthinkable, nightmarish storm. No time now even to sleep. He had to think. If only his head would stop throbbing, maybe he could make it through the day and somehow move Henry off the property during the night.

The blood. He still needed to check the border of the pool for blood. Kneeling, he inspected the stairs and handrail, and then from there hobbled along on all fours like a wounded bear, his eyes focused on the charcoal-gray stone coping, section by section, until he'd journeyed the entire perimeter and, surprisingly, found nothing.

Staggering to his feet sapped the last wisp of

175

his energy. The stabbing pain in his skull nearly blinded him. He reached back to touch the wound, his pulse suddenly racing as he flashed to the moment he'd awoken on the lawn and squinted at his own blood on his hand.

*Who the hell hit me? Aside from Tiffany and her friend, who else would have been here late at night?* He looked toward the spot on the lakeside lawn where the memory ended, wiping sweat from his face with the back of his hand, now even more confused. *And how were they right behind me, right there to knock me out a second after Angelique and I fell to the ground?*

He gripped the handrail like a crutch. He needed to rest, needed to think.

*Whoever it was, they must have seen me with Henry . . . Oh my God . . . Someone knows . . .*

Time passed as Leo sat cockeyed on one of the lounge chairs beside the pool with an elbow on one knee and the bag of ice pressed to the back of his head, staring at the water, his vision like that of an old television set with poor reception, blurring between two channels. Closing one eye, for a moment he saw only an empty pool, its soft surface sheened by morning light swirling away from the return jets. In the next moment, day abruptly returned to night and Henry floated there a few yards away, once again under a veil of moonlight, once again with arms outstretched;

176

though now, instead of panic, Leo felt what he could only guess might be the palm of a benevolent hand on his shoulder, leading him to the warm water with the silver tray in hand, toward a living, breathing image of Henry.

Straining to block the morning birdsongs from his mind, Leo closed both eyes and let the ice pack fall from his wound, now hunched in a position similar to that of Rodin's *The Thinker*, spellbound by the vivid, cinematic delusion playing behind his eyelids. He breathed in the slow-motion scene, recalling it all now in detail—the feel of the grass beneath his feet as he approached the water, the soft serenade of crickets as he set down the bottle and tray and stepped into the water with a film of steam whirling at his calves. Henry floating a few yards away, swiveling from his back and fanning his arms, gently kicking, his eyes beaming as he swam closer to the stairs, smiling while he kept his head low in the shallow end and coyly asked if Leo cared to join him. And the night had gone on from there without a false note, hour after hour had been a perfectly orchestrated water dance, until—

Voices of men speaking Spanish sounded in the distance, and a moment after, motors of landscaping machines ripped to life. Leo's elbow slipped from his knee and he tumbled from the chair. Lying on the grass, he stared at the vacant pool, the light of the fully risen sun now reflecting the nearby oak branches in the faintly swirling current. He pushed himself up and leaned against the chair, looking in the direction of the woods, where his epic trek with Henry had ended just before dawn. No help was on the way. Henry was out there, wrapped in a blanket. Dead.

# SIXTEEN

Gina had planned on a tiny catnap between the meeting and her drive to work, but after sleeping so little the night before, the nap consisted of a few odd minutes of tortured dreams and three smacks of the snooze button. She dragged herself out of bed and stood before the full-length mirror hanging from her closet door. Her hair was matted on one side and frizzed out with static on the other. She looked like an aging groupie in her old Pink Floyd T-shirt and her favorite pair of blue-and-white-polka-dot pajama pants. Her reflection stared back with red puffy eyes. She'd been rubbing them throughout the night and during the past half hour while praying for sleep that hadn't come. An hour or so ago, in the meeting, she couldn't recall anyone mentioning insomnia or how this insidious side effect not only thwarted any attempts at rest in early sobriety, but also emboldened her inner critic, who'd picked her apart while she tossed and turned and sweated against the sheets.

She left the mirror and peered out the window at the driveway, relieved not to see Ray's truck. A second after, her stomach sank when she registered the absence of Corey's pickup as well.

No big secret that he went out drinking with

his friends, but as far as she knew he'd never stayed out all night without at least sending a text. She checked her cell phone. No messages. Anger welled up as she imagined him showing up late to work at the Sheffields', or hungover, or both. Then she pictured him unconscious in an overturned truck with blood on his face, and rushed into the hall and swung open her sons' bedroom door.

"Dylan, wake up."

His head turned on the pillow and he groaned, "What time is it?"

"It's early, and I have to leave soon. Where's Corey?"

"I don't know. I texted him that we were at the hospital but didn't see him last night."

"He didn't say where he was going? Sit up for a minute, open your eyes."

"Jeez, Ma." He pushed the tangled strands of hair from his face and shoved the blanket from his shoulders. "I have no idea where he is. I haven't seen him for, like, a week. Can I go back to sleep, please?"

She stomped out without closing the door, returned to her bedroom and pulled open the dresser drawers, piecing together the clothes for her twelve-hour workday. She should've gotten out of bed when her alarm first went off or not even bothered to lie down at all. Twenty minutes or so before she had to be in the car, so no time for a real breakfast. She'd call Corey while she drove.

First things she saw in the shower were Ray's disposable razor and dandruff shampoo sitting on the edge of the tub in the corner. *Goddamn him,* she thought, *how could he leave me like that on the bed for Dylan to find me?* She threw Ray's things into the bathroom trash can before stepping under the showerhead. All that remained now were those goddamned boxes by the back door, his jackets in the closet and one dresser drawer still stuffed with clothes. If he didn't get it all by the end of the weekend—and this was a promise to herself—she'd toss everything into the woods down the road. Or better yet, into the fucking ocean.

The shower curtain whipped closed and she positioned herself beneath the hot water. Her neck hurt. Her stomach grumbled. She needed coffee as much as a person had ever needed it. Twelve hours of work ahead of her. Twelve hours of smiling through frantic arranging and cleaning and pandering to the woman of the house, and that twelfth hour could stretch to a thirteenth, maybe more depending on Sheila's mood. Gina had signed on to slave away summer after summer, but always with a bottle of wine as the reward after these marathon days, sometimes also with a secret drink or two during work. How she'd managed to not take a drink during the past hour this morning, after thinking about it so intensely in the church parking lot, she had no idea. The water temperature from the shower steadily decreased, as it always did after a couple minutes, so she turned the Cold off and tried to appreciate the last minute of diminishing warmth.

As soon as she stepped out of the tub she heard someone knocking loudly on the front door. A moment later she froze in place when she heard Ray calling from the doorway, "Coming in," followed by his heavy footsteps in the living room. Swallowing hard, she stared at the puddle forming around her feet. *He must have broken in,* she thought, since she'd already changed the locks. Exhausted even by the thought of dealing with him, she quickly wrapped a towel around her body and cracked the bathroom door.

Ray's boots came stomping into the hall as Dylan's voice carried from his room. "Why won't anyone let me sleep!"

Ray answered with all the charm of a drill sergeant, "Rough fuckin' life you got here, *bed-wetter.*" A second later he stopped abruptly when Gina stepped into the hall as she imagined her new sponsor would, like a mama bear about to maul someone who'd come too close to her cub.

"Hey," he said, sounding surprised to see her.

"What did you just say to Dylan?"

"Oh, that? That was nothing. Playing with him is all." He turned his head and called out, "We're good, right, Dyl?"

Dylan muttered from his bedroom, "You are such a *dick*," and before Ray could react, Gina shoved a finger against his chest.

"You shouldn't be here."

"He's tired, so I'll forget he said that," Ray said, folding his arms. "Needed a ladder for the job site, and since you keep hounding me I thought I'd grab some clothes while I was here."

Gina felt nauseous, thinking back to how weak she'd been the last time he knocked on the door, kissing him, almost sleeping with him. "Don't ever talk to my son like that again," she said, pushing past him and entering the bedroom they'd shared for nearly three years. He followed while she spoke. "I've been asking you to get your stuff all week, and you show up unannounced right before my first day of hell weekend? *And* you insult Dylan, in *my* fucking house!"

"Jesus, G. Calm the fuck down."

"You left me for dead yesterday, do you realize that?"

"Drunk and dead are two very different things, honey pie."

"What are you even doing here? You don't live here anymore! You know what, I don't have time for this. Just get the hell out. I'm too tired to look at your face, let alone to deal with your bullshit."

"Christ sakes, first you tell me to leave when I don't have anywhere to go, it takes me a little time to get situated these past months, and then out of the blue you're all like, *Get your shit out right away or I'm dumping it on the curb?* Real nice. I've been sleeping on Jimmy's goddamned pull-out couch for how many weeks? My back is killing me. On top of that—you know, technically, I haven't said I'll give you a divorce."

"Are you fucking high?"

"Whether I am or not, I think we still have some talking to do, don't you?"

He grabbed her by the arm and she shoved him away.

"Don't touch me."

"You weren't saying that yesterday, *honey*."

"I'm saying it now. Do not—ever—touch me again. And don't ever come in this house again, either, or I'm calling the cops."

Ray scratched the side of his head and stared, refolding his arms.

She looked more closely at the redness in his eyes. "Jesus, you really are high, aren't you?"

"Who gives a shit if I am?"

She muttered, "Dylan is right, you are such a dick," while throwing clothes back into the drawer and slamming it shut, then faced him as she shouted, "And for your information, I don't need you to *give* me a divorce! What's wrong with you?"

"You haven't been a treat the whole time yourself, Gina."

"Don't let the door hit you on the ass on your way out."

She continued dressing, sliding on shorts, a collared shirt, socks and her work sneakers, trying to ignore him while he lingered and stared, annoyed that now, of all times, he finally wanted to talk. With her bag over her shoulder and keys in hand, she stepped into Dylan's room to tell him she was leaving and that she loved him.

"Love you, too," he mumbled from beneath the blanket.

Then she hustled through the living room, calling back, "You're trespassing, Ray! If I don't see you leave before I pull out of the driveway, you can spend your morning talking to the cops. And take these boxes on your way out, or so help me God, I'm setting them on fire when I get back tonight!"

Moving with hurried steps along the cracked cement walkway, fuming, she pulled out her phone, amazed at how crappy her first official day sober had started off. Worried about leaving Ray inside with Dylan, she dialed 911, but waited to press the send button. He wanted this. He enjoyed this, the drama, the arguments, and it damn sure hadn't been a coincidence that he'd come by the morning of her first holiday weekend at the estate.

She deleted the three digits from the phone screen, recalling what Maryanne had said just after the meeting—about how she could restart her day anytime she wanted. Probably easier said than done, but supposedly all she had to do was take a deep breath and allow herself a second to pause. She could choose to change her perspective. With that thought she breathed in and scanned her unkempt front yard.

She noticed some of the crocuses already full-grown and ripe with color, and then plenty of other signs of springtime and the coming summer all around—squirrels scampering across the patchy lawn and along tree branches, blooms on the bushes, full green leaves on the oaks and sunlight filtering through. Even as her marriage and drinking had fizzled to an end, and Ray seemed more unhinged by the day, all this beauty surrounded her.

But that flicker of serenity was snuffed out as Ray trailed her to her car. She felt him hovering like a storm cloud when she slid into the driver's seat, the stench of weed and cigarette smoke creeping in. She gripped the side handle and pulled but he held her door open.

"Let go," she said.

He looked on blankly.

She pulled hard but the door didn't budge. "Let go, Ray," she said again with a long sigh. "I mean it."

He continued staring. She pulled even harder and he yanked it open wider.

"Don't you get it, G? I can leave if I want to, but you . . . *You* don't get to leave *me*." He angled his body between her and the door, leaned in and ran his finger along her cheek.

"Don't do that!" She leaned away, frightened by his confidence and this oblivious attempt at affection. Two months ago they'd parted as strangers. Yesterday had been a colossal mistake. He didn't get to touch her anymore. Never again. He'd left her half-dead, for God's sake. She looked out the windshield, hoping he'd realize the pointlessness of holding her hostage—and that's exactly what this was, a hostage situation, and she hated him for it. "I was serious when I said I'd call the cops, Ray. You're really going to push it that far?"

No answer, of course. And to think she'd actually thought she loved this maniac for a while there. He was sick on so many levels, but then again, she needed help as much as he did. Choosing to be with him in the first place proved that.

The right-hand number on her dashboard clock changed. She was already late. Glacially slow, another full minute passed with neither of them speaking, his eyes like bloodshot marbles glaring less than a foot from her face.

She finally broke the silence by shouting, "Fine, I'm dialing the police!"

As if he'd just awoken from a spell, he unfurled his grip from the top of the door, then repeated,

"You don't leave me," sounding deadly serious, and gently pressed it closed.

She turned her head and fumbled with the gearshift, her eyes watering. She didn't want him to see how badly he'd scared her, or to know that his words had just now dropped inside her stomach like stones. She had to get away. With him eyeing her through the driver's-side window, she reversed, feeling as though she'd been punched.

She didn't want to drive off until she saw him leaving, though, not with Dylan inside, so she shifted into Park just after reaching the street, her car idling perpendicular to the driveway while she watched him walk toward the shed and then prop his extension ladder on his shoulder. Looking through her passenger-side window, she hated him more by the second for making her late for work, though much more for scaring her, for acting like a bully in her own home, where she'd made the mortgage payments all by herself every month they'd been together, where her son now lay in his bed.

From the opposite end of the driveway, Ray saw her staring and flashed that damned smirk of his, raising his hand as if to say *I'll see you later*.

Gina shifted into Drive but kept her foot on the brake, staring, as Ray took the key to her house from his pocket and pointed it like a gun to his temple, then jerked his head to the side, pretending to blow his brains out. "Get it?" he yelled, with his hands cupped around his mouth. "You've got the key to my heart, baby! And like the reverend said, till *death* do us fucking part! *Ha-ha-ha-ha-ha-ha!*"

Nearly choking on her tongue, she floored it down the block. Just before the Stop sign she slammed on the brake, skidding before parking at an odd angle by the curb. *I need to change the locks again,* she thought. *And no backup keys anywhere he can find them.* As soon as she could see straight she flipped open her phone, thinking she'd call the police, but then for some reason she pulled up her new sponsor's number instead.

On the second ring Maryanne answered, "Hey, hon. How are ya?"

Gina had been holding back tears purely out of pride, hating Ray for having power over her enough to affect her so viscerally, but now Maryanne's innocuous question hit her like a fist in her chest. She stuttered out the basic summary of the past half hour. "My son didn't come home last night, and my husband, who's about to be my ex-husband, I think he just threatened to kill me if I leave him—or maybe that he'd kill himself? I'm not—"

"Whoa, stop. He threatened to kill you?"

"I don't know," she said, and kept speaking through hyphenated breaths. "Maybe. I'm not sure if he has a gun. Never thought about it till now. But he scared me."

"Has he ever hit you?"

"I don't want to get into any of that right now." The memory of Ray punching her in the stomach during their last drunken blowout a couple months back suddenly registered as if it were happening right then, the physical pain returning in a wave. She couldn't get any air.

"If he did threaten you, you really should report him, dear," Maryanne said, sounding extra motherly. "Maybe get a restraining order."

"I don't know, maybe. I probably should. But right now I'm late for work, and today is my first day sober in I don't even know how long, so I pretty much feel like a chicken running around with its head chopped off. I slept maybe an hour last night, and even though I quit smoking when the boys were little, I want a cigarette like you wouldn't believe." Sucking in a deeper breath, she unclenched her hand from the steering wheel. "Sorry. How are you?"

"Can't complain. We should get back to what you said about your ex-husband, though. I have some experience with this and want to help."

Gina wrestled a stick of gum from its wrapper, stuck it in her mouth and chewed quickly until she'd slathered the surface of her tongue with mint. "So, any advice on staying sober?"

"First of all, take another deep breath. I'm

190

serious. I want to hear it. Breathe in, breathe out. Go ahead."

She felt the urge to snap at Maryanne, but realized how irrational that would be, also how crazy she must have sounded. "Okay," she said, "here goes." Her lungs filled slowly, loudly enough for Maryanne to hear, and then the same on the out breath. "How was that?"

"Excellent. Now how do you feel?"

She watched a sparrow leap from a branch and join three others on the telephone wire across the street, the sky cloudless and bright blue behind them.

"Honestly, I don't know. I feel numb, or in shock more than anything. This morning is off to a rough start."

"You need to get to work, huh?"

"I should be driving now if I'm going to get there a little after when I'm supposed to get there. So, yeah. Speeding might need to happen."

"Well, don't get a ticket. That's all you need now."

"Are you laughing?"

"It's not at you, dear. I just know exactly how you're feeling."

"This is strange for me. Here I am rambling all this crap to you over the phone at eight in the morning and I hardly know you."

"It takes a little getting used to, trusting someone. I get that. But all that matters now is that you take one thing at a time and do what you need to do, which is to get to work, don't drink while you're there, and either call me or get to a meeting right after. Long as you don't drink today, you'll be all right, I promise. I'll be at work myself, but call me anytime if you feel overwhelmed, and if you can't call, then say the Serenity Prayer to yourself. You'll be amazed how pausing to say that short prayer can take a lot of the power out of whatever stress you have going on, and it helps to remind you what you can or can't do about the situation. Take the day in bite-size pieces. Half an hour at a time. Fifteen minutes. Get through the morning, make it to lunch, then the afternoon. You get what I'm saying. Later today we can talk more about you filing a restraining order, but for now just know that you're not alone. Okay, hon?"

Gina wiped her eyes. "Okay, thanks."

"Good. Now put both hands on the wheel, focus on the road and get your sober ass to work."

She hung up and did as she was told, placed both hands on the steering wheel and pulled away from the curb, but a few feet along she stopped once more when her phone rang. Hoping to hear from Corey, she looked at the screen.

*A call from Leo Sheffield? I can't answer now,* she thought. *Whatever mess you need me to clean up for you, Leo, it can wait till I get there.*

A moment after the ringing ceased she dialed

Corey's cell number, but the call went straight to his voice mail. Gina's mouth hung open. She couldn't think of a thing to say. Instead, she set down her phone and gripped the wheel until her knuckles turned white, chewing her gum. She'd be angry if he came to work late, livid if he missed the day. How could she blame him, though? She'd been so far from perfect, especially these past few months. She'd let her boys down. How could she expect them to be there for her? She needed to start driving, but redialed her son's number first, and this time left a message: "Core, it's Mom. I hope you're okay. Anyway, I'll see you at the Sheffields'. I love you."

Fifteen minutes later, after nibbling her nails for most of the drive, she turned off Gin Lane at the stone lions, passed through the Sheffields' gates and drove down the driveway to the wide parking lot next to the kitchen. The landscaping crew had finished their work and now bustled around the lot loading their mowers and weed-whackers onto the trailers with wood-slatted sides, none of them paying her any mind as she shuffled past with her phone to her ear, listening to Leo Sheffield's voice mail: "Gina," he said, sounding as though his throat had been scraped raw. "I need your help." The pause that followed went on so long she thought he'd forgotten to hang up, then he added, "You're the only one I could call," and a second later the message ended.

She replayed it, even more confused as to what the hell he was calling about the second time around, overwhelmed by everything when she entered the kitchen and found her coworkers. Her face stretched into the falsest of smiles and she greeted them both even before the screen door slapped closed. "Sorry I'm a few minutes late. Any updates?"

Josie, her second in command of the house, shrugged but continued polishing silverware, while the chef, Michael, looked on with a grin while hunched over a cutting board.

"Sheila called my cell about an hour ago," Michael said, expertly slicing a yellow bell pepper at a wicked pace. "They're going to be ten for dinner tonight, not eight."

Seated on the opposite side of the granite-topped center island, Josie set down the gleaming spoon she'd been working on and then forcefully rubbed a dab of silver polish up and down the tines of an antique salad fork. Her mouth pursed into her signature smirk, which Gina knew meant she had gossip to share.

"Missus S also said that Mr. Sheffield came out last night," she said, "but when he didn't come downstairs early for his coffee like he usually would, I figured he was just sleeping in." She looked toward the door to the hall and then leaned closer, speaking softer. "A few minutes ago I went outside and found him sitting in a chair by the pool—and holy cow did he look rough. Sit for a sec, G. Have a coffee before the fun begins." Josie returned the final piece of silverware to the velvet-lined case, closed its hardwood top and fastened the brass clips. "Oh, and when Corey shows up, Missus S wants him to wipe down all the wicker chairs on the porch and run a mop over the boards. When's he getting here?"

"He should be here any minute."

Gina slid her phone into her pocket and turned her head to find Mr. Sheffield entering the kitchen from the hall, looking dead tired, his hand pressing something to the back of his head.

"Good morning, sir," Michael said, glancing up from the cutting board, and Josie and Gina both echoed the same greeting.

Mr. Sheffield answered, "Good morning," though his voice had a gravelly edge, just as it had in the voice-mail message, and his eyes seemed to be focused somewhere far off outside the kitchen windows. He released his hand from his head and Gina noticed what he'd been pressing there—a bloodstained dishcloth wrapped around a plastic bag with partially melted ice cubes sloshing inside.

He began tilting to the right with his arm out, as if to catch hold of the door jamb, wavered for a moment and then took a half step toward her, but staggered sideways. Gina shouted as she lunged for him; then all at once they stumbled together through a blur of flailing arms, her coffee mug shattered and the ice pack and bloody cloth dropped to the floor.

# SEVENTEEN

"I had a rather embarrassing accident," Leo said, gazing down at the jagged pieces of the mug and the spilled coffee steaming on the floor, painfully self-conscious that Gina had just run to his aid and now strained under his weight to steady him.

Her shoulder beneath his armpit kept him propped up long enough for the treble in his eardrums to dissipate and the vertigo to fade, though the nightmare that had plagued him all morning returned like water through a breaching dam, a torturous montage of images—Henry in the pool, his own desperate thrusts to resuscitate him, that haunting look of surprise before he'd closed his bulging eyes, then pulling him across the lawn, farther and farther from the house, deeper inside the darkness below the faraway pine boughs, and finally dropping his wrapped body in the woods, apologizing as he staggered around and blindly covered him with needles. Despite his drunkenness at the time, he remembered it all too vividly, the haunting series of hours that he knew no amount of drinking would ever allow him to forget.

Gina picked up the bag of ice and bloody cloth from the floor, looked at him for a moment and then gently pulled his head forward.

"My God," she said, sounding horrified, "what happened?"

"I decided to make the drive out late last night," he said, easing away from her to lean against the door jamb. "It's almost too stupid to say out loud. I decided to have a dip in the pool, and when I stepped out I slipped on the top step and hit my head hard enough that I bled a bit. Nothing to worry about, though."

"Why aren't you at the hospital?"

"I've been icing it for a while now and the swelling seems to be going down. I'll be all right after getting some rest."

Gina eyed him the way his mother used to when he was a boy and he'd done something reckless or just plain dumb. That unblinking stare. The unspoken disappointment. He hadn't showered yet, either, which only occurred to him when she brought the back of her hand to her nose. "Bend over again," she said. "Let me get a better look at it."

Leo complied, glad he'd thought to explain away any blood beside the pool, but feeling less confident in his cover story with each passing second. All the goddamned cocaine still so present in his bloodstream kept his pulse pumping at an uncomfortable pace. The paranoia inescapable. His jaw clenched as she placed her fingers on his scalp and inspected the wound. The buzz from the booze had mostly worn off, enough for the hangover to take hold, anyway, which included a god-awful headache that he imagined would have been there head wound or not, something akin to diamond-tipped daggers slowly puncturing his brain through the temples.

Gina let go and faced him. She placed a hand on his cheek and forced him to look at her, speaking as though she were in fact his mother and he an especially dimwitted child. "All right, so this is actually a very serious wound you have here," she said. "And you're absolutely going to need stitches, Mr. Sheffield. Come with me." She took his arm and began leading him through the kitchen. "So we're walking now, right? Don't worry. I've got you. I see that look, and I know what you want to say but you can just skip it. You don't have a choice in this. I'm taking you to the hospital, and I don't want to hear a word about it."

"I feel like such a fool," Leo said, feigning a smile for Michael and Josie as he walked beside Gina to the kitchen door. She led him by the arm onto the landing and down the three wooden stairs while commenting on his appearance, harping at him over the obvious point that he looked as though he hadn't slept. Then she stopped walking and stared more intensely.

"What was that message you left me this morning about?"

He looked at her, though found it a challenge

to focus. She'd worked for him all these years, trudging competently through what must have been interminable days when Sheila demanded every little thing be done the moment she mentioned it. Gina had never complained. She also knew so much about them, about him, and during all that time she'd kept his private life private, and even backed him up on his occasional lie. Despite her issues with drinking a bit too much on the property at the end of her shifts here and there, and her tragic decision to marry a deadbeat who apparently siphoned what little money she had—no wonder she always needed loans—he'd trusted her. But this secret he couldn't trust her with. Not her. Not anyone.

"Forget about it, it's not important," he said, hoping that some additional details might make the story more believable. "And you're right, I was awake all night. Had to catch up on some work before the guests arrived today. And this here," he said, pointing at the back of his head, "was a freak accident." The lie barely left his mouth and had already thrown him even further off his axis, probably because more truth had leaked out than he'd intended. His injury *had* been a result of an accident, though the result of Henry's accident, not his. The wound, he realized now, was the scarlet letter he'd wear throughout the weekend, a visual reminder of his sin, the violent penalty for losing his mind and attacking his daughter's oldest friend. Someone had hit him, and *goddamn,* they sure as hell had hit him hard. Not knowing who'd attacked him had been eating away at his sanity ever since he'd regained consciousness on the lawn, and now drained what little energy he'd had left, so he admitted that he needed to lean on Gina like a crutch for another moment.

"It's better that you stayed awake," she said, straining under his weight. "If you have a concussion, and you most likely do by the looks of your head, I've heard you could die in your sleep. Not sure why, but that's what I've heard." Her voice drifted in his mind and settled like autumn leaves on a forest floor, her next words nothing more than a backdrop of low-tone static.

Although he still felt light-headed and dizzy, he would have gladly paid a million dollars to skip the trip to the emergency room—more than a million to avoid the doctor's questions about his coke-fueled heartbeat, the wound, the reek of whiskey and sweat seeping from his pores. If only he could skip everything. But no, he couldn't. The day ahead rolled out before him like a scroll. After the hospital, all the impending greetings and conversations with the guests would be way too much to handle. He needed to shut himself away and hibernate through the hangover, and as soon as possible figure out a way to get Henry somewhere safer. He'd spend some time with the kids, sure, but the rest of them—the socialite neighbors, the yes-men and ass-kissers from the company, the dilettantes and country club rats—they could all go fuck themselves. He'd lost someone he cared about, horribly, suddenly. And Henry was still out there. A ticking bomb. How could he play host and sit through Sheila's epic dinner parties, let alone keep his shit together?

Gina managed to hold him upright until they reached the edge of the driveway, but with their first steps onto the beach stones he encouraged her to let him stand on his own.

"Give me a minute," he said. Mired in self-pity, he heard the crunching of tires on the driveway and gazed to his left. He squinted at the beams and needles of light gleaming against a chrome bumper, and then, more forcefully than he'd meant to, he shirked Gina's hand from his forearm as the tall iron gates began swiveling closed and the limo pulled ahead.

Oh Jesus, no. He'd forgotten to call Pete and cancel Henry's pickup.

"Excuse me a moment, Gina." He left her there, and with awkward steps ambled down the center of the shale-and-pebble-covered drive, the morning sun too bright to see beyond a fierce haze, his hands raised with palms out to signal for Pete to stop the car. As soon as his driver pressed the brake, Leo picked up his pace and made it to the side window before Pete could step out.

Leo turned and saw Gina walking over and then turned back to the window as it powered down.

"Hell, damn it," he said to Pete, "I'm so sorry, I should've called. My guest decided to meet friends for breakfast and he's going to stay with them for the weekend. I feel awful that you made the trip all the way out here for no reason. And on a goddamned holiday weekend no less."

"Oh, that's okay, sir. My apologies for getting here late. I should have planned for the extra drive time with so many people on their way out on the LIE. It would have made a lot more sense to take you up on your offer to put me up in a motel for the night out here."

Leo tried to grin. "You're on time by my watch."

"Not quite, sir. You asked me to be here over an hour ago to pick up—"

"It's fine," Leo said. "Really." Then he glanced at Gina, who'd been standing beside him and had obviously overheard that a guest had been at the house last night.

"Well, I hope your friend wasn't inconvenienced," Pete said. "I could have at least driven him wherever he's staying for the weekend. I left three hours ago, but apparently so did half of Manhattan." He leaned to the side, looked past Leo and added, "Nice to see you, Gina. How are things?"

She rested a hand on Leo's shoulder as she

answered, "All's well. Should be a great weekend here. Just making the final preparations before the rest of the guests arrive."

Leo reached out to steady himself against the front quarter panel. Her hand slid from his shoulder. Calling her and leaving that pathetic message had been a huge mistake. She hadn't asked about the guest, hadn't even given him a sideways look, but she knew him well enough to see through his lie, and now that she knew someone else had come out with him from the city she'd think more about his cryptic call and scrutinize his head wound even closer. Although she and Pete had minimal knowledge about the events of the night, much more limited than Angelique and the faceless person who'd knocked him out, at least four people already knew of Henry's existence at the estate. And Leo had no alibi. Not even a plausible cover story as to why Henry had come here in the dead of night, or where he went.

The limo's black paint radiated furnace heat into his palm, the morning already much hotter than a typical Memorial Day weekend and humid as hell. He faced east, blinded by the sun blazing directly in his line of sight. He needed a shower, and three or four Valium, and then ten or twelve hours of comatose sleep, and then—most of all—a feasible plan to move Henry. A string of questions, many of which he'd grappled with throughout the night, suddenly hit him like buckshot. If he hadn't given Henry so much coke and all that booze, would he still be alive? Had the person who'd knocked him out done something to Henry first? How could he transport Henry's body off the property without anyone noticing? Where could he take him? His palm was melting, his knees buckling. He needed Gina to let him stay here rather than go to the hospital, and for his driver to turn the limo around, and to leave. Why was Pete staring at him like that?

"Are you all right, Mr. Sheffield?"

"Fine. Why do you ask?"

"You're pale, sir. And sweating."

Pete's words resonated with a mild echo. Leo removed his hand from the limo, intending to walk with Gina toward her car after a final exchange, and then, hopefully, find the magic words to wriggle out of the trip to the hospital.

"I had a fall last night," he said. "Gina thinks I should get the once-over from a doctor, and she was about to drive me to the ER to see if I need stitches, but I'll be fine. Thanks for asking. Sorry again for the mix-up this morning." He pulled his billfold from his front pocket and peeled off two hundred-dollar bills and held them out. How much had he given Pete the night before? Five hundred? A thousand? More? That part of the night remained a blur. "Please take this for your trouble."

"No need for that," Pete said. "But I'd be happy to drive you to the hospital." He nodded at Gina. "You can stay. I've got him."

"I may have to wait, though," Leo said, wincing as a bead of sweat came rolling down from his forehead into his eye. "Could be hours before a doctor sees me."

"That's what you pay me for," Pete said. "No sense in taking her away from whatever she would be doing here."

"You're sure?" Gina said. "I don't mind taking him."

"Positive. Hop on in, Mr. Sheffield."

The weekend hadn't even begun and Leo already preferred the idea of lying down beside Henry in the woods and never getting up. Sheila would be arriving much too soon, as would Andy and Clay. Tiffany had slept through all the drama last night, otherwise she wouldn't still be asleep now in her bed; but Angelique might tell his daughter sometime today exactly why she'd fled, and then what? Yet another awful what-if to worry about, whether his daughter would know anything of last night's insanity and confront him today. And then, of course, in the evening the guests for the first dinner party would be decked out and chatty, trickling in two-by-two like animals boarding the ark. How could he keep them from venturing around the property? He couldn't. And they'd all be buzzed, some of them drunk. What if someone wandered into the woods?

Leo tucked his denim button-down into his khakis, squinting with his hand up to shade his eyes, thinking he must look as wrung out and wrecked as he felt. What if instead of the hospital he went to the airport? He could hop on a plane and disappear. Not to one of his vacation houses or condos in Hawaii or Coconut Grove or out on the Cape, though. To truly vanish he'd have to avoid any place where he owned property. He'd pay cash for everything, grow a beard, buy a new identity. He could try Fiji, maybe Thailand, or what the hell, Morocco. His name could dissolve in any one of those places easily enough, right? Plus, he had accounts down in the Caymans that no one knew about, plenty of money to live well for ten lifetimes. But whichever spot on the globe he chose, it had to be a country without extradition. He'd make sure to check on that. Otherwise he might live out the rest of his life in a cell.

"Sir?" Pete reached out from the car window and tapped his arm.

"Sorry, I'm a bit overtired. You were saying?"

"We should get going."

"I'd hate to take up any more of your day waiting around for me for God knows how long in a hospital parking lot," he said, blinking more to keep the sweat from trickling in. He didn't want to leave the property with Henry laid out in the woods only twenty or thirty yards from that stretch of the lawn out there, and dreaded the idea of spending the next hour or two or more in the ER. "Gina, I'm not sure we even need to do this right now."

"Not another word out of you," she said, placing a hand on his back and edging him over to the limo's side door. "Arguing with me on this is pointless."

With Leo inside, she thanked Pete, and then kept her arms folded as the car swung around the lot, offering a quick wave at the tinted glass when they passed. Pete drove along the driveway at roughly one mile per hour, with the divider down, and Leo sat on the black leather bench seat in back facing the windshield, on edge to begin with since he and Henry had ridden together in this very same compartment less than twelve hours ago, then even more tense when he saw an older model pickup pulling forward through the open gates, effectively blocking the drive.

Leo gripped his knees and bent forward, his teeth grinding. He'd been here plenty of times since he and Henry started up, coming down from the coke, but this degree of discomfort was altogether new. His thoughts turned to the detox nightmares of unfortunate strangers, a swell of empathy for the addicts who panhandled outside his office building and all the other drug users who couldn't hack this part, the coming down. Then came a sudden surge of understanding for Henry, and all the other suicidal ones. They'd felt as he felt today. He understood their impulse to end it all, which rose up in him now as a desperate wish to feel nothing. He needed to get it together, snuff the sullen line of thinking and get through the goddamned trip to the goddamned hospital and then get through the rest of the goddamned day.

A glare from one of the bronze chess pieces summoned Leo's attention to the left. Then he saw something altogether inexplicable— Angelique standing next to one of the pawns, staring at his car. His mouth hung open. He rubbed his eyes, hoping he was hallucinating.

"No," he said, cringing at his own shredded voice.

Pete looked up into the rearview mirror and answered, "I'm sorry, sir?"

Leo cleared his throat and wiped sweat from his brow before answering. "No—I was saying, what I mean to say is, there's *no* way you're not taking something extra for this."

"Really, sir—"

"You don't want to argue with me on this, Pete."

"Yes, sir."

With his driver still eyeing him from the mirror, he clumsily poured four fingers of Scotch and slugged it in one gulp before his focus returned to Angelique. She'd been his daughter's closest friend for years. She'd come to the apartment and the estate hundreds of times. But what must she think of him now? Last night he'd been a madman, a monster. He'd scared her and she'd screamed. She'd seen Henry floating limp and lifeless in the pool. After all that, why would she return here now? For Tiffany? To tell her in detail about the whole awful mess? To try to convince her to leave with her? She should have run away, stayed far away . . . called the police. Come to think of it, God only knew how Tiffany hadn't awoken . . . Or how none of the neighbors had heard Angelique pleading for help, or if they had, why they hadn't done anything in response to a girl screaming in the night. Could it have been a neighbor who'd struck him from behind and left him unconscious on the lawn? Fucking hell, how many people knew about Henry?

He felt sick, a tuning fork effect vibrating along his arms and legs and his skull pounding as his finger pressed a button on the side console and the tinted window lowered halfway. Twenty, maybe twenty-five yards from him, Angelique stood as still as the bronze pawn beside her. Leo sat frozen in his seat, stunned by the sight of her, mystified as to why she was standing barefoot and alone on that section of the north lawn. They stared at each other, locked in that tension like animals at a watering hole—one predator, one prey, but who could say which was which now? Angelique was a few paces too far away for him to decipher her expression, though close enough to trigger a resurrection of the memory—the bright moon, Leo looking up and discovering her on the balcony, her hands gripping the railing, her mouth open in disbelief while she looked down at him waist-deep in the shallow end of the pool, holding Henry by the waist, his arms splayed and floating Christlike on the water.

The unexpected sight of her had sparked so much more paranoia. This girl on his property could ruin everything. She'd seen too much. While he dreaded the idea of even looking her in the eye, no way around it now, he had to get back from the hospital as soon as possible and deal with her today.

# EIGHTEEN

Ten minutes earlier Corey had pulled over beside the hedge wall a few yards down from the Sheffields' driveway and held Angelique's hand, doing his best to reassure her while the engine idled and she listened intently with her knees up and her arms clasped around her shins.

"Just remember, he's not going to hurt you," he said. "And I'll be here to make sure you're okay, so try not to worry too much. He's shitting himself right now about everything that happened last night, so really—you have all the power."

"I know," she said. "I think it's just hitting me that we didn't sleep at all. My eyes aren't focusing."

He touched her arm so she would look at him, meaning to convey that they'd both get through this and the hard part would be over soon. They leaned closer and Corey kissed her cheek, hoping to calm her fidgety hands when he took them in his and lightly squeezed, and for another minute or so they kept their foreheads pressed together, the lack of sleep taking its toll on them both.

"You ready?" he said, and she nodded slowly. They both looked out the windshield at two landscaping company trucks leaving the estate, and just after they'd driven out of sight Corey eased the truck ahead along the edge of the road and parked beside one of the lions. She opened her door and stepped out, typed the code on the keypad and the gate began to swing inward, the hinges whining while she ran back, pulled his sweatshirt over her head and handed it to him through his window. "I'll find you in a little while," she said over her shoulder, already hurrying through the opening and over to the right, following the first step of the plan, which was to skirt the perimeter of the lawn and make it back inside while staying relatively out of sight. Her safety from Mr. Sheffield, he figured, would be that much more assured once she met up with Tiffany.

After waiting long enough that he'd imagined her already entering the house, he pulled ahead and retyped the gate code. A few yards along the driveway a glare coincided with an extra layer of sound, the crunch of other tires, and in a flash he saw the limo's front bumper rounding the curve beside the hedgerow. The driver applied the brakes, and Corey did as well. He briefly considered driving onto the lawn to let them pass, but then shoved the gearshift into Reverse. Although Angelique had had about a ten-minute head start, for some reason she still stood in clear view over by the chess pieces, close enough for Corey to assume that if Leo Sheffield happened to be riding in the limo he'd already seen her.

He backed his truck out, paused briefly to look

both ways and reversed over to a patch of grass across the street. Parked there, he waited with his head down, staring at his hands. He didn't want Leo to see him in profile if he passed by with his window down, definitely didn't want to make eye contact—the moment when Corey had swung the stone cherub and cracked the rich man's skull suddenly so alive in his mind. While the limo drove past, his knee bounced anxiously. He cracked his knuckles one by one and counted to ten before lifting his head and looking into the side-view mirror. The brake lights engaged as the car swung around the bend. He exhaled just after it disappeared, wondering if Mr. Sheffield had been inside.

A few minutes later he entered the kitchen to the sounds of a vacuum cleaner in the distance and low-volume jazz on the radio. He found Michael hunched over a large shiny mixing bowl, whisking something when he looked up to meet Corey's eyes. The noise from the other room cut out, and soon after Josie came bounding in from the elbow-shaped hall that connected the kitchen to the dining room, carrying the vacuum under one arm. Her face hardened when she saw him in the doorway.

"Your mom wants you to wipe down all the wicker furniture and to carry the cushions out from the sunporch. She wasn't happy when she got here."

"Why isn't she happy? I'm not late, am I?"

"Checked your phone at all?"

Josie didn't wait for his answer. She cut him off by simply depositing the vacuum in the corner and leaving the room. Michael kept his head angled toward the mixing bowl, but with his eyes up, whisking away with that metallic scraping sound, and like Josie, without any hint of a smile. The jazz saxophone spiraled on behind him. Corey had known them both for years and had liked them well enough, but today he resented them. They'd judged him as soon as he walked in, must have been judging him even before he got here. If they only knew a fraction of what had gone down overnight . . .

He left the kitchen with a roll of paper towels and a spray bottle full of the all-natural citrus cleaner that Sheila Sheffield preferred for the outdoor furniture. Passing through the living room, he stopped beside one of the screen doors to the porch when he heard his mother speaking in a hushed tone and saw her outside through the windows. "No, I promise. I won't drink," she said. Silence followed before she answered the person on the phone. "I will." Another pause, then she ended the call, saying, "Thanks again. You, too."

She entered the living room as though blown in by a strong wind, stopping short as soon as she saw him. "So, you made it," she said, hands on her hips. "I called you three times this morning."

"Yeah, sorry. My battery died."

"You had me worried, Core." He noticed her eyes were red and watery. She ran a finger under each one and then crossed the room and hugged him, and after an awkward moment when he let go but she didn't, she spoke over his shoulder. "Where were you last night? You never came home."

"Just out with friends."

Gina kept on holding him there with a tight grip until he started to feel self-conscious.

"Ma," he said, gently breaking the hug, "you okay?"

"I'm just relieved you're all right."

"Who were you on the phone with just now?"

"I feel like I haven't seen you for weeks."

"I've been out a lot, I know."

His mother looked tired, more than likely hungover. He hadn't been home at all lately aside from the quiet hours when she and Dylan slept, and only a meager handful of words had passed between them since he'd cleaned the upper floors earlier in the week and left the window unlatched so he could break into the Sheffield estate. Why had she sidestepped when he asked about her phone call? She wouldn't make that kind of promise about not drinking to Ray, and no other names came to mind.

"Anyway," Gina said, "you're going out to

prep the porch furniture now, right?" He nodded, and she kept talking while moving toward the kitchen and straightening things along the way, tamping the magazines into a tighter fan on the snub-footed mahogany table in the center of the room, primping cushions on both the designer sofas. "Soon as you're done with that, we could use you in here. They'll all start arriving in a couple hours. Oh, and something else you should know—Mr. Sheffield had a fall last night."

"A fall? Is he all right?" He'd feigned surprise but had no confidence in his performance. He didn't want her to look at him, so he turned and grabbed two cushions for the outdoor furniture from the stack in the corner.

"He's heading to the emergency room now but should be back soon. When he is, let's make sure to pay extra attention to him and see that he has whatever he needs, okay? Okay." And with that she zipped out of the room.

Relieved to hear that Mr. Sheffield had already spun a cover story, Corey left the house through the screen door with the warped hinges and got right to work, spraying the orange-scented cleaner on one of the white wicker ottomans and rubbing traces of mildew and dust from the creases, thinking back to a few minutes ago. Mr. Sheffield had been on his way to the hospital then, so he must have seen Angelique in the yard. She should talk to him this afternoon. The sooner the better, because she could take off as soon as Leo came through with the money, and aside from wanting to get her out of this crazy stressful situation as soon as humanly possible, the sooner Corey could stop what he'd just begun doing—rubbing mildew from rich people's stupid fucking outdoor furniture—the better.

He continued cleaning for the next half hour, working up a sweat. For May, this heat flirted with record highs. The thermometer tacked on the corner porch beam had leveled off at the mark halfway between eighty and ninety degrees and it was still only midmorning. Plus, the humidity made it feel much hotter, the air so thick he imagined a Louisiana bayou in the dead of summer wouldn't be much worse. He rose from his knees, twisted side to side to crack his back and ran his arm along his brow. Sweat trickled off his fingers. He looked down at the small bed of red tulips below the porch rail where he'd landed last night after jumping off the roof, two of which had been crushed, a few others snapped higher up on their stems.

His throat tightened. He squinted, hoping that the gray incongruity on the grass by the retaining wall had been an illusion. He'd tossed the cherub into the bushes a few yards from where Mr. Sheffield had fallen, so it made no sense for it to be out in the open there on the lawn. Even if his eyes were playing tricks on him and the bloody cherub still lay somewhere in the bushes, how stupid he was to forget to remove it from the property. He'd have to run down there and heave it into the lake, or else risk someone finding it and connecting it to Leo's bashed-up head. Then he remembered the landscapers had been on their way out a couple minutes before he pulled into the driveway with Angelique. Someone must have moved the statue from the bushes to the edge of the lawn while they did whatever work over there. But none of those guys would have looked closely at it, right? His eyes grew heavier while he squinted, figuring that what he thought he'd seen must have been an optical illusion with all that light reflecting off the lake, since, as far as he could tell, nothing lay out there now. Unlike the other side of the property with all the sculptures, this wide slope down to the lake and the willow trees had no decorations, nothing but a blank acre or two of green grass.

His heartbeat seemed to thump now inside his bones as the facts of the day streaked through. Right then a doctor was probably sewing Leo Sheffield's scalp with a needle and thread, the guy Corey had nearly killed. Soon he would return from the hospital, and soon after that his guests would begin arriving in their limousines from the city. And Angelique, she'd looked like she was in shock out there on the other side of the property, standing beside the bronze pawn, staring at Leo's car. They'd both witnessed a death and neither had reported it to the cops. They hadn't slept. It was getting harder and harder to think straight, though one thing was for sure—everything depended on how they handled things for the rest of the day. *Everything* depended on their next few choices.

He ground his fists against his eyelids, blinking away the aftereffects of too much sun, his head turning at the sound of the screen door opening. Tiffany shuffled out, cradling an oversize mug in her hands, dressed in pajama pants and a tank top covered in dabs and smears of dried paint, her blond hair wild with static.

"Have you seen my friend?" she asked, peering over at him while blowing steam from the coffee, sounding a touch annoyed. "You know, the pretty one, Angelique."

"Yeah, a little while ago. I saw her walking out by the tennis courts."

She held the mug to her bottom lip as though it had been glued there, blowing on it some more before tilting it for a tiny sip and facing the lake. "Any of my family here yet?" Her voice sounded distant, as though she'd been talking to herself or didn't care about the answer.

"Your father is. I heard he came out early."

"He did? Why haven't I seen him, then?"

"My mom told me he fell and hit his head last night, and that he's at the hospital now to get a couple stitches."

Tiffany turned to look at him. "He fell? Where? When?"

"I didn't get any details. Just that he hit his head."

"He was out here last night?"

"Yeah, I guess."

A vein began twitching along his left temple as her eyelids lowered and she looked at him over the mug's rim. Hearing that her father may have been at the house when she'd been passed out had obviously surprised her. The rest of the night's details were so over-the-top insane she wouldn't have believed a word, not without seeing his cell phone photos of her daddy's boyfriend floating dead in the pool or his body out in the pines. Even then she still might not believe Mr. Sheffield had had anything to do with it. Corey watched Tiffany finish her sip and stretch with her back arched, the mug high in one hand, the tank top rising to reveal both her pierced belly button and the aquamarine frill along the rim of her underwear. Then she zeroed in on his eyes with an unblinking stare, lowering her arms and releasing a subtle sound he imagined she'd make in bed when a guy touched her just right, disguising it as a yawn. She seemed to enjoy making him uncomfortable, and kept at it, grinning as she blew the steam again.

Corey's mouth and throat had gone dry. Standing in front of her, sweating, with a spray bottle in hand, he felt incredibly awkward. He said something about the heat and flinched midsentence as his voice cracked. In the throes of full-on panic mode, he pointed at her paint-spattered shirt and added, "You working on a new painting?"

"Thinking about it," she said. "What's my mom got you doing, scrubbing the wicker?"

"Yeah, then mopping the porch."

"What a bitch."

Corey knew better than to agree, but didn't know what else to say. Of all the Sheffields, Tiffany had been the only one who ever acknowledged the menial quality of his tasks at the estate, the vocalization of which now somehow made it even worse. He wished she hadn't noticed. Even more, if he had to do this stupid shit, he wished she'd leave him alone while he did it.

"Well," she added after a long pause, "hope they're at least paying you okay."

All he could do was shrug. His eyelids had grown so heavy, as if for the past minute she'd been swinging a watch from side to side, holding him at her command. He felt he might fall down from exhaustion by the time she pulled the screen door open, and then in a blink, she vanished into the house.

Feeling as though he'd passed out on his feet and had fallen into one of those bizarre dreams where you believe it's all real, even as you know it can't possibly be, he sprayed the next wicker chair and half-heartedly began wiping. He needed to sleep, if only for an hour, to realign his glitching thoughts and let his body recharge. A wave of dizziness buckled his knees and he gripped the porch rail to keep from stumbling. Easing down to kneel, he scanned the lawn once more to search for the cherub, but once again found nothing but wide-open space, nothing but green grass and a few geese waddling along the bulkhead.

He didn't have enough energy to stand up yet, and besides, he needed to think through his next move. The fucking wicker could wait, and he might even be able to skip it without anyone noticing. The night had been way too crazy, way too long. He needed to find Angelique and make sure she was all right. They needed to talk through the plan one more time before she demanded the money from Leo. His eyelids lowered like slowly drawn shades. He would stay here on his knees, sleep for a minute, maybe two. He needed to rest his eyes at least; he needed a break from this punishing light, shimmering on the lake like mercury.

# NINETEEN

With a stack of dinner plates cradled to her chest, Gina went clattering from the kitchen to the long oak table in the dining room and set them down to answer the house phone. Sheila Sheffield's voice came through on the speaker setting, shrunken and tinny.

"Gina, hello. Our car is about five minutes out. Have your boy meet us at the roundabout to bring in the bags, will you?"

"Of course, Missus Sheffield."

"Beautiful weather to start the weekend, isn't it?"

"Yes, wonderful."

"I've heard reports that a storm may pass over us on Sunday, but—"

The line crackled with static, then went silent.

"Missus Sheffield, are you still there?"

"Correction. We're actually about two minutes out now, not five."

"Alright, that's great. Corey and I will be outside to greet you when you pull in."

"Until then," she said, and hung up.

Gina hurried into the living room with the phone still pressed to her ear and the dial tone droning on, thankful that Sheila hadn't inquired about her husband. Hearing that Leo had gone to the emergency room would surely launch her into a fit of neurosis, not so much because of his injury but for the detour from her meticulously plotted weekend plans. Lowering the phone, Gina spotted Tiffany's friend out on the porch talking with Corey, the two standing a bit too close to one another. Then she noticed Angelique's fingers clasp around his hand. What the hell was this? *He's MIA overnight and now instead of working he's holding hands with this spoiled rich girl?*

"Corey," she snapped, "Missus Sheffield is pulling in now. I need you outside."

"Okay," he said, and she watched Angelique scurry off the porch toward the pool. The pills in Gina's pocketbook had been prescribed for anxiety, and while her sponsor might disagree, she decided this day justified taking a few more than the prescription advised, and if need be, maybe a few more throughout the hours leading up to dinner.

She and Corey exited the kitchen just in time to greet the arrivals and to offer polite military-style waves at the passing limousine. Still facing the car, Gina edged closer to her son. "So, you and Tiffany's friend are holding hands now?"

Corey lowered his hand as soon as the car passed and shrugged. "She's cool."

"Just be smart, Core. They're not like us."

Then, even before the driveway gates finished closing, another limo swung from the road into

225

the entrance. Gina waved at the second one as Corey approached the first. Pete stepped out, opened the passenger door, and Leo Sheffield emerged. The other limo pulled in beside him, blocking Gina's view until she made her way over and found Sheila Sheffield standing on the bed of pebbles between the cars, speaking to her husband and inspecting his bandaged head like an interrogator. Measuring a mere five feet tall, Sheila was a postmenopausal woman with the short-cropped haircut of a little boy, yet, as far as Gina was concerned, she seemed to stand much taller since she also had the forceful personality of a rooster.

Gina's eyes met Leo's while Sheila continued pecking at him.

"You look like an invalid with that on your head. What will our guests think?"

"Your concern is really touching, dear."

Sheila was already walking away from him as their two sons, Clayton and Andy, exited the limo she'd arrived in, followed by Andy's longtime girlfriend, Gretchen, a stunning long-legged brunette from Switzerland, whom Gina had exchanged no more than ten words with in as many years and who'd made no lasting impression other than the high-maintenance requests for particular soaps and conditioners and lotions, which Gina made special trips to buy during the bustle of crazy weekends like this one.

The seldom-discussed fact about Gretchen was that she smoked pot in the third-floor bathrooms whenever she spent the night at the estate. And then there was the more relevant fact, which no one would ever state but everyone knew: Sheila wouldn't spit on her son's girlfriend if she were on fire.

Her other son's sheepdog, Polly, loped off toward the ivy-covered archway that separated the parking lot (which Sheila insisted on calling the roundabout) from the lakeside lawn and began sniffing around the tulips. Clay called Polly back but the dog paid no attention. Leo stared at Gina and mouthed the words *Please help me,* and she nodded so slightly only he would have seen.

The Sheffield boys then took turns hugging their father and commenting on the square of gauze taped over the fresh stitches on the back of his head, playfully mocking him.

"I won't hug you too hard, Dad," Andy said. "Wouldn't want you to lose your balance again and break a hip this time."

"Stand back, everyone," Clay yelped, "Fred Astaire is going to show us how it's done."

Leo took his grown sons in a dual headlock, the three of them jostling and chuckling in the middle of the lot. "Lovey," he said to Sheila, "where exactly did we go wrong with these two?"

Rather than responding to her husband, Sheila began rattling off instructions for Corey, pointing at the growing row of luggage and bags the driver had been piling beside the limousine and stating where each piece needed to go.

"Yes, ma'am," Corey said like a well-trained cadet when she'd finished, taking two of Sheila's bags by their handles. Gina picked up two of the others destined for the master bedroom and walked ahead of him, looking over her shoulder at the dog as it destroyed more flowers, and at the Sheffield men leaning against one of the limousines like the preppiest preppy-ass street gang of all time. Sheila had turned away and now spoke on her cell phone to a food vendor as though her gourmet cheese order were a matter of life and death. Andy's freakishly tall girlfriend stood outside the mix, as usual, in cutoff jean shorts and a silk blouse with spaghetti straps, her eyes covered by Armani sunglasses while she maintained a frozen pose and stared in the direction of the dog.

After Gina helped Corey drop off the bags in the master bedroom and he headed downstairs for the next batch, she retrieved her own bag from the kitchen and slipped into the bathroom down the hall, intent on swallowing not one but two extra Xanax. The pills sat cradled in her palm, the faucet running. One day sober. Was one day enough time to fret over having to reset her sobriety date tomorrow? She had to admit she'd abused them as much as she'd abused alcohol over the past months, rarely taking the prescribed dose, often swallowing an amount by dinnertime that, when mixed with wine, shoved her into the shadowy neverland of a blackout an hour or so before the late-night talk shows began.

Her train of thought derailed in the gurgling sound of water entering the drain, and then she was revisited by a series of visceral memories with Ray, his grip on her throat the night before she kicked him out, the bruises on her stomach the next day, that awful laugh and the gesture in the driveway with his finger and her spare key pointed at his head like a gun. Maryanne was right—she needed to get the restraining order right away. The water kept on running, the pills still cradled in her palm. *This loneliness,* she thought, *should be classified as a disease.* She shut off the faucet and returned the orange bottle to her bag, but kept the two loose pills in her pocket. She wouldn't take them. Not yet, anyway. Knowing she had access to them whenever she needed them might just do the trick.

The rest of the morning hours passed like a feverish dream while Gina busied herself with a litany of preparations and last-minute inspections of the bedrooms and bathrooms on all three floors of the house. Meanwhile, ten or twelve of the guests had arrived from the city, some already sipping their first or second drink of the weekend, most of them settled in with the Sheffield kids in the lounge chairs surrounding the pool.

Gina made her way downstairs and into the dining room, expecting to work on the place settings and flower arrangements for the dinner table without having to feign interest in a guest's remarks or volley with them for the sake of chitchat. But as soon as she took the first plate from the stack, she heard Sheila and Leo arguing in hushed voices from the other side of the closed glass door of the sunroom. She watched them in profile. Although she knew she should move from their view before Sheila turned and caught her eavesdropping through the glass, the desire to hear their conversation pulled her closer, to within a few feet of the door.

"My head hurts, honey. Can we table this until after I've rested for a few hours?"

"It's a simple yes or no, Leo."

"I've already answered."

"So you drove out here in the middle of the night, by yourself, instead of coming today with your family."

"Yes, just like I said before I left. Is wanting some time alone so unfathomable?"

"And if I ask Pete if you were by yourself in the car, what do you suppose he'll say?"

"That I was! How many times do I have to defend myself to you? I don't have a mistress!"

"I know you're hiding something. Was Gina here when you arrived last night? Did you two get to have some *private* time?"

"This is exhausting."

"I've never understood your affection for her."

"Gina is an employee, nothing more. Stop this nonsense, and be nice to her for a change."

"You're a son of a bitch."

"And you're—"

"Go ahead, Leo. Say it."

"What's the point. We've said all this enough times already, and I'm in no shape to go toe-to-toe with you today. My head is fucking killing me."

Gina scooted over to one of the lakeside windows, pulled a chamois cloth from her back pocket and began wiping down the sill and frame, already regretting what she'd overheard, appalled that Sheila suspected that she and Leo might have some sort of romantic connection. She also knew Leo hadn't come out from the city alone, though he'd used the male pronoun when they stood outside with Pete. Referring to his mysterious guest, he'd said *he* had already left. Why Leo wanted to keep that person a secret from Sheila, it didn't really matter. Gina didn't want to find herself facing Sheila's questions, having to decide whether to blow his cover or reinforce more than one of his lies at once—buying her a conciliatory gift on his behalf, whenever she could escape the estate with Leo's credit card in hand, would be plenty.

To her right, Tiffany and Angelique came strolling in. A moment after, to her left, Sheila flung the sunroom's glass door open and entered the dining room with quick steps, scowling.

"Something wrong, Mom?" Tiffany asked.

"Your father's a big fat liar, but aside from that, everything's fine."

"I feel for you," Tiffany said. "Must be tough being a martyr all the time."

"I love you, too," Sheila said, exhaling loudly. "Please tell me that's your first glass of wine today."

"Sure, if it's what you want to hear. *Mother,* this is my very first glass."

"Cut the shit, honey. Let's be good hosts and visit with everyone."

Tiffany laughed and held the wineglass to her lip. "You really want to risk me saying what I think of them? You can handle chatting with the upper-crusties on your own, can't you?"

"*Now,* Tiffany."

Gina averted her eyes and moved a few feet closer to the corner and ran the cloth along the tall cherrywood window frame, hoping that by facing away they would pay her no mind. This tactic had worked well over the years—keep your head down and appear engrossed in some menial task so as not to invite the awkwardness. Be invisible so they won't realize their family drama has been witnessed, so they don't engage you in artificial conversation, so you won't have to play along and add yet another decorative layer to the lie. The lie being that their life at the estate qualified as a real-life *Town & Country* exposé in the making, rather than a toxic zone of bickering and resentment and little drops of poison.

She sensed Sheila and the girls leaving the room through the hall by the kitchen, but then glanced over her shoulder and found that Angelique had remained standing beside the dining table, looking toward the sunroom, her face flushed red and her jaw stressed as though she'd just been slapped. Across from her, Leo stood in the doorway. He and Angelique stared at one another with an intensity that made Gina wish she could tiptoe out of the room unnoticed, but instead she continued on with the cleaning charade, wiping the same immaculate strip of wood with her head down, reciting affirmations to herself, knowing that although they hadn't vocalized any recognition of her presence, the two must have been aware of her. She'd have to wait them out.

Angelique's footsteps trailed off in the direction of the living room, followed by the floorboards creaking behind her under Leo's weight. Gina turned slightly as Leo stopped the girl in the doorway and took her by the arm. She shrugged his hand away and whisper-shouted at him with a finger in his face. The only word Gina could make out was *don't*. And neither said another word before they left the dining room.

Gina paused, looking out the window at the bright runway of light shimmering off the lake and the handful of guests milling about the lawn in shorts and polo shirts, bathing suits and sarongs. What the hell had she just witnessed? Had Leo Sheffield been having an affair with his daughter's best friend? He was closing in on sixty and she was only eighteen or nineteen. Not that such a huge age difference mattered to some men. Rich and powerful men like Leo sauntered down the streets of the Hamptons all summer long with their trophy wives and flavors of the month at their sides, but this girl had practically grown up with the Sheffields, and Gina knew Leo well, or so she'd thought . . .

She pushed her hair away from her face and held it there, questioning her instincts about what she'd just seen and heard. Despite the terribly tense interaction with Angelique just now, Leo just didn't seem the type to either do anything so reckless or to cross such a fraught moral line. Still, that shirk of his arm and their body language—something was all wrong. The thought of him waiting for her to be of age, or worse, so much worse, the idea that maybe they'd begun having sex even before she'd turned eighteen, made Gina sick. But if anything like that *had* happened, wouldn't she have noticed something before? They'd had plenty of female guests at the estate over the years, some of them beautiful enough to be models, a few of them actual models, and Leo had never shown interest in any of them, let alone a girl as young as Angelique. Still, Gina couldn't think of another explanation for the emotional intensity of that interaction.

The longer she thought about it, though, the more she felt a key piece had eluded her. If Leo had been meeting Angelique in secret, then why did he also want to keep the unnamed male guest a secret from Sheila? And why had he left that cryptic voice-mail message before Gina arrived at work? His slip-and-fall story reeked of bullshit. Who the hell had Pete driven out here last night, before Leo's head got all bashed up—a friend of Angelique's? Did the man from the limo hit Leo in retaliation after he'd done something to her? All these questions made the hand-holding on the porch so much stranger and more troubling. She worried that Corey had stumbled into a spiderweb; that Angelique had been spinning him all morning and already had him wrapped around her finger, planning to use him for some shady purpose. She worried that her son had been blinded by infatuation, high on the idea that this pretty girl from the Upper East Side or wherever she lived had taken an interest.

She had to get out of the house for a minute and clear her head. The only task she could think of that justified some time alone outside was cutting tulips in the flower garden to add to the already lush dining room arrangements, so she trekked out from the kitchen with a pair of shears and a bucket and crossed the lawn amid the sounds of tipsy guests, her head turned to the left to catch glimpses of them. Gretchen's long, slender frame lay out on a blanket-covered chaise like a life-size Barbie with sunglasses, Andy Sheffield sunning himself beside her, a half-dozen others standing in the shallow end or dangling their legs in the water, everyone other than Gretchen laughing when Clay's sheepdog scampered onto the diving board and launched herself into the pool.

"Naughty girl, Polly!" Clay yelled, already cackling along with the rest of them. Gina stood still and watched from a distance as the dog paddled the length of the pool. Clay pulled what appeared to be a soggy plastic sandwich bag from her mouth right after she climbed the steps and told her she was naughty again, admonishing her for chewing on trash as she ran over to the row of chairs. His dog then shook water from her shaggy coat and sprayed everyone lounging there, sending some of them scampering back onto the lawn, squealing and shouting at her to stop. Andy laughed harder than Gina had ever witnessed, holding his stomach, meekly reaching his other hand out to console his distraught, uptight girlfriend, and at the same time Clay lunged to grab the sopping-wet dog by the collar, but missed. So then, of course, Polly made a beeline back to the diving board and took flight, all four paws outstretched when she hit the water with another huge splash.

The stasis in her legs relented and Gina walked on, entering the flower garden between one of the wrought-iron benches and the sundial. She kept walking until the path led her down a slope, where she soon found herself concealed by taller shrubs and the series of wooden structures with wisteria, thick as moss, clinging to the slats and beams. She set down the bucket, slid her hand to the base of her pocket and palmed the two loose pills, knowing she shouldn't take them but knowing just as well that she'd already made up her mind. *I need these,* she thought, and placed the pills on her tongue. But before she managed to swallow them she stepped back, startled by someone whispering loudly from behind the thick row of privet to her right.

"There's no excuse, I know," she heard Mr. Sheffield say, his voice about half its normal volume. "Please accept my apology. I'm begging you. On the lives of everyone I love, I'm so sorry I scared you like that. I've acted horribly, but you have to believe me. If I'd been in my right mind—you have to know, I would never hurt you."

Gina sank to the soil. On her hands and knees and with the pills tucked beside her molars, she listened to Angelique's response. "My boyfriend thinks we should turn you over to the cops."

"Please, you have to talk to him. Convince him not to say anything."

"Don't touch me!"

"Shh! Alright, Jesus, I'm sorry." Leo's voice shrank to a whisper. "But you have to convince him to keep quiet. Think of Tiffany. Think of what it would do to her to hear any of this."

"I don't want to tell anyone about last night, but we need money."

"You're blackmailing me?"

"I'm just telling you how this can all go away."

In the brief silence, Gina swallowed the pills and felt a sudden need to pee. He'd apologized for hurting her, but that could mean so many things. Had he hit her? Forced himself on her? Gina's gut told her it was the latter. Could Leo Sheffield really have assaulted a teenaged girl? The tone of their conversation implied that he had, and certain moments and phrases also triggered Gina to wonder if Angelique might be pregnant. Maybe she'd mentioned the money as a payoff for keeping her pregnancy a secret. Maybe some of it would pay for an abortion.

"All you have are accusations," Leo whispered forcefully. "And I could press charges against him for assault just as easily."

Gina crawled next to the row of privet, rose to her feet and found a sliver between the bushes where she could see the two of them in profile.

"He took pictures," Angelique said.

"He what?"

"Photos."

"What are you talking about?"

"Of your friend, in the pool, while you were getting another bottle and that blanket in the house. We know what you did, and we have the pictures to prove it."

Mr. Sheffield stared with glazed eyes. "Well, then," he said. "Guess you got me." Sweat rolled along his jaw and gathered at his chin during a long, intense pause. Then he went on, speaking in an unsettling monotone. "So exactly how much do you and your bloodsucking accomplice want to keep quiet?"

Angelique took a second to push her hair back before answering, then leveled her eyes at him. "One million."

"Seriously?"

Gina watched him raise an eyebrow, and for a brief flash she thought he may have grinned. But then his face went slack once more.

"Done," he said. "You'll have it tomorrow night."

"Tonight would be better."

"You realize how fucking difficult it is to get a million dollars in cash together when all the banks are closed? I'll have it tomorrow. Here, just after sunset."

"Fine," she said, "but one more thing. I don't want to see you till then. Don't even look at me after we leave the garden—not till you hand over the money."

Leo brought his hands to his face and exhaled so loudly it resembled a growl, then quickly reached out and grabbed her arm. She shoved his hand off. "I told you, don't ever fucking touch me again."

"Sorry, but hold on a minute. What assurances can you give me that you and this guy with the photos will keep quiet? And how do I know you won't ask for more?"

"Sucks being at someone else's mercy, doesn't it? Kind of feels like someone just tackled you and pinned you to the ground?"

Gina had to get away before they left their hiding spot. She wished she hadn't heard any of this, and definitely didn't want to hear another word. What the hell had Angelique meant about photos of Leo's *friend* in the pool? Sweating as she moved along the path, she thought again about the unnamed man from the limo and Leo calling her phone so early in the morning, asking for help. Then she thought back to Corey and Angelique holding hands, hoping her son had become the girl's confidant and nothing more. Could Corey have had a hand in what happened to Leo? No, she decided right away, he couldn't have. He'd been out doing whatever he usually did, probably drinking with his friends, not here at the estate in the middle of the night. The man in the limo, he must have been the one. But who was he?

She gathered the shears and bucket and frantically clipped a variety of tulips, hurrying to finish so she could return to the house. Leo claimed his head wound had come from slipping next to the pool, but Gina feared the truth involved the man Pete had mentioned, who may or may not be some boyfriend of Angelique's, who may or may not have foiled Leo's attempted rape or assaulted him as retribution for some such sick behavior with her in the past. Whatever the ugly truth, none of this made any sense. She'd worked for Leo Sheffield since her boys were little and had respected him all the while. On more than one drunken night at the estate he'd confided a paternal affection, stating that he thought of her as more than an employee, almost as family. But what she'd heard Angelique say just now, coupled with the girl's reaction to Leo touching her in the dining room, it all seemed to point to some sort of assault. How hadn't Gina seen the evil in him during all these years? How had he managed to hide his dark side so well?

With her bucket of flowers, she approached the end of the path, her heart beating in her throat. She leaned her head out from the flower-covered archway and saw the Sheffield boys and seven or eight guests still lollygagging poolside. The wide patch of lawn between the garden and the kitchen entrance looked clear, but it would take plenty of steps to get there. She focused on the distant doorway, preparing to walk a reasonable pace across the lawn—but then, with her very first step, she met Leo head-on, her hands out to avoid colliding with him as he came stomping with his head down from the other side of the curved privet wall. He stopped, and after staring for a moment with sweat dribbling down his forehead, he placed a hand on her arm.

"Gina," he said, out of breath. "I think I need to lie down."

She exhaled, eyeing him until he hung his head and brought his palms to his face. With her arms crossed and the bucket dangling below her elbow, she spoke as she would to one of her kids when they'd done something disappointing, formulating a sentence she never imagined saying to him.

"First," she said, "I think you'd better tell me what the hell that whole conversation with Angelique just now was about."

Leo tilted his head back and released an exasperated sigh. Then he faced her and responded with zero emotion. "I don't know where to start." Over his shoulder, Gina saw Angelique walking away from them, toward the chess pieces and the much larger sculptures.

"I need to sleep awhile," he said, taking an awkward step to the side. "Help me upstairs, and if you promise to keep it between us, tonight I'll tell you the whole thing. Everything that's been going on."

"Not sure I can promise the keeping-the-secret part. Not this time. Not until I hear the full story."

"Fair enough," he said, looking gut-shot.

"If you hurt that girl, she has every right to report you."

"It's a much more complicated situation than you can possibly imagine."

"Well, I feel sick over what I just heard." She took his arm as if yanking a child away from fire, and together they started toward the kitchen door. "I can see you're not well, so I'll have some mercy for now and let you sleep first. But you're going to tell me *everything* when you wake up."

He looked at the ground and nodded, the very personification of shame as she let him enter the kitchen ahead of her. The screen door slapped closed and she plodded alongside him past Josie and Michael, both of them preoccupied with their own chores while she helped him into the hall and up the stairs and finally into the master bedroom.

With Leo under the covers, she stood in the doorway and looked at him lying there on his side, facing the opposite wall, the square of gauze taped to his head discolored with a brownish-red splotch where his wound had suppurated at the stitch line. This man had shown so many kindnesses to her. He'd given her all those small loans, which were really gifts that he kept secret from his wife. He'd sat with her on the kitchen steps a number of nights last summer, and sometime around Fourth of July weekend calmly encouraged her to open up about her troubles with Ray. The contrast between those intimate conversations and the deeply disturbing one she'd overheard in the garden with Angelique was stunning. How could this be the same man? What had he done to his daughter's friend?

She closed the bedroom door and walked downstairs in a daze, then wandered along the ground floor even more detached, as though sleepwalking, first passing by Tiffany, who sat cross-legged on the living room rug with a giant sketch pad in her lap, then past a white-haired couple who said hello and stared at Gina when she didn't say anything in response. As she passed the kitchen doorway, Josie called out to her, asking for help with something, but her voice hardly registered, as if she'd spoken from a remote frequency, like a distress signal from a desert island through layers of radio static.

Gina kept wandering, barely aware of her surroundings until she stopped beside the deep sink in the hall between the dining room and kitchen and hunched over. A sheen of sweat coated her face. Her hand shook as the faucet handle turned. She cupped her fingers under the rushing stream. *I can't do this,* she thought, meaning sobriety, then realized she meant her job as well, as she ladled the cold water to her lips.

# TWENTY

By dinnertime, Corey had finished his shift at the estate and finally returned home for a nap. After an hour of coma-like sleep in his bed, he awoke to his brother telling him that Mick was on the phone, and then, as he sat up, Dylan handed him a shiny new key to the front door.

"Wait, why do we have new keys?"

"Mom had someone change the locks today, so Ray can't just walk in anymore."

Corey squinted at the dust-coated clock on his bureau, groggy as hell when he took Dylan's cell phone and said to Mick, "What's up. I'm sleeping."

"Yo, I need you to drive me to Layne's for a bag. I'll smoke you up for it."

"Sorry, can't. I gotta be somewhere in a little while."

"Ah, come on, man. How about I spot you a couple of fat spliffs just for the quick run over there? Then, you know, I'll just need you to drop me at the bonfire—before you take off for wherever the fuck you need to be."

Corey looked at the clock once more, relieved that he still had some time before he was supposed to pick up Angelique, and reluctantly agreed.

A half hour later, with Dylan wedged in the middle and Mick in the passenger seat, Corey downshifted his pickup as they went snaking through dense woods, bouncing and swerving down Layne's long dirt driveway with muddy water splashing up the tires from the deeper, wider holes. He slowed where a space opened up in the woods and rolled to a stop in front of the porch light glaring above the rickety screen door. A late-eighties Crown Vic with a cracked windshield and a slightly newer Corolla with a missing hubcap were parked at angles by the house. They belonged to a couple of the local burnouts Corey had known most of his life, guys so perpetually stoned that at times they could be mistaken for furniture. But the pimped-out black Ford pickup off to the right belonged to Ray, and for Ray to end up out there scoring weed or whatever else from Layne, Corey figured he must already be coked to the gills and wasted from hours of pints and bourbons at Gilligan's.

One of the knuckles on his right hand cracked when he unconsciously tightened it into a fist. His other hand tilted back the tallboy can of Bud he'd been holding between his legs. He finished it off while opening his driver's-side door, and he and Mick stepped out.

Although he'd told his brother to wait for them, Dylan hopped out of the truck and grabbed his arm. "Hang on, Core. Ray's inside. You sure you want to go in?"

"Yeah, I'll be fine."

"You didn't see how crazy he looked today, though. Mom even told me she's getting a restraining order."

"Good," Corey said.

"Just don't get into it with him, alright? It's not worth it."

A sea of crickets chirped all around them, their backdrop broken by the metallic whine of the screen door's hinges, and the heavy clomping sound when Layne, their forty-year-old weed dealer, stepped out. Dressed in his usual dirty white tank and jeans, his sleeves of tattoos exposed, his feet in unlaced work boots, he stood staring at them from the lopsided porch, grinning as he raised a pipe to his mouth. He flicked his lighter and touched the flame to the bowl, stifled a cough and released a plume.

Corey nudged his brother's shoulder to convey that everything would be okay, and joined Mick on the path to the house. The two walked up the slatted old porch steps and each fist-bumped Layne, who greeted them through another burst of smoke from his lungs, each of his words squeezed while he continued the long exhale. "What, just you two? Where're the girls?"

Mick shook his head and clapped him on the shoulder. "You're a bad man, my friend. I'm ashamed to be associated with you. Let me get a hit of that."

Layne's laughter resumed, a choppy, goatlike sound that scared most people who didn't know him and weirded out practically every girl he ever encountered. Mick lit the bowl and with his elbow swung open the screen door, and the three of them entered the front room.

Red-faced and red-eyed, Ray smiled from his couch seat and raised a hand. "Well, well. Looky who we got here. Hey, *tough guy*. Long time no see."

Corey kept his hands in his jean pockets, concerned that he might finally haul off on him otherwise. "You're not funny."

His smile already fading, Ray leaned back with his arm slung along the top of the couch. "Okeydoke, then, whatcha up to, tough guy? Checking up on me?"

"I don't give a shit what you do," Corey said. "And stop fucking calling me that."

Ray held a green long-necked bottle gripped between his thumb and two fingers, and tilted it back as he leaned forward and rested his elbows on his knees. "Your mom ask about me? She's missing me now, huh?" His smile returned, but went unacknowledged as Corey and Mick followed Layne down the hall to his bedroom, where he kept his stash in a bowling ball bag in the closet.

The deal took less than a minute, and with his quarter-ounce bag of hydro stuffed in his pocket, Mick entered the front room first and opened the screen door. Corey trailed closely behind and tried not to make eye contact with Ray again, thinking no good at all could come from it, but his soon-to-be ex-stepdad quickly stood from the couch and blocked his path, stinking like a brewery floor when he placed a hand on Corey's shoulder and leaned in as if to tell him a secret.

"Shouldn't do drugs, Core," he whispered, his eyes bulging.

"Like you're one to talk."

"Hey," he said with a rush of anger, "let me tell you something. I can handle my shit. And you're just a piss-ant kid who's living at home, and I'm the sucker who went and married your crazy fucked-in-the-head mom."

"Yeah? Well, she kicked your loser ass out. And guess what—*No,* she doesn't fucking miss you. None of us do."

"Why you always gotta be such a little prick." He leaned closer, his forehead almost touching Corey's. "Huh? What was that? Speak into the mic." He tapped Corey's head with his knuckle. "Answer me. Why you always—gotta be—such a little—bitty . . . *prick.*"

Tempted to shove Ray's arm to the side or bull his way past, Corey leveled his stare.

He'd promised Dylan.

*Be the bigger man.*

And he was also about to meet up with Angelique.

*He's not worth it.*

He took a step toward the door, feeling calmer but still ready for a fight. "This's been fun and all," he said, "but I'm out." He managed to squeeze past Ray, and with the next step he shoved the screen door open.

Halfway to his truck, Ray jogged up from behind and grabbed him by the shoulder. "Hold up. Fucking hear me out for a minute." He let go when Corey turned and let the crickets answer for him. Then he hoisted his bottle for another sip but saw that it was empty and dropped it on the ground, quick to grab Corey again by his shirt. "You didn't answer my question in there."

"Dude, take your fucking hands off me."

"You can go, *after* you tell me why you're such a fucking little prick to me all the time."

"I only have one thing left to say to you," Corey said, shoving him and taking a step back, too sick of holding the anger in to censor himself anymore. "Fuck-the-fuck off, Ray. Forever."

Ray's eyes blazed as he stepped toward him. Corey kept backing away.

"You think you can talk to me like that and just walk off?" Ray's voice had risen, oddly high-pitched, his jaw flexing and nostrils flared when he reached back to his beltline. "You think you're tough, huh?" Then suddenly his hand thrust forward and the barrel of a black handgun was aimed dead-center between Corey's eyes. "Who's the fucking tough guy now?"

Corey raised his hands. "Whoa, chill," he said, taking a half step back. "You're not gonna shoot me. Just put that shit down."

"Look at my face and tell me I'm lying."

The truck doors opened and Mick and Dylan stepped out, his brother saying, "Hey, let's just go, Core, alright? We'll just go now, Ray."

"Not till your prick older brother says he's sorry."

Corey stepped backward, slowly, wedging his hands in his pockets without breaking eye contact. As Mick and Dylan returned to the truck through the passenger-side door and gently pulled it shut, he crept around to the driver's side, still looking at the drunk and strung-out guy with the gun pointed at his head. Standing beside his door, he raised his hand, unsure if Ray had slid into a blackout or had snapped, possibly now in the midst of a total mental breakdown. With his palm out he offered a casual wave, hoping to diffuse the bombs in Ray's eyes, and called out as calmly as he could, "I'll see ya, Ray."

That's when the gun finally shifted away from him, but only slightly. Ray pulled the trigger— *Bang! Bang! Bang!*—three bullets shot into an oak trunk a few feet from Corey's front bumper, the bark splintering off close enough for some to graze his cheek.

Mick whispered loudly, "Get the fuck in, man!" and without a moment's hesitation Corey ducked in, turned his key, flipped on the headlights and jammed down on the clutch, shifting into Reverse, his back tires spinning even before his door swung closed. Ray fired again into the woods, shouting between shots, "See you soon, tough guy!"

After he'd whipped the truck around, in the rearview Corey kept his focus on the drunk, coked-up maniac behind him who hadn't moved from that spot in front of Layne's house and also hadn't lowered the gun. Moths fluttered around the bare bulb over the porch while he yelled something incoherent, his frame shrinking in the mirror as the truck sped away—though if the gun had a fully loaded clip, not fast enough. Flooring it across the uneven ground and shallow mud puddles, Corey saw Ray step forward and level the gun at the truck's rear window. "Mick, get down!" he yelled, pushing his brother's head forward just as Ray fired the gun once more.

The bullet blasted the driver's-side mirror and sent it dangling by a wire. The boys shouted all at once.

"Holy fuck!"

"Go, man!"

"Fucking shit!"

With the tires spinning and the chassis rocking

and creaking, the pickup raced into the mouth of the dirt drive, the three of them thrown wildly about as the gun fired one last time and a tree branch splintered off to the right.

No one made a sound once they were finally swallowed by the woods, safely out of sight. Dylan had his knees angled away from the gearshift, he and Mick both with their hands pressed flat against the dashboard while Corey kept the pedal to the floor. The tires churned up a steady spray of pebbles and the axles went slamming and jockeying from one deep depression to another, until suddenly the woods opened up at the road.

Once they were cruising for a minute, Dylan faced the windshield and muttered, "What a fuckin' nut-bag."

Then Mick leaned behind him to catch Corey's eye. "Hey, you good?"

He kept looking straight ahead, lit a cigarette before he answered. "What do you mean?"

"I mean with Ray."

He shrugged. His tongue felt swollen. The headlights slashed across the oaks bordering the road as they leaned into a curve. Even if he could have spoken then, he had no words. Had it ever been good with Ray around? Had he, Corey, ever been *good?* Other than the one long night he'd spent with Angelique at the ocean, after she leaned in and kissed him, he couldn't remember a time when all his muscles weren't tight, as if his natural state had always been to walk through life braced for the next lightning strike. Just now Ray had held his life in his hand, and drunk as he was, Corey—or his brother—could have been killed before ever knowing anything outside this suffocating place. How stupid would it have been to die there tonight?

He considered telling Gina about this in the morning, but then thought about how Dylan had described her shuffling into the house last night after her time in the hospital. Hearing that Ray had threatened him with a gun and went so far as to fire it toward both her sons would only send her the rest of the way over the edge. She'd told Dylan she was getting a restraining order, so she must already know that her ex had officially flown off the rails. Maybe that would keep her and Dylan safe from now on. Otherwise, Corey wouldn't be able to leave. And he was hoping Angelique might consider leaving with him instead of on her own. Goddamn . . . He needed to escape this place . . . this crazy townie bullshit that he'd been enduring here his entire fucking life.

The road was all curves until he slowed and made a left turn toward the bay. He had to drop off Mick and Dylan at the dead-end road nearby where some of the surfers and other burners had a bonfire going, and then hightail it to Southampton to meet Angelique outside the Sheffields' gates. She'd be waiting there in twenty minutes. He could make it there in fifteen.

Tonight they'd talk out the money exchange with Leo and toss around ideas about where she should go once she had it. Could he go with her? Whether she felt comfortable with him taking off with her or not, he couldn't imagine staying here one more day. And after being at the estate since early that morning and confronting Mr. Sheffield so many hours ago, Angelique probably needed to get away just as much as Corey needed to get back to her. And like him, he imagined, she wouldn't be able to breathe a full breath until she did.

# TWENTY-ONE

Leo awoke in his bed, confused by the faint voices outside the windows until he recognized them as Sheila and a handful of her friends chatting ground-level on the lake side of the house. He squinted at the French doors and through the space between the drapes above the balcony railing. The dark sky and general stillness inside the house oriented him enough to assume that he'd slept through dinner, rising now after many of the kids' friends and his company employees had departed and the six or eight remaining guests had transitioned to brandy and cognac and port wines out on the porch.

He pressed his hand to the bandage taped to the back of his head, quick needle stabs resuming along the track of stitches when he eased his legs over and pressed his feet to the hardwood. With his robe slipped on, he stepped as quietly as he could across the bedroom floor while Sheila and the guests maintained their steady murmuring outside. It hadn't even been a full twenty-four hours since Henry's death, but Leo couldn't leave him in the pines much longer. Someone could so easily wander out there, and now, Gina had overheard his conversation with Angelique and wanted the full story. He had to move Henry

257

off the property—tonight, if possible—but how?

Entering the hall by the soft red haze from the night-light plugged in at the baseboard, he stepped toes-first along the creaking floorboards, his arm extended toward the banister like a drowning man reaching for a lifeline, and step by step he crept even more cautiously down the stairs. Thankfully, no one reentered the house while Leo rifled through kitchen drawers for a flashlight. He eased the kitchen door closed behind him and loped across the lawn under the cover of darkness, toward the archway in the garden wall where he'd stumbled into Gina that afternoon. He figured that at this late hour she must have gone for the night, but if she hadn't, and if she knew he'd left his bed, she'd push him to tell her everything.

The thought of confessing to her that he'd dragged Henry to the farthest corner of the property and left him there—dead—triggered him to pick up his pace past the sculptures and tennis courts. Then he pushed harder, running, suddenly terrified that his father's voice would transmogrify from his conscience once more. Braced for another psychological beating, he looked over his shoulder toward the house and the pool and the lake receding in the distance. He needed to get to Henry, but just as much, he needed to outrun the old man. Propelled by the desperate hope of avoiding his father's ghostly descent from the treetops or ascent from the soil, Leo pressed on, his robe flapping behind, his head throbbing so intensely beneath the bandage that he feared he might pass out. Dizzy as hell, he finally slowed just before the pine boughs, which loomed as a jagged border to the star-dotted sky.

He veered from the lawn and advanced until the heavy canopy of limbs covered him and blocked the view of the house. When he reached the area where he'd tried to dig, he flicked the flashlight on and followed the cone of light along the route he'd taken while dragging Henry into the woods. The path, he could see now, would be far too easy for a curious guest to follow; he'd left a drag trail through the fallen needles, over the root-gnarled ground, all the way from the lawn to the densely wooded property line.

He'd intended to leave Henry as well hidden as possible, but damn, what a piss-poor job he'd done to conceal him in the dark. He knelt down and swept the flashlight beam along Henry's body. The loose blanket no longer fully covered his head, and a sizable scrap of the wool was missing after it somehow had been torn away. Scanning his surroundings, Leo found items strewn around that he had no memory of leaving behind, each of which could be cataloged as evidence—the shovel, the empty Glenlivet bottle, the garbage bag with Henry's cell phone and wallet and his clothes spilled out on the ground—

each item undoubtedly covered by dozens of Leo's fingerprints.

The flashlight returned to Henry's face, his half-closed eye, his slack bottom lip, the pine needles crosshatched over his ear. For quite some time, Leo stared at him through a watery blur, as though rain had begun sliding down a windowpane, while his memory steadily pieced back together a film reel summary of the day they'd met . . . the company party on that cold, windy evening before the Thanksgiving holiday. One of the less-than-memorable employees introducing Henry and a minute later excusing himself to freshen his drink, leaving Leo to stand there with the smiling young man. The attraction on his side he'd tried to ignore. No one at Seri-Corp knew Leo preferred the company of men to begin with, and then, as the boss, he also had to tread extra cautiously as far as flirting with an employee of any gender. As handsome as Henry was, Leo assumed he had a girlfriend, or possibly a boyfriend, though even if he didn't, surely a good-looking man in his midtwenties wasn't thinking about Leo as he would have hoped.

But then they spoke for the next few minutes about . . . well, it didn't matter what they spoke about . . . Leo quickly picked up on Henry's signs, his light touches on Leo's arm when he laughed, his prolonged eye contact and sustained smile, his charming compliments. And then, before Leo even realized what was happening, Henry dropped the volume of his voice, leaned in and said, "I'm free tonight, if you'd like to speak some more in private," and without any hesitation Leo agreed that they should meet. And for all the months since then a blank space stood in his memory between that thrilling moment and the slow-motion sequence two hours later, when Leo opened the door of the presidential suite and slipped the Do Not Disturb sign on the knob, the closing of the door, the dead bolt in place, the silence before their first kiss, and the lack of words during the dreamlike hours that followed. No man had ever felt as lucky as Leo had that night—or as unlucky when, hours later, they had to part ways.

Leo leaned closer and slid the blanket back over Henry's head, but then immediately jolted backward when a burst of electronic music sent him falling to his hip, the flashlight beam slashing wildly over the pine trunks and the ground as he crawled like a starving dog over to the bag of clothes and hurriedly emptied all the contents. The techno beat continued blaring from the pine needles beside him. Henry's ring tone played for another few intense heartbeats while Leo searched the ground. Then, mercifully, it went silent just as he found the damned phone.

Leo squinted and discovered the name **Mom** and the words **Missed Call** highlighted on the screen. He checked the phone's menu bar and swallowed against the lump in his throat when he saw the litany of notifications—ten other missed calls, fourteen unread texts, nine unheard voice mails. Henry had been missed—missed by people who cared about him, the most frequent caller and texter being his mother. But Leo had called this week, too, and there were plenty of his old messages listed in the queue as well. He'd need to erase every one of them, starting with any voice mails Henry may have saved, then all his incriminating texts—and there would be tons of them—somewhere in the neighborhood of a hundred sex texts, way too many playful phrases with words like *kiss* and *suck* and *fuck,* and hundreds more that at least implied a romantic relationship, hundreds of Henry and Leo's private flirtations waiting like grenades without pins.

*I'm in hell,* Leo thought, realizing he also needed to erase the same scroll of evidence from his own phone—the long, damning text thread, the voice mails, the explicit emails, every single photo, no matter how benign any may have seemed before. He decided to listen to Henry's nine voice mails first, though, to know who'd called him and to see what they'd said, starting with the message Henry's mother just left.

"It's me again," the woman said, her voice shaky as she went on. "You said you'd check in at least once a day . . . Please, Henry. Call me . . . I need to

262

know you're okay." Silence filled the recording for another few seconds, as if she'd waited for him to answer, before finally hanging up.

Leo's eyes watered as he scrolled through the other voice mails. Two of the messages had come from unknown numbers earlier that afternoon, the first of those from a solicitor, but the second one stunned him and sent an awful chill along the length of his spine. "Hello," the recorded voice said. "This is Detective James Faraday, calling for Henry Beauchamp. We've received a missing person's report from a Mrs. Lorraine Beauchamp—your mother—who informed us that you were recently admitted to Brooklyn Mount Sinai Hospital for psychiatric observation, and that during the past week since you were discharged she's been unable to contact you. If you could please contact me at the following number when you get this message, that would be a great help." The detective proceeded to leave his number, the same one Leo had seen listed next to the voice mail.

The moment the recording ended he erased it. His throat felt swollen. He angled the flashlight toward the body. Henry's mother must have reported him missing even before he came out here to the estate. Why hadn't he just called her back? A new streak of pain penetrated Leo's skull. He thought about calling a car to drive him to the airport. He thought of the gun in his safe upstairs.

The energy drained from his limbs. His heartbeat seemed to slow, as if his life force were trickling out and seeping into the ground. He imagined himself a lost hiker on a frozen mountainside, laid out on ice, too tired to continue on, wanting only to sleep.

Acceptance washed through. He wouldn't be able to cover this up, not for long, and the idea of fleeing dissipated like smoke in a breeze. He hung his head. All along, the crude plan to disappear had been nothing more than a desperate dream. They would lock him up either way.

With the flashlight aimed at the ground, he looked over at the vague lump in the darkness. The detective's message meant someone *would* come here eventually. The missing person's report made it official now. Leo crawled toward Henry's body, weighted down by the same crushing sadness he'd felt when he dragged him out here, though now also feeling a surprising swell of anger. Kneeling next to the body, he leaned forward and groaned, doubting for the first time that Henry's death had really been accidental. Perhaps he'd simply followed through with his suicide attempt that had landed him in the psych ward earlier in the week, though to do so here would amount to intentionally setting Leo up for a long, hard fall.

A breath of wind permeated the woods as he leaned closer to the blanket covering Henry's head and whispered, "Did you plan all this? Is this payback for me not returning your *I love you?*"

He started sobbing, but then couldn't breathe. He wasn't sure if he even wanted to breathe anymore. *No,* he thought—*no more self-pity! Man up!* He returned to his feet, wobbly, dizzy. Only the weak-willed threw in the towel without first fighting with everything they had, and Leo was anything but weak. His father had made sure of that. He still had time. Suicide was *not* the only option. He wouldn't just curl up and die, not yet, anyway. First things first; he had to focus on erasing every damning word he and Henry had ever said to each other that still remained on either of their phones.

His thumbs worked frantically for a moment until the menu question on Henry's screen arose: **Erase entire conversation?** Box checked. Yes. All texts erased. Alright, next—the six saved voice-mail messages from Leo, saved under the moniker **Papa Sheff**, all deleted. He needed to wipe away every electronic trace of his connection to Henry, then take out the battery and smash it with a hammer, along with the sim card and the rest of the phone—obliterate it before Detective Faraday pinpointed its signal here—

*Shit. They can track this thing with GPS.* The phone felt radioactive in his hand as he flipped it over and clawed at it to remove it from its case.

He paused, unsure if he'd heard something moving in the woods. Then he knew he hadn't imagined it. Branches rustled behind him. His head turned sharply away from the sideways cone of light beaming at his feet. More rustling, followed by sounds like snapping twigs, like footsteps. He squeezed Henry's phone tighter, squinting at the darkness.

"Mr. Sheffield? What are you doing out here?"

He fumbled with the flashlight and aimed it at the drag trail, saw nothing at first but then lengthened the beam. Her white sneakers, her legs and cargo shorts came into focus.

She stepped closer, into the light.

"Gina," he said, turning quickly toward Henry and then back to face her. "Let me explain."

# TWENTY-TWO

Gina had been sitting in the dark, nipping from a bottle of Grey Goose in one of the vacant third-floor bedrooms, too afraid of bumping into Sheila to journey out to her car and finally leave for the night. She'd been thinking the same thought for nearly an hour: *Five more minutes, then I'll make a run for the kitchen door.* Though now, after drinking shot after shot of straight liquor and forcing her eyelids to remain open, she'd also become wary of driving at all.

Mired down, feeling stuck in the dark bedroom thanks to her own drunken stupidity, she happened to be looking out the window when Leo left the house from the kitchen door dressed in nothing but his red silk robe and slippers. She opened her eyes wider and watched him shuffle across the lawn until he reached the sculptures, leaning closer to the windowpane when he began jogging with an awkward gait away from the house.

Drunk and high from too many pills, she imagined his reason for venturing so far from the house after dark—to meet up with Angelique, either to pay her off or to revisit their tense conversation in the garden earlier that afternoon. She slugged a much heftier gulp from the vodka bottle and stood up, intent on confronting him. If he tried to fire her, so be it. He'd done something terrible and she knew it. She was untouchable.

She set the bottle on the windowsill, left the bedroom and staggered along the hall, then hurried down the two flights of stairs, pausing momentarily at the ground floor landing to listen to Sheila and her socialite friends babbling bullshit on the lake side of the house, their voices wafting in through the screen doors. After bumbling against the walls of the hallway, she entered the kitchen and immediately clattered into the copper cookware that Michael had left overturned on the center island, cursing under her breath as she stepped much more carefully the rest of the way to the door.

Once outside, she paced next to the pine boughs, off-balance, wandering along the dark tree line, knowing he was out there somewhere but not yet seeing or hearing any trace of him. Then a glow of light winked and splintered through the branches deep in the woods and pulled her from the lawn.

She followed a rough path between the trunks where the pine needles had been swept aside and soon spotted him about twenty yards ahead with his back to her. From there she crept toward him cautiously, expecting to find him with Angelique, maybe with a sack of cash passing between them. But instead, she found her long-time boss alone, hunched over in his robe. A liquor bottle lay beside him on the ground, along with some scattered clothes—a pair of pants and a crumpled white shirt, a jacket sleeve draped from a garbage bag—and a bit farther back, a shovel laid out beside some sort of mound—something oblong and lumpy wrapped in a blanket. She rubbed her eyes, confused by everything, the low light from his flashlight making it difficult to gauge the overall scene as she approached. With her next step, he turned. As if speaking inside a dream, she asked him what he was doing out there.

"Gina," he said, flashing the light at her feet and then raising it up, straight into her eyes. "Let me explain."

The dreaminess of the scene faded quickly and she snapped at him, "Where is she!"

Tripping over a thick root as she stumbled closer, tempted to punch his face once she stood over him, she fought through her own slurring as all the pent-up anxiety came rushing out in anger.

"You did something awful to Angelique. I know you did, so don't even try to deny it. I thought I knew you, but you're nothing more than a predator." She paused, then shouted, "Say something, you two-faced piece of shit!"

Leo stayed on his knees, his face shrouded in shadow. Gina hovered over him for a moment, swayed and then kicked his thigh. "Start talking!"

"She isn't here," he said, his body shaking as

though electrodes had begun zapping him from neck to knees. "There's so much. I'm sorry . . . It's just too much. I can't even think anymore."

She kicked him again, harder, and he bent even closer to the ground. The vodka had loosened her, eroded her usual filter, empowering her now to speak to him as she'd never done before. She felt absolutely righteous in her indignation for this man who'd fooled her so completely for so many years, and had no desire to hold back anymore. "You said you'd tell me the whole story, so you're going to fucking tell it all. Now!"

With his head down, Leo answered meekly, "Just look around. Nothing matters anymore. I'm going to hell." He dropped the flashlight at Gina's feet and buckled at his waist. "I'm in hell already," he said, and fell into an awful fit of sobbing, rocking forward and back and muttering pleas for forgiveness. Gina picked up the flashlight and directed the beam at the dirty bandage taped to the back of his head, and then his face, his red eyes, wet cheeks, snot running from his nose. *He looks like shit,* she thought, and then felt compelled to say so.

"Leo," she said, conscious of the fact that this was the first time in twelve years that she'd ever called him by his first name. "You should see yourself. Mr. Fortune-Five-Hundred CEO, Mr. I've got a mansion in the Hamptons and a ridiculous penthouse and everything else in the world a person could ever dream of having. You should really see yourself right now. You look like hammered shit."

He could fire her, sure, but at this point who the hell cared. She wouldn't work for a predator, and if Angelique needed backup when she pressed charges, Gina would testify. She'd say whatever needed to be said. *From now on,* she decided, *these abusers are all going to answer for their crimes.*

Leo kept sobbing while she swept the ground with the flashlight, shining it over the random things scattered about. Looking closer at the pieces of a suit, she felt goose bumps rise along her arms. And the shovel—why was there a shovel out here? She stepped a bit farther, straining her eyes as she approached the mound. It had an especially odd shape, elongated but also with strange curved sections. Something hidden, wrapped in a blanket. She moved closer. With each step she took, the shrinking cone of light clarified the shape more and more. The blanket itself, when she got a better look at it, was familiar—the afghan from Leo and Sheila's master bedroom.

*Wait,* she thought, *what's it wrapped around— is that—no—it can't be—an ear, a hand?* She gasped, too shocked to scream.

"It was an accident," Leo said directly behind her.

271

She swiveled so quickly she dropped the flashlight, spiraled down and fell to her side. Before she could even get to her feet the adrenaline sent her scrambling away from both Leo and the body, moving into the darkness of the woods, struggling on all fours like a wounded fox being pursued by a vicious pack of hounds. She sensed Leo moving toward her, right behind her, heard his feet crunching over the dry needles a moment before he grabbed her by the arm.

"Please wait," he begged as she broke free. "It really *was* an accident."

She couldn't see well enough to locate the path or even to know which direction to run. She felt him beside her and slapped at the darkness, connecting with nothing, still struggling to stand as she stumbled along on hands and knees. He grabbed her again and cinched his arms around her in a tight hug. She fell to her thigh, his hand clamped over her mouth as she just now thought to scream, the two of them flailing in the pine needles until he wrestled her to her side and pressed his weight down. She kept wailing into his hand, screaming for help from unknown depths, worked her jaw and managed to bite his finger, and yet still he kept his hand clamped there.

"There's more to it than you think," he said, whispering intensely next to her ear. "Just let me explain."

With his hand pressed so tightly over her mouth, she could hardly breathe. She'd caught him with a dead body. She knew now that he needed to silence her, that he wasn't simply trying to subdue her; he was trying to kill her. The most primal part of her, the survival instinct, kept her punching and clawing at him, while he struggled to keep her from screaming, wedged to the ground.

"Please, let me say this," he said more desperately. "Hold still for a second and listen!" She squirmed more but he kept her pinned. She had no leverage. Her only chance now was to wriggle her head until she could bite his finger again.

"Stop! Just let me say what I have to say, and then I'll let you up," he wheezed, then went on in a softer tone, though at a much more frantic pace. "Do whatever you want after I let you go—just hear me out first. Henry, my friend over there, he came out here with me Thursday night. Pete drove us from the city. It was late when we arrived. We were doing drugs. We drank too much. When I was in the house and he was out by the pool, he had a terrible accident. I don't even really know what happened, but he died, and I was so distraught, so drunk, I wasn't in my right mind when I brought him out here."

Although Gina couldn't muster another scream with his palm holding her mouth closed and partially covering her nose, the lack of oxygen panicked her even more and she tried to push him off her in a few quick moves, kicking, grasping at pine needles and throwing them where she guessed his face might be.

"Please stop," he said, breathing heavily, sounding exhausted. "Please just listen to me and then I'll let go. I promise I won't hurt you. And you need to believe me—I didn't hurt Henry, either. He was a friend, a good friend. I may have even loved him. I don't know anymore. But whether I loved him or not, I cared for him. We cared for one another. He'd had issues before we met, and this week he'd tried to kill himself. I brought him out here so we could have one good night together before I had to pretend to be someone I'm not for the rest of the summer. I was in the house getting us something to eat, then found him in the pool. He wasn't breathing. I tried, I swear to you I did everything I could, but I was drunk, very drunk . . . I probably hadn't even gotten to him in time for mouth-to-mouth to make any difference. He was dead. I was alone with him, and he was dead. I hid him out here in a moment of panic. That's the truth. I didn't know what else to do."

After a pause, he added, "On the lives of my kids, I didn't kill him. I would never have even hurt him. Just like I'd never hurt you. *Never*."

Gina hadn't intended to listen, but since she'd

been forced to lie there pressed beneath him, unable to move, his story had seeped in regardless, detail by detail. The dead man under the blanket, whose name Leo said was Henry, their secret affair, the accident, his whole bizarre story— while Leo had been speaking she'd witnessed the disastrous chain of events from Thursday night as if watching a sped-up movie reel—it was all too crazy and too detailed to be a lie.

"And the rest of it," Leo said, finally releasing some pressure from his hand over her mouth. "The conversation you heard today. That was another part of this whole fucking awful mess. See, Angelique was here Thursday night, too."

While he paused to catch his breath, Gina shouted into his hand and squirmed to get him off her, though much more out of frustration now than fear.

"She saw me with Henry in the pool just after he died," he said. "But she misread what she'd seen, and when she ran off I went into a sort of autopilot mode and chased her. I needed to explain to her what I'm explaining to you now—that it had been an accident. This whole nightmare started with an accident. And then somehow it escalated into something so much worse. I chased her, she was screaming. I tackled her. I didn't know what to do. I'd just held my dead lover in my arms . . . and I was so drunk. So insanely drunk."

During this last bit of his story, Gina had been lulled into a drowsy state, hating him still for scaring the shit out of her, but she also couldn't imagine him killing someone. She believed everything he'd said, even felt a twinge of pity for him now. Her assumption about him forcing himself on Tiffany's friend had been so far from the truth. The truth hadn't involved any predatory, pedophilic evildoing—only tragedy. The world of the past few days, for everyone in her life, was just so damned sad. She sobbed quietly. For the man in the blanket, for Corey and Dylan, for herself—maybe even for Leo.

"Last things to tell you," he said, still breathing unevenly. "Someone hit me from behind just after Angelique and I fell to the ground, knocked me out cold. Whoever it was, she referred to him as her boyfriend, and now the two of them, they want money to keep quiet about Henry. I can't prove it had been an accident, and supposedly they have photos. But that's not even the worst part. Henry's mother reported him missing. He's only been here for the past twenty-four hours, but supposedly she hadn't heard from him all week, long enough for a detective to take the case and to call his phone. I listened to that message, too. No one's seen him since Pete dropped us off, and even though I begged him not to, I know Henry told his mother about me. He was excited to tell her I'd invited him out here—he'd told me as much in the car. Sooner or later, all the detective will have to go on is that Henry was supposed to be here. I'm in an impossible position, Gina. I'm sorry for this, for everything. I'll stop now. I'm going to take my hand away. Just please don't scream. Please. Don't scream."

# SATURDAY

# TWENTY-THREE

Throughout the morning guests arrived at the Sheffield estate in limousines and luxury cars, and Corey tried to will away the encroaching delirium from lack of sleep while trudging up the stairs a half-dozen times loaded down with suitcases, satchels, garment bags and carryalls. Aside from a brief nap sometime around sunrise, he and Angelique had stayed awake all night again, talking about the craziness with Ray outside Layne's house, then about their plan for the money handoff with Leo, though mostly they spent the night listening to the ocean waves, huddled together under a blanket on the sand.

Out of breath and sweating, he passed by some of the new arrivals and others who'd spent the previous night in the guest bedrooms, most of them already decked out in awful yuppie-wear—the tennis shorts or white slacks or khakis with a sharp crease ironed down the center, collared T-shirts (also ironed) or designer button-downs (also ironed) rolled just above the wrists or tied at the belly button. And worst of all, those few with sweaters draped over their shoulders, the sweater arms loosely folded at their chests, a layer that served absolutely no purpose in the unseasonable heat other than to advertise the obvious—that the person wearing the sweater like a bright white stole was rich, and today they'd dressed in their *Hamptons-wear.*

Corey had been doing his best to bat away hateful thoughts, recalling that here and there during the summers he'd worked at the estate a certain guest hadn't been so bad, some had even been nice to him. But today the lack of sleep opened him to the old resentments, and they welled up over and over, especially after he'd recognized that none of the guests seemed to notice his existence at all once they'd handed off their bags. Despite his efforts to think about something else, this sense of invisibility gnawed at him. It also occurred to him that no one in his real life had ever spent a day as these people were spending theirs today—waited on hand and foot, yawning poolside, bored in paradise.

After he'd finally hauled the last two bags from the porch to a third-floor bedroom and returned downstairs to see what other tasks Mrs. Sheffield had in store for him, he passed by two middle-aged couples munching on breakfast snacks in the sunroom and overheard fragments of their conversation about how awful the holiday traffic had been when they left the city, the four of them exchanging complaints about how they'd endured a four-hour crucible all the way up the Long Island Expressway, Sunrise Highway and finally Montauk Highway. Widening his search for Sheila, he passed by other guests, some with even more distance in their eyes, some wandering the downstairs rooms and a few scattered pairs strolling outside toward the pool with mimosas in hand. They all had an oddly dazed look, as though they'd volunteered to while the day away as extras in an incredibly boring film, killing time before the next meal by lounging poolside or moving from the sunshine to a patch of shade, or vice versa. Nothing to do and nowhere to be, and yet they complained to each other about the people in their lives or the state of things in their companies, though more often than not they complained to the help, sometimes to Corey, though usually to Gina or Josie, their complaints loosely veiled as requests.

It wasn't a good feeling, loathing each and every guest and the Sheffields themselves—especially Leo Sheffield for what he'd done to Angelique—but Corey continued wearing his servant-boy mask as he plodded along the lawn toward Sheila, who'd waved at him from the porch steps, taking some solace as he imagined Leo pacing back and forth in the master bedroom, his feet licked by the flames of his own private level of hell.

"I have a very important task for you," Sheila said, pointing at the muddy paw prints Clay's dog had tracked across the painted floorboards. "We need to rectify this situation, wouldn't you say? Our guests should be able to walk barefoot without fear of infection."

Corey looked down at the paw prints and called her a psycho in his head. Lack of sleep made it much more difficult to hide his disdain, but then he thought of Angelique receiving a million dollars of the Sheffields' family fortune and managed to smile as he answered, "I'm on it. You can rely on me, Missus S."

She led him inside the house to a supply closet, handed him a large metal bucket and explained which environmentally friendly soap to use, emphasizing more than once the importance of his mission. A few minutes later, he carried the sloshing bucket of soapy water, a mop and two oversize beach towels out to the porch, sweating as he got to work. Because the old-fashioned bucket didn't come equipped with a wringer, each pass Corey made with the mop left the porch sopping wet and dangerously slippery from the soap. To counter that, Sheila expected him to get on his hands and knees every ten feet or so and rub the porch boards dry with the towels until the entire fifty-foot length gleamed once more.

He was ten minutes into swabbing and drying the boards like a pirate ship's deckhand when the jingling of dog tags pulled Corey's attention from the section of floor he'd been rubbing with the towel. Polly shook pool water from her thick coat, looked right at him and then charged back and forth across the nearest flowerbeds, then veered toward the porch, already too close to the steps for him to have any chance of altering her course. He stood and tilted his head from side to side to crack his neck. The dog's tongue flapped and slobbered, and she appeared to be smiling as she thundered past, stamping out a new track of brown paw prints down the entire length of painted boards. Polly made it to the opposite end, launched from the steps and circled quickly on the lawn before scampering back up. She charged right at him, splotching a whole new trail of tracks in her wake, which for Corey was the last straw—he lunged to grab her but fell hard on his knees and elbows, and she rumbled past, barely escaping his outstretched hand.

Without thinking, he dropped his towel and chased after her, leaping to his right off the steps and then streaking across the grass along the side of the house as though someone were chasing him, running as fast as he ever had. From behind, some of the people by the pool whistled and cheered him on as the dog picked up speed through the lawn ornaments and chess pieces. Corey began to suck wind even before he passed the final bronze bishop and rook, but he continued pushing, refusing to let up as he followed Polly's trail past the tennis courts and the toolshed. His lungs burned, his legs felt shaky and yet he couldn't slow down. Why was he chasing this stupid dog? The question sapped his energy as though someone suddenly pulled a plug, and he slowed to a jog. A few wobbly steps later, it occurred to him that the dog wasn't merely playing with him and enjoying the chase, she'd been running toward a specific destination. She wanted him to follow her to that spot way out in the woods where he'd watched Leo dragging his friend. The dog was leading him there, to the body.

Fueled by a curiosity he couldn't ignore, he quickened his pace into the woods between some of the wider pine trunks, and after a minute, in the distance, he saw the mound over by the neighbors' dark hedge wall. Polly crouched beside the body, her tags jingling like mad as she growled and tugged at the corner of the blanket, tearing the fabric. Corey approached her and tried to shoo her away, but the dog had her front paws dug in for leverage, pulling and ripping the blanket more with each thrust of her jaw until suddenly a scrap tore free.

Polly bounded past in a blur, once again just beyond Corey's reach. He fell to his hands and knees and watched her run full-stride through the woods with the scrap in her mouth, with no energy left to follow. She had too big a lead, and he knew her trajectory, anyhow—straight back across the acres of lawn. Easy enough to assume that she would first celebrate her theft by tramping her dirty paws all along the porch, and then would likely show off her newfound treasure to the sunbathers by the pool. *Leo,* he thought, *you're so fucked.*

Exhausted, with his head tipped forward, Corey covered his nose against the smell as he crept the last couple feet and then stood beside the body, horrified to find it only partially covered by the blanket. Three of Henry's mottled fingers lay curled above the dirt, his bare shoulder and the left half of his face exposed. The dead man's wrinkled eyelid, thankfully, still remained mostly closed, but the purplish spiderweb of capillaries along his skin and the pine needles stuck to his open lips were disturbing enough. He'd watched Mr. Sheffield kiss this young guy, both before *and* after his death. Leo definitely hadn't killed him; even so, the sight of this poor guy lying here like trash felt so wrong that Corey considered saying, *The hell with the money, just call the police.*

But then something beyond the promise of a huge payday for Angelique and the possibility of escaping with her that night compelled him to let the universe decide how it all should go, as a mosquito-like thought pierced his conscience—a clear vision of Leo behind bars for a murder he hadn't committed and which hadn't actually occurred. Corey hurriedly pulled the blanket over Henry's clawed hand and head, then scuttled around gathering piles of pine needles and spreading them over the body until he'd effectively camouflaged it so much better than Leo had.

He couldn't remain out here another minute. Sheila Sheffield would be looking for him, livid when she saw crisscrossing tracks of Polly's paw prints all along the porch. Little did she know that, if not for his complicity in keeping her husband's secret, the estate would be a crime scene within the hour, a breaking news story. National, maybe even international news. He felt no affection for this family, no discernable sympathy or respect, so why did he feel such a strong obligation to protect the guy who'd scared the hell out of Angelique? He had no answer beyond two facts: first, Leo had been decent to Gina over the years; second, Leo hadn't hurt Henry at all, so it would just be wrong for him to be hauled off to prison for murder.

He backed away from the body, his hand still over his nose.

*I'm not protecting him much longer, though,* he thought, and started toward the house with two comforting thoughts playing in his head on a loop: *As soon as he hands over the cash to Angelique, we're gone . . . After that, Leo's on his own.*

# TWENTY-FOUR

Leo paced in his bedroom after going through his messages. The same detective who'd called Henry had left a voice mail for him. Detective Faraday conveyed the details of Henry's disappearance, the fact that Henry's mother had searched his apartment and found Leo's number, and finally ended the call with a stern "Please call me as soon as possible." Leo tossed the phone on the bed, yanked the balcony doors open and was met by a humid morning breeze. Gina knew about Henry now. This detective awaited his response. Angelique wanted a million dollars in exchange for her silence and for not releasing the photos her co-blackmailer had taken the night Henry died. Leo had far less than a full million in the wall safe, and no solid option as to how to get his hands on the rest, even less of an idea of who to ask to bring another seven or eight hundred thousand here from the city by nightfall.

He poured four fingers of Scotch and pulled one of the antique Victorian-era chairs that no one ever sat on from the bedroom to the balcony and slumped down. Sipping his drink with his chin in his hand, he gazed out through the wrought-iron bars and watched the guests milling around between the porch steps and the pool. Sooner or later, one or two of them would no doubt wander out to the other side of the property, drunk or horny or just curious to explore. Sooner or later, Angelique and her partner would decide to break their word and screw him. Sooner or later, Gina might decide to follow her conscience and call the cops. And worst of all, sooner—rather than later—if his phone call wasn't returned, Detective Faraday *would* pull up to the intercom at the gates and ask to be let in.

Looking out through the balcony bars, he felt trapped, caged, imprisoned. His father's words returned in conjunction with the pounding in his temples: *Be a man . . . No son of mine . . .* You *represent* me *when you go out into the world.* Leonard Sr. had never haunted him so persistently, his voice itself the original prison.

Leo focused on his two sons lying out on lounge chairs alongside the pool, hoping to avoid his father's voice by observing them. Andy had all the traits of a stereotypical man's man, the gorgeous girlfriend on his arm to boot. And yet Clay had remained single most of his young life, never with a serious girlfriend at all. The sensitive son, the one who preferred dolls to toy soldiers as a child, just as Leo had—for years now he'd been more interested in his dog, Polly, than in dating women.

Leonard Sr. had beaten Leo into a sort of brainwashed submission after he'd showed some of the same affectations Clay had displayed early on and never felt the need to suppress. He'd forced Leo to deny his true nature prior to his death, and that denial had remained entrenched within him for all the decades since. For nearly sixty years now, not only had Leo never vocalized to anyone that he was gay, he'd never even allowed the thought to linger, not even when alone with Henry.

*My father, for all his fury,* Leo thought, *did he hate me for mirroring what he'd denied in himself?* He stared through the balcony bars for another minute, focused on Clay more than the others, hoping his son might live a much freer life than he had, when suddenly a commotion arose down below. Most everyone bordering the pool began whooping and hollering as Polly darted past, followed by Corey running after her, both of them racing at top speed toward the north side of the property.

Leo stood and gripped his rocks glass. From his high vantage point he watched Gina's son chasing the dog across the acres to his right, through the sculptures and past the tennis courts and between the old-growth oaks on the way to the pines. He gripped his glass tighter, realizing where Polly was headed.

He held his breath as the dog and the boy grew smaller and smaller, approaching the literal skeleton in Leo's secret closet. Then, one after the other, the two tiny bodies way out there veered sharply into the woods and disappeared. Leo felt an intense pressure from head to toe, as if he'd entered a deep-sea trench and kept on descending, the surrounding water squeezing the oxygen from his lungs, his brain, from each and every blood vessel. His grip loosened. His glass slipped through his fingers. He couldn't bear to look down. He took a step back as his sons and the dozen or so guests beside the pool sharply turned their heads toward the balcony in unison, alerted by the sound of smashing glass.

He had to head out there, head Corey off the trail if possible; if there was still any time. If the boy had already seen Henry's body, Leo would need to hold him off in the woods long enough to explain, to plead, to bribe him if need be. Still in his robe and slippers, Leo double-timed his way downstairs and out of the seemingly empty house through a screen door on the opposite end from the sunbathers by the pool. He jogged while glancing over his shoulder every few steps, hoping nobody had seen him, though the one person he'd most hoped to avoid appeared in his periphery a moment before she ordered him to stop.

"Leo, where do you think you're going?" Sheila yelled, walking toward him from behind at such a pace that she might as well have been running, since she easily caught up to him as soon as he paused. "Leo!" she shouted, now a mere few feet from him.

"What's wrong with you?" he shouted back at her, feeling as though she'd snared him by the ankle.

"What's wrong with *me?* We have guests here, not to mention your children! You look like a mental patient running across the yard in your robe, and with that ridiculous bandage on your head! Have you gone insane, is that it? Should I have you committed?"

"I've been cooped up in the bedroom, dear. I just wanted to get some air."

Gina's son had disappeared into the woods and had been there far too long already. Sheila's tensed brows and wide eyes held Leo in place. He kept his head turned away from her while she spoke for what felt like a lifetime. Then his stomach seemed to fill with snakes, a bitter taste like venom rising in his throat as the dog ran full-bore along the tree line with something hanging from her muzzle.

Sheila grabbed his wrist. "Did you hear a word I just said?"

He didn't answer. He was too preoccupied by the sight of Corey leaving the woods and walking the same line the dog had run. Sheila repeated her question, and when he still didn't respond, she stormed off. He watched her cross the lawn and reenter the house through the kitchen, then shifted his focus to Gina's son, whose head had just turned toward him.

They shared a moment of long-distance eye contact and then Corey quickly looked away, walking faster with his head down as he passed by the pool and finally hooked left onto the porch and disappeared.

Leo brought his hands to his face, gritting his teeth just before he heard himself whimper.

Any second now the world would end.

# TWENTY-FIVE

Lunch was served on two long tables in the backyard. The Sheffield children and twenty guests ate their chicken Caesar salad, poached salmon, couscous, roasted vegetables, melon slices and berries, while Mrs. Sheffield played helicopter host, hovering tableside and chatting everyone up. Corey made eye contact with Angelique as she and Tiffany took their plates around the house to the porch, and she seemed to understand by his expression that he wanted her to find him in a little while. He had seen Mr. Sheffield only briefly, just after he had returned from the woods, but otherwise hadn't seen him leave his room all day.

When the midday meal ended, Corey worked alongside Michael and Josie. As a team, they broke everything down, transferred the uneaten food to containers and stored the leftovers in the two industrial refrigerators, folded the chairs and the table legs and stacked them all against the side of the house. During lunch Angelique had returned stealthily and whispered as she walked past him, "Meet me in the garden as soon as you finish."

Now that he'd carried the last table with Josie, and the Sheffields and their guests appeared content to luxuriate in their food comas for a while, he had one of those rare windows of downtime when he'd be able to slip away.

He found Angelique sitting on a bench in the garden, smoking a cigarette. The dark red grooves below her eyes, he imagined, had come after she'd rubbed them raw. She offered her cigarette pack and lighter and scooched over to make space for him to sit.

"So," she said, exhaling smoke, "how you holding up?"

"Getting kinda loopy from not sleeping," he said, "but otherwise I'm okay. What's the latest with Leo?"

"Nothing new, which is probably good. This bench is actually the spot where we're supposed to meet tonight when he brings the money."

"Did he say what time?"

"Just said to meet here after dinner, around sunset."

"You still think I should meet him instead of you?"

"Definitely. I don't want to be alone with him again."

Corey let her words settle before reaching for her hand. When she responded with a light squeeze of his fingers, he asked, "How're you holding up overall?"

She took a long drag and held it for a while before breathing it back out. "I'll be a lot better after we leave."

"You're still sure you want me to come with you?"

"Yeah, and I'm glad you want to. This would be so much crazier if I had to figure it all out alone." She breathed out another plume of smoke. "I wish you weren't stuck working, so we could go somewhere else till he hands over the money, maybe sleep for a while. I don't even know how you're functioning at this point." She laced her fingers with his while staring straight ahead. A moment later she dropped her cigarette to the dirt and rubbed it dead with her heel. "When we leave tonight, let's stop off at the ocean for a little while, okay? Before we start driving for real, I mean—wherever we decide to go."

Corey exhaled smoke as he answered, "Sure," and squeezed her hand. Then he turned and saw her eyes watering over. "What's wrong?"

"I'm not even sure anymore," she said, laughing for a second. "All of this is just so crazy. It's like my life ended two nights ago and now everything's an unknown, but my old life was sort of over when my mom went into the hospital and I knew she wouldn't be coming home. It's just scary now not to have any idea where I'll be tomorrow, or next week, or next month. But then there's you . . . I've been sitting here for the last half hour thinking about what I felt when I saw you, right after you hit him and pushed him off me. I felt safe in a way I don't think I'd ever

297

felt before, like you were my guardian angel or something. Which is crazy because we still hardly know each other."

She wiped her eyes and faced him.

"I know I said I wouldn't, but can I ask now? Why *were* you here that night? It's all right to tell me. I trust you, no matter what you say."

Corey's mouth went dry, even drier after he took a long drag from his cigarette. *Should I tell her the truth? What else can I really say?* The excuse he'd prepared—that he'd left his wallet here when he'd been cleaning with Gina and had just returned to retrieve it at one o'clock in the morning—was stupid. And more than that, he didn't want to lie to her. *Well,* he thought, *I guess this is it.*

"I didn't expect to see you when I first came here," he said, and paused to swallow. "That's probably where I should start, Thursday night. I don't know, maybe I should start further back. See, I had this idea last summer after I thought about how lots of these mansions are empty most of the year. I thought maybe I could sneak in and tour a house every once in a while, you know, and slip out without anyone knowing. So I did that a few times at the end of last summer, and then a few more times this month. I wasn't breaking in to steal anything. Not until Thursday, anyway. So I was in the house when you and Tiffany happened to show up. You two came in, and I climbed out the window just before you would've caught me. Shit, you must think I'm such a loser."

She angled her head so he would look her in the eyes.

"I definitely don't think you're a loser. Just so you know, I'm not judging you at all for planning to rob Tiff's parents, and I won't, so don't worry about that. It's not awesome, but it's also not the worst thing I've ever heard. I'm just really curious why you were still here when Tiff's dad was in the pool with that guy, when he chased me."

It was too hot to think. No clue how to answer. A bumblebee buzzed past and then circled around them as she touched his arm and added, "You can tell me. I hope you feel you can."

Beads of sweat rolled down his back. His eyelids had squeezed down to slits against the sun and the brutally bright shade of blue pulsing overhead. The flower petals were baking all around him, dying of thirst and shriveling against their stems. He couldn't tell her the whole truth, not now. What good would it do to confess that he'd sat on the roof Thursday night, and here and there had peeked through the windows, melting all over again each time he caught a glimpse of her face? There was just no good way to phrase that.

She broke the stillness by cocking her head and

asking, "So when you broke in here, what were you going to steal?"

"I'm not really sure. I guess it didn't matter. I don't know if this makes any sense, but I think I wanted to take something from them because they have so much and they still don't pay my mom very well. I sort of talked myself into that being an excuse to break in in the first place."

"So you've broken into a bunch of other houses out here, but never stole anything?"

"Yeah, I just snuck in and snuck out. Usually pranked the people before I left. You know, like putting salt in their milk, or moving a painting from one room to another. I'm not sure why I kept doing it except that it was a rush."

He finished his confession expecting her to at least look at him sideways, maybe even to tell him not to talk to her anymore, but instead she surprised him with a tired smile.

"How many times have you done it?"

"Six or seven, maybe eight."

"How many times was someone home?"

"Five or six. Most of the times someone was there."

"Jeez, you're crazy! But you must be pretty good at it if no one ever caught you."

"I didn't want to sound all cocky about it, but yeah, I'm really good at it."

Both wearing grins and squinting against the sun, they stared ahead at the mouth of the garden path. He took her hand and spoke just above a whisper. "I'm really glad you want me to come with you." She clasped her fingers more snuggly around his and leaned to the side to rest her head against his shoulder, but a moment later sat up straight as Gina came into view.

"Here you are," she said to Corey, her hands moving to her hips. "If you want to keep this job, Missus Sheffield needs you to mop the paw prints from the porch again. Right now."

# TWENTY-SIX

An hour later, Gina walked the length of the third-floor hall and veered into a guest bathroom, locking the door behind her. She closed the toilet lid and sat, removed the baggie of pills from her pocket and held it up at eye level to re-count the remaining Klonopins she'd purchased last night at the bar, her mind still so clouded by the insanity in the woods. Leo Sheffield had let her up after telling his story and then completely fell apart into a blubbering mess, begging her not to tell anyone about Henry—the man in the blanket, the man he'd been cheating on Sheila with and may have even loved, the man who now existed in her mind only as the dead body on the property. And then at some point, while on his knees, with his arms wrapped around her legs and his face against her feet, he'd offered her money. A lot of money, just to keep quiet. She'd told him she needed sleep, said she would sleep on it, and then had left the pines feeling like a total zombie. With so much vodka and so many pills in her bloodstream, and after all she'd heard while he held her down—after what she'd *seen*—the drive home from Southampton had passed in a blur. She still had only the haziest recollection of stopping at the bar, drinking more and buying these pills. Then no memory at all of the second leg of the drive, or entering her house, or getting into bed. And ever since returning to this house, for the past five or six hours she'd been operating purely on auto-function, a numb automaton performing housekeeper and staff management duties, too confused to feel any fear or anger or whatever emotions she should have been feeling. What would a *normal* person feel in such a screwed-up situation?

Her tolerance had grown out of control without her pausing to think about it until now. She'd already swallowed three Klonopins with her morning coffee and had seven left. She needed to ration the rest—maybe take one more now, two in the late afternoon, two or three during the dinner party . . . She just needed to make sure to save at least one for the lakeside soiree. As they always did for each of the big holiday weekends, the Sheffields had invited her to join the party after dinner; though, as Gina saw it, the invitation to socialize with the guests she'd spent the past two days and nights serving wasn't a generous gesture as much as an obligation. Sheila expected her not only to be there but to shine with gratitude, to be the gracious employee on display. Her part in the party would be to mingle and chat and show how thankful she was to be socializing with her betters. What a fucking treat. And meanwhile, how would Leo play his part? Would he seek her out? The thought overwhelmed her.

Leaning forward, she brought her hands to her face and whispered a prayer. "If you're listening, if you can get me through today . . . I promise, after this weekend I'll stop everything. No more pills. No more drinking, either. I'll call Maryanne, and on Tuesday I'll start detoxing at home, and then—I really hope—there won't be a next time. God, *please* just let me get through this day. I promise, after this I'll try to stay clean. I just need this now."

After swallowing two more pills, Gina checked her eyes in the mirror—the whites were a bit red, the lids heavy. Not great, but not tragic. She exited the bathroom and walked the hall, trying to appear casual while concentrating on keeping her balance with each step, forcing a smile and saying hello to a few guests as she passed by. She held the banister on her way down the first flight of stairs. She then made it halfway down the second-floor hall before she had to pause in a doorway to greet Gretchen and Andy, who sat in comfortable oversize chairs, facing one another with magazines and coffees.

"Can I get either of you anything?"

Gretchen didn't acknowledge her, but after a short silence the Sheffields' eldest son turned the page of his *Architectural Digest* as he answered, "No thanks, Gina," barely raising his eyes from the magazine when he added, "I think my mother is looking for you, though."

"Thanks, I'll track her down."

Gina left the doorway wishing she could hide from Sheila for a few hours. She'd lied to herself in the bathroom; she wouldn't make it through the day. She should just get in her car and drive off before dealing with the twenty-two place settings she still needed to complete for dinner, before the sixteen invited guests and the family and Angelique sat down to the six-course meal, which would later need to be cleared one by one, and all that wine to pour, and then a dozen or more guests expected to roll in throughout the night.

A little farther down the hall she heard Corey speaking softly to someone from behind a closed bedroom door, then recognized Angelique's voice. Gina raised a fist, and with her knuckles poised to knock she angled her head so her ear hovered less than an inch from the wood.

She leaned even closer until her ear pressed against the door. For some reason, the quiet on the other side that followed bothered her even more than the troubling snippet of conversation she'd just overheard, Corey saying something about them taking off earlier than they'd planned—if Leo already had the money.

They'd been holding hands on the porch. She'd heard Angelique mention a boyfriend who'd taken photos. She'd convinced herself that the unnamed man from the limo had been the one who'd hurt her boss, but Thursday night, when Leo had been wounded, Corey hadn't been home.

She tried the doorknob and found it locked. Her head tipped forward suddenly and struck the door. "Corey," she called out, rapping her knuckles on the wood. "You finished with the porch? I need you downstairs."

"Yeah, Ma. Just helping to rearrange some furniture in here. Be right out."

She waited, her blood pressure rising. Then she turned her head as a door down the hall opened and a man around Leo's age emerged, speaking loudly with a cell phone to his ear. "Tell him to set up a conference call later in the week," he barked. "Yes, that's correct. I'll be in Southampton until Monday evening. The weather's marvelous now, but I've heard we could see some rain sometime tomorrow, possibly even some thundershowers . . . I know, of all the weekends. Anyway, I'll have my cell if he needs any more info before we're all back in the office . . . Correct. You, too. Ciao."

Gina hadn't realized she'd been staring at him until he pocketed his phone and raised his hand to offer a dead-fish sort of wave. "Fantastic lunch today."

"So glad you liked it," she said. "I'll be sure to tell the chef."

"Delicious," he said, adjusting the braided belt around the waistband of his shorts. "Save me a dance at the party tonight, would you?"

The long silence and his unbroken stare said everything: apparently, *she* was delicious. And to make it even more awkward and gross, he had the nerve to wink on his way down the stairs. Ugh. With the white-hot heat of a thousand blowtorches, goddamn it did she hate it when her employers' bloated old guests flirted with her. Didn't he get that she couldn't answer his disgusting advance honestly, that she was basically a captive here? Yep, of course he did. He knew the situation exactly. Wealthy letches like him believed themselves immune to sexual harassment standards the average person was expected to abide by. They could buy whatever they wanted, or at least pay off whomever they needed to after crossing the line. That guy had gone downstairs with a smile on his stupid face, knowing he could say almost anything to Gina in this vacationland and get away with it. She was just the help, after all.

*Save you a dance,* she thought. *Not a chance, asshole. If you're lucky, I might not kick you in the balls.*

Gina could have snapped at the jowly old creep, but thanks to the pills, he didn't matter . . . Not even worth thinking about now that an optimal amount of opiates had just dissolved in her blood and a hundred tiny suns had begun pulsing beneath her skin . . . Her eyelids lowered to slits and she forced them wider, staring at the vacant spot where Mr. Sheffield's corporate crony had leered at her. How could she be expected to do this job sober? How else could she pander to these people and smile? What's more, how could she even *be* here, knowing there was a corpse outside?

The unreality of that thought struck like a fist. She pressed both hands to her chest, exhaled a long breath and simultaneously heard her own whispered words, "What the hell am I going to do?" When no answer followed she faced the bedroom door and knocked again. "Corey, come on. I don't have all day."

Finally, the door opened and her son stood before her. Gina felt her heart beating faster once again as their eyes met and he quickly looked at the floor. Angelique sat on the bed with her face behind her hair, nervously picking at her thumbnail. None of the furniture had been rearranged.

Gina stepped back and waved Corey into the hall. "You mopped the porch, right?"

"Yeah," he said, and made a show of exhaling with a huff, "even though it looked fine to begin with."

"I'm not surprised, but we do as she asks, right?"

Corey slowly shook his head.

"I need you to go out to the shed and get all the tiki torches, the big citronella candles, and bring it all to the side of the house by the porch. After that, come find me in the kitchen. Josie could use your help, but Missus Sheffield also might have something else for you to do by then."

Corey turned back to Angelique as he answered, "Okay, Ma, I'm on it." And the girl looked up with her hands in her lap, her eyes glassy, her thin frame curled inward and tensed like a timid fawn.

"Sorry to sidetrack him, Mrs. Halpern. He's been helping me."

"That's all right, dear. And you can call me Gina, like always."

Corey walked the hall ahead of her surprisingly fast, as though trying to escape, but she jogged to catch up and grabbed his arm. "Wait," she said, huddling with him at the top of the stairs. "What the hell were you two talking about in there?"

"Nothing," he said, though he still couldn't look at her, and just then Sheila exited the master bedroom to their left.

"Oh good, I found you," Sheila said to Gina, and a moment after she began talking, Corey slipped down the stairs.

Once Sheila left her, Gina held the banister tighter than usual, stepping down the stairs as if they were a slippery moss-covered slope, feeling as though she might not be able to hold back a scream. When she finally reached the bottom, she made more of an effort to keep her eyes open and said hello to a woman entering the house through a screen door—Barbara, one of Sheila's wealthier nonprofit cohorts, whose eyes Gina had never seen, as she always kept half her face blacked-out by oversize Jackie O sunglasses.

Barbara paused to ask, "Any updates on that storm that might be passing through tomorrow?"

She'd caught Gina off guard. "There's a storm forecasted, or forecast?" She slipped into nervous laughter. "Sorry, I haven't been keeping track of the weather."

"I see," Barbara said warily, walking off before Gina could pull together a friendly parting comment.

Back in the kitchen, even as her obsessive thoughts about Corey's involvement with Angelique and Leo continued flaring, the next few hours passed in a blur. She'd worked within the eye of a whirling holiday weekend enough times to function on cruise control, sidestepping disaster like a ballerina until finally being allowed to leave for the night, frazzled and exhausted. The chaos was oddly comforting today. As long as she stayed in perpetual motion in the midst of everyone bustling around her, she could hide out in the open.

By early evening she knew she needed to avoid close interactions, as she imagined she may have secretly gulped a few too many fingers of vodka and taken a few too many pills to convincingly pass as one hundred percent sober. It had taken a concerted effort to focus when coordinating with the party tent people and the extra waitstaff, but she'd otherwise mainly kept her head down and her hands busy with the charcuterie boards and hors d'oeuvres trays, answering yes or no to questions from Sheila or Josie or Michael, or from the random guests who wandered through the kitchen to pick at the plates of gourmet ingredients scattered about.

After swallowing all but two of the pills and refilling her thermos with vodka and a splash of cranberry juice once—or had it been twice?— she realized she may have overdone it a tad. But a couple hours from now the drinks would be flowing freely, and then no one would notice and no one would care if she had her own cocktail in hand or if she appeared a little tipsy. Just ride it out until then, that's all she had to do.

Mr. Sheffield had been conspicuously absent at dinner. As far as Gina knew, he hadn't left his room all day; he hadn't shown his face to anyone since the two of them exited the woods many hours before sunrise, just after he'd begged her to keep his secret. He'd been decent to her over the years, but even if his story were true—that the man out there had died in an accident—shouldn't she call the police? Shouldn't Leo? How long could a dead body on the property be kept secret?

Later in the night, she went upstairs to change into her turquoise summer dress and strappy shoes. She had, thankfully, somehow made it through the twenty-person dinner without spilling anything on anyone or saying something inappropriate. Now, she looked at her phone and saw that Ray had called four times in half as many hours. Doing her best to block him from her mind, she quickly erased his voice mails without bothering to listen. She swayed on her way out of the bathroom, and from there balanced herself with her free hand, gripping chair backs and pressing against the edge of the long dining table until she made it to the lake side of the house. She exited through a screen door and stepped onto the porch, feeling like an alien amid the classical music and boisterous guests, struck by the odors of expensive perfumes and citronella candles and the glitter of jewelry dangling from earlobes and draped above well-tanned cleavage.

Excusing herself, she slid by a married couple—a woman in a sequined cocktail dress and her husband in a gray Armani suit—then had an unfortunate moment of eye contact with the creep who'd asked her to save him a dance. With a wobble here and a wobble there she slipped around a dense cluster of well-dressed guests and hurried down the porch steps to the wide entrance of the party tent, only to recoil in disgust when she looked back and saw the creep adjusting his belt once again, laughing along with two other Ted Kennedy look-alikes, then saying something while raising his glass and—*eew*—winking again.

Her dress felt too thin. Everyone else seemed engrossed in conversation while she stood alone, smoothing down the fabric on her hip and pretending to read something from her phone. *I have to get out of here,* she thought, then flashed a smile at one of the waiters passing by with a silver hors d'oeuvre tray, remembering the only aspect of the party that held any appeal—the wet bar. She politely fought her way over, as if swimming there, the thick bass from three cellos drowning out all the voices until the bartender shouted back, asking her to repeat her drink order.

Sometime later, with yet another lovely drink in hand, Gina felt a haze spread all around her. A man in a snappy blue sport coat who'd been smiling suddenly frowned and walked off. A blink later a woman with big teeth and a mole on her chin squinted at her and said something unbecoming. Gina fantasized about spitting at someone, smiled when she imagined whipping down someone's slacks from behind. Then she drifted from the party while standing perfectly still, recalling and then reliving one of the more intense arguments with Ray, yelling back at him this time.

Her eyes snapped open as Sheila said something to her and grabbed her shoulder. She may or may not have answered her question before Sheila disappeared in a blur. The bartender handed Gina another drink. She said, "Huzzah," raised it high, then drank, wiping some dribbled liquid from her chest and her dress.

She looked around. Voices blended. Faces warped, mouths and eyes exaggerated, as if the tent were lined with funhouse mirrors. What time was it? How long had she been out here?

*I should find someplace to lie down,* she thought, sipping her new vodka tonic and turning, the scene blurring as though she were riding a slowly spinning merry-go-round. Stunned by the sight of him staring at her, she accidentally swallowed an ice cube—then, squinting, she took a wobbly step back.

For the first time all day, she and Leo stood face-to-face.

He looked as though he'd slept in his clothes, and the ball cap on his head had a sideways tilt. His overall appearance, along with his hangdog expression, told her all she needed to know. He obviously hadn't come downstairs to join the party. He'd come outside for no other reason than to talk to her.

# TWENTY-SEVEN

Sheila summoned Leo from his hiding place, obviously irate as she banged on their locked bedroom door with the side of her fist and ordered him downstairs to address the "Gina situation." He gripped the edge of the mattress while she shouted through the door and spelled out the reasons why Leo could no longer use his injury as an excuse to remain holed up in their bedroom. Gina had drunk far too much and was stumbling around; she'd been muttering nasty things at the guests, making a spectacle of herself. Basically ruining the party. Sounding incensed, Sheila finally demanded, "Leo, you need to tell her to leave. She's an embarrassment. If you don't take care of this, I will. But if you leave it up to me, I'm going to tell her never to come back."

"I'll be down," he said, with his mouth beside the door, though he would have preferred a root canal or an audit by the IRS; anything to avoid going down to the party.

"And you can go back to forgetting about any exchange of toasts between us tomorrow night. You and your pet housekeeper have already relegated this weekend to a crisis management exercise—at best."

Once she stormed off, Leo threw on the

wrinkled shirt and khakis he'd worn to the hospital and slipped a ball cap with his company logo over his freshly stitched head. He descended the stairs, slowly walked through the downstairs rooms and eased the creaking screen door open, exiting the house as some shadow version of his previous self, with timid steps, brimming with paranoia. The mock chandeliers hanging from the porch ceiling and tent canopy blazed like spotlights. He squinted, hoping to locate Gina right away and to skip any interactions with the guests. The headache he'd had upstairs was already a hundred times worse, as the musicians were in the midst of playing a string-heavy movement with far too many high notes, the violins especially torturous as they screeched out arpeggios. He avoided eye contact, well aware that he looked like shit. Hungry, dehydrated, he felt shaky, hollow. Stepping from the screen door, he tried to ignore the sense that he was now a freak show attraction and everyone in the vicinity had noticed him.

He located Gina a few feet beyond the entrance of the massive tent, bent over with both elbows on the bar. She turned from the bartender with her drink at her lips and faced him, stumbled back, staring at him, expressionless, eyes glassy. He braced for what she might say in front of everyone, imagining what she could shout out. She was drunk, and a drunk person always had far less of a filter. Any second now, she'd ruin a lot more than Sheila's goddamned party.

He took a cautious step toward her. She shook her head disapprovingly, and then, rather than saying anything, she shoved him aside and awkwardly skirted past. She left the tent and climbed the steps with a limping gait, using the handrail as a crutch, and then stumbled along like a pinball through the crowd of guests on the left-hand side of the porch until she disappeared. From over his shoulder, speaking above the orchestra, the bartender asked if he wanted a drink. Leo didn't answer. His attention had been drawn to Clay's dog, the sound of her tags jingling as she weaved through the well-dressed crowd with her tail wagging and some sort of cloth clamped in her mouth.

Then his eyes focused on the doorway above the porch steps, directly in front of him, where Angelique gazed at him from the other side. Another figure stood in the screen-covered space beside her. Corey. Leo's thoughts returned to earlier in the day, the moments before he'd broken his glass on the balcony, the sense of urgency, the T. S. Eliot line about the world's demise looping through his mind when Sheila stopped him on the lawn. Corey had followed the dog out into the pines, so now he must know about Henry, too. He must have seen his body out there . . . Had to have seen him . . . And now he and Angelique stood like ghosts in the doorway, staring down at him, side by side.

Leo reached up and pressed his hand to the back of his ball cap where it covered his stitches. The orchestra music and voices of the party faded. During all these torturous hours since regaining consciousness on the lawn, he'd had no idea who'd been with Angelique Thursday night. Recalling now what she'd said in the garden—that her boyfriend took photos and thought they should call the cops—he removed the cap from his head and pressed the wound harder, until the pain filled his vision with tracers.

Tiffany approached dressed in her grungiest paint-spattered overalls and a black bra, with a burning cigarette stuck in an extremely long, old-fashioned filter, which she demonstrably extended from one hand while swishing a brandy snifter in the other.

Her friend and Gina's son left the screen door frame the same moment she asked, "You okay, Dad?"

"Sure," he answered, grinning at his daughter's affront to the otherwise well-dressed affair. "And what does your mother think of you being out here in this outfit?"

"She said that if she hadn't given birth to me she would doubt that I was hers."

"Sounds like something she would say."

318

"You sure you're all right, *sport?* You look a little spaced-out."

"Not one hundred percent," Leo said, "but a little better than before." He rested a hand on his daughter's shoulder and gave her a peck on the cheek as he headed back toward the house, toward the doorway where Angelique and Corey had been, finally with an idea of who might have hit him.

# TWENTY-EIGHT

With her vodka tonic in hand, Gina left Leo without a word and wandered away from the party toward the flames of the tiki torches that Corey had staked into a wide semicircle around the lawn. The alcohol and pills and the flapping torch fire beside her all began to effectively smudge the ambient noise and the features of most of the faces of the guests on the porch, and meanwhile the music also helped to dilute whatever traces of anxiety would have otherwise remained. Leo wanted reassurance, but she had nothing left to give. She wanted to forget all that he'd said and all that she'd seen in the woods last night. She needed to be alone and to drink her drink without a mask. Out there on the lawn, she could do as she pleased. Clear her mind. Forget about Leo. Forget about Ray. Just drink. Listen to the music. And drink some more.

After a while, the orchestra's instruments seemed to liquefy. She lost all sense of time. Her eyelids flitted as she stood beside the softly dancing torch flame. She sank down to sit on her heels, watching a blurry group of women bedecked in designer gowns, listening to one of them ramble in a high-pitched voice about the most extravagant party she'd ever attended during her summers in the Hamptons, at someplace she kept referring to as "The Castle." *Jesus, they're awful,* Gina thought, leaning forward with a hand flat on the grass, trying to sip her drink, wishing she had a chair or even a blanket to sit on.

Just then she spotted Tiffany pantomiming the women she'd been watching. "Mmm-hmm, darling," Tiffany said, while stepping past them with her long cigarette holder poised at her lip. "Isn't it grand, darling? Yes, by all means, to think that we're the problem with the world, and somehow the world is our oyster. And even more delicious—" she paused to smoke theatrically "—that oyster of ours is always just waiting to be *shucked.*"

One of the women must have noticed Tiffany's antics, and turned to face her, head cocked. "Are you speaking to us, dear?"

And Tiffany replied with a flourish, "Horrible hag says what?"

"What?" The woman was stern-faced now, as were the others. Tiffany answered by pinching the sides of her decrepit overalls, the cigarette holder and snifter balanced in her hands as she sank down to curtsy. Then she meandered away from them across the lawn, with her middle finger extended over one shoulder, and approached Gina, laughing as the two made eye contact.

Gina raised her glass and smiled wide, about to call out to her, *Thank you!* But then a loud voice derailed her thought and forced her eyes to open wider, and at the same time spun Tiffany around—Leo shouting at his son from the corner of the porch, "Clayton, put the damn dog inside the house!"

Gina stood and took a wobbly step closer, away from the torch fire, and a few steps later passed by Tiffany, who'd corkscrewed down to her knees while tilting back the snifter to lick the final drops of brown liquor from the rim. Walking a hazy line to the porch, Gina locked her gaze on Leo's bandaged head, watching him try to wrestle something away from Polly. The dog had a piece of fabric in her mouth and Leo finally yanked it away from her right before she bolted off down the steps. Polly ran by Gina and nearly plowed over Tiffany before hooking left toward the lake and fading into the darkness, and Leo raised his hand, looking as though he intended to call out, either to her or his drunk daughter or the dog. But no words escaped his mouth. He looked down at the cloth he'd wrestled from Polly's jaw. His mouth went slack. He let the cloth slip from his hand.

Something was wrong with him. She took another step as Leo reeled for a moment and staggered toward her. He clutched the railing where it met the corner post. Gina staggered a bit herself but managed to keep her balance, and after a few steps went from walking to running toward him. Leo's face tightened severely, his legs giving out, his left hand curled like a claw. She reached him just as he released the corner post, though not in time to catch him. Gasping, with his right palm pressed to his chest, he slumped down as though he'd been shot.

Heads turned. Andy Sheffield shouted, "Dad!" hurrying over and falling to his knees beside Gina, who held his father in her arms and felt suddenly sober enough to assess the situation and to delegate.

"I think he's having a heart attack," she said, with her hand on Leo's cheek. "Call an ambulance. And find your mother." Andy stood up looking stunned, and when he didn't move right away, Gina yelled, "Call 911! *Now!*" The music drowned out her voice as it intensified, continuing its climb into a crescendo.

Most of the guests hadn't yet noticed Leo's collapse. But the group of women Gina had been critically analyzing from the lawn had, and were on their way over as Leo's son raced across the porch and pushed his way through others with their backs to the scene. Gina heard him call out to his mother and watched Sheila turn with a look of annoyance a moment before she heard Andy's plea. "Is there a doctor here? We need a doctor!" The music stopped. A loud murmur followed.

Gina held Leo in her arms with her back against the railing spindles and tried to steer him away from panicking by keeping a hand on his face and whispering that everything would be all right, help would be there soon; he would be fine. He didn't react to her touch, or her words. He merely gazed up at her, his face tight, his eyes wide. She stayed with him, cradling him like that until Tiffany asked to take her place.

Gina stepped aside, and was five or ten steps removed from the horde of socialites and the grown Sheffield children huddled around her boss when the strands of lights seemed to bulge, twinkling from post to post and all along the railing, the bodies of the bystanders morphing to fit her doubling vision and then her fish-eye-lens point of view. Her head lolled to the side as she knelt and picked up the torn scrap of cloth that Leo had dropped. It took her a second to realize why the pattern and material seemed so familiar—it was a dirty, ragged corner of one of the blankets from the Sheffields' master bedroom. She turned toward the lake, thoroughly confused as to how the dog had this in her mouth in the first place, but also why it seemed to terrify Leo. Then she recalled how Leo's friend had been wrapped in the woods, wrapped in the blanket from upstairs.

She looked over at Leo in Tiffany's arms, surrounded by worried guests and his two sons. Nothing about these past few days made any sense, and if he died tonight it would make even less sense to continue working here. With her elbows on the porch rail and the swatch from the blanket in her hand, Gina slid into a deeply reflective spell, recalling a montage of moments at this estate during the past twelve years. If he died tonight, this life she'd known for so long would end. If he died tonight, who would be the unlucky one to discover the man Leo had laid out in the woods?

Sometime later, the ambulance arrived. The flurry of emergency medical technicians on the porch pulled Gina back to the present, and the first thing she fixated on was that Sheila appeared incredibly calm—businesslike rather than distraught in her chitchat with fretful guests. A minute or two passed before Gina reached her breaking point, so sickened when she heard Sheila tell the musicians to continue playing— after it seemed Leo would live—that she muttered something caustic enough to make the woman to her right gasp. And worse, when one of the cellists held his bow at his side and expressed concern, pointing out the obvious fact that Leo was still being seen to by the paramedics, Sheila went so far as to threaten not paying them if they didn't cue back up.

Once the music started again, Gina grabbed the arm of a man standing beside her, unable to keep her criticism of Sheila to herself. "You believe that shit? What a heartless *bitch*."

"Are you sure it's a good idea to speak that way about your employer?" the aging James Bond–type asked.

Gina shut one eye to see him more clearly. "You're all disgusting," she said.

"Pardon me?"

"Exactly, thank you for asking. I hereby pardon you, sir."

The man walked off right when a waiter came by with a tray of champagne glasses, and Gina clamped her phone under her armpit, taking two glasses before whirling around with one in each hand. She squinted at the man she'd just spoken to, who'd sought out Sheila. Both looked at her like some sort of circus oddity, Sheila shaking her head, the 007 impersonator nodding with a sympathetic expression. Meanwhile, with Vivaldi playing, Tiffany, Andy and Clay rose from their knees a few feet from their father, Tiffany looking especially terrified while the paramedics finished prepping him on the gurney and a path cleared.

Gina gulped down the champagne in her right hand and then the champagne in her left, and dropped the empty glasses onto the lawn, unconcerned whether Sheila was still watching. Then she backpedaled out of the way and stood on the grass, barely breathing while the paramedics carried Leo past her to the ambulance. The orchestra played on as she wandered behind the procession of onlookers, and once she reached the wide parking area she squinted through the blur and saw Corey and Angelique getting into his pickup. She couldn't navigate the field of beautiful people fast enough to reach him before the ambulance pulled away and he tailed closely behind. Guests kept getting in her way, asking if she knew what had happened to Leo, and she kept shrugging, answering that she didn't know, finally pushing Barbara with the Jackie O glasses to the side, feeling that she needed to get to Corey *now*—or else something terrible might happen.

Intending to run, she jogged along the edge of the driveway in a spacey zigzag, while the Sheffield kids and many of the guests moved in the same direction, like the best-dressed herd imaginable, as though they'd all been lassoed and tugged by the ambulance heading toward the gates. She curled off and faced the lawn sculptures, thinking she should call Maryanne. She'd had a few drinks during these long shifts at work in years past, but she'd never been anywhere near this drunk, and definitely never so strung out. She opened her phone and saw that Maryanne had been one of her missed calls. In full relapse, she couldn't work up the courage to call her back.

The ambulance pulled through the gates and set its siren blaring, Corey tailgating the flashing lights to the road. Gina remembered why she'd wandered out this far and resumed jogging along the driveway rocks with uneven steps, yelling at his rear bumper, but way too late. Corey was gone. She reached the gates just after they closed, gripped the bars and hung her head, staring at her shoes, listening to the siren fade. Then her phone buzzed, alerting her that she had a new text. Blinking wildly until she could see clearly, she assumed it would be from Maryanne—but instead, the message had come from Ray.

What's with the ambulance?

Huh? What the hell was he talking about? Another text came through.

U look tired. Nice dress tho.

Gina angled her head to look from side to side through the bars.

Yeah I see U.

She stepped back.

C what happens when U don't answer my calls.

Her throat constricted. She couldn't get enough air. He was out there somewhere in the shadows. She hadn't had time to go to the police to get the restraining order yet. She turned to find that everyone who'd followed the ambulance had already made their way back to the house, the emptiness of the lawn making it even harder to breathe. She took a few quick steps away from the gates, her ankles bending on the driveway stones as she imagined her head centered in crosshairs. Running now, another text sent vibrations into her hand. Then another. As soon as she read them, she wished she hadn't.

**U can run
but U can't hide.**

# SUNDAY

# TWENTY-NINE

Despite Leo's medical drama, on Sheila's insistence, all the guests who'd been invited to stay for the full weekend still occupied the estate the following morning. As it turned out, Leo hadn't actually had a heart attack. The ER doctor's best guess had been that he'd had an anxiety attack, possibly some residual dizziness from the head wound and the concussion he'd sustained Thursday night. But after his vitals were monitored for twelve hours, nothing out of the ordinary appeared to be going on with either his heart or his brain. Aside from giving him a prescription for Valium and strongly recommending bed rest for the remainder of the holiday, the doctor released Leo into his wife's care.

Their short car ride home passed with only a few terse words spoken, mostly by Sheila, about half of which focused on the "Gina situation." As soon as they were upstairs and she'd watched him settle into bed, Sheila turned to the doorway, where Corey stood awaiting instructions, and told her husband, "Gina's son can take care of you for now." Looking from one face to the other, she added, "And for the rest of the day you two are going to work together to ensure that Leo doesn't have any more *accidents*. Can we agree on this?"

Leo made eye contact with Corey and raised an eyebrow. "Looks like you're stuck with me for a while."

Corey looked either stoned or badly in need of sleep. His eyes were bloodshot, his eyelids heavy, and he kept shifting his weight from one foot to the other. He held his hands clasped at his waist, fidgeting with the bottom of his T-shirt.

"I'll get you whatever you need, Mr. Sheffield," he said. "Everyone's just glad you're all right."

"You're a good man, Corey. We're lucky to have you and your mom here."

Sheila glared at him with folded arms. She wanted to fire Gina, but Leo hadn't equivocated at all before he said no, and then said it again, much louder, for good measure. So now, on top of the crazy logistics he needed to sort through to stay out of prison, his wife was royally pissed at him. A point she emphasized on her way out of the room with Corey in tow, as she spoke to Leo like a child: "Since you didn't eat breakfast, I'll have him bring something up from the kitchen. Don't even think about moving from that bed."

Gina appeared in the doorway just after Sheila led Corey out, with the portable home phone pressed against her stomach, her eyes down. "Sorry to bother you, Mr. Sheffield," she said, glancing over her shoulder as she stepped into the room. "You have a phone call."

"Take a message, please."

She looked back into the hallway and moved closer to the bed, her hand pressed tightly over the phone receiver when she leaned down to whisper, "It's a detective, the one who called your cell. I tried to explain that you haven't been well and are in bed, but he's pressing."

Leo squinted at her, feeling cornered, trapped in the bed. "What exactly did he say?"

She looked over at the doorway once more and then back. "Everything, I guess. More than you told me when I found you in the woods, anyway."

"Jesus," Leo whispered, "just tell me what the fuck he said."

Gina glared at him. "He said a man named Henry Beauchamp had been released from the hospital a week ago and is missing. His mother asked him to check in with her once a day but she hasn't heard from him since Monday. He's not at his apartment, and the last she knew he was excited about coming out here for the weekend. The detective wants to know if you've seen him—after he asked me if *I've* seen him. He said he called twice already and left messages, and if you don't get on the line now he'll have to make the drive out from the city tomorrow."

They stared at one another until Gina added, "Just talk to him."

Leo tilted his head back and released the longest sigh of his life. "I'm sleeping. Try to make him understand that I'm not well. Take his number and tell him I'll call back later."

"What if he doesn't wait and decides to drive out today?"

"Please, I can't deal with any more hypotheticals. I need to think. Take a message. Say I'll call him back later today."

Gina stared for what was probably only a few seconds, but for Leo it seemed she'd held him underwater for a full minute by the time she spoke.

"Alright," she said, and continued staring as she uncovered the receiver and placed the phone to her mouth. "Yes, hello? I'm sorry to make you wait so long. Yes, he's sleeping now but should be awake in the next few hours." She turned and gave Leo another hard stare on her way out, her voice fading as he sat up straighter to hear. "Of course," she said, "let me just get a pen . . ."

Leo shoved the blanket aside and swung his legs over. He set his feet on the floor, his eyes focused on the Impressionist-era countryside painting in front of the wall safe. He had a quarter mil locked in there . . . nowhere near the full amount he'd promised Angelique. He could run off right now without a word to anyone, take the cash, his passport, the bank codes in the Caymans, call for a car to pick him up and head straight to the airport. The painting's porch-fronted cottage and pastoral grasses pulled him in. The peaceful scene suddenly terrified him. He'd hardly even noticed it hanging there for all these years, and definitely had never thought about how the cottage exposed in all that wide-open space evoked a sense of loneliness, vulnerability, or how the windswept grasses held so much anxiety in their stems.

He looked closer at the cottage's dilapidated porch rails and its rickety wooden door. That's what it all came down to—trapped there in the sun-drenched slats and posts, in their rough texture, Leo felt what the artist must have felt, imagined him speaking from the other side of the closed cottage door. Stuck inside, sick with loneliness, the painter had been crippled by his fear of the outside world but also too afraid of death to end it all. And because of this fear he'd lived day after day imprisoned in his own home, separated from the sunlight.

Leo had never paid much mind to the art Sheila had selected for the summerhouse, and sure as hell had never bothered to appreciate this one. It had always served a simple purpose—to hide his reinforced steel vault, where the gold watch he'd given to Henry now lay locked behind tumblers and dials. His safe, where a copy of his most recently amended will also was housed, along

337

with the boxes of nine-millimeter bullets and—
of course—his gun. If he didn't figure out how
to move Henry soon, if some miraculous solution
didn't come to pass, the money in there wouldn't
matter. The gun would be his reason to turn the
dials. The only thing left to reach for.

# THIRTY

With the bedroom door closed, Corey spent the next half hour on a chair in the corner making small talk, while Leo Sheffield sat in bed with a fresh bandage on the back of his head, nibbling on cheese and crackers and spooning chicken barley soup into his mouth. Eventually, he asked about the boy's plans now that he'd graduated high school.

"I was thinking of enrolling in clown college," Corey said. "I hear there's always a need for more good clowns."

Mr. Sheffield grinned and brought his napkin up to wipe the soup dribbling from his chin.

"I didn't expect you to say something funny when I had my mouth full."

"Sorry about that, sir."

"No, not at all. I think I needed that. I haven't even cracked a smile since Thursday night. You heard about my little accident Thursday night, right?"

He lowered his spoon and set the food tray to the side.

"I'm finished with this," he said, which Corey assumed meant he should come over and take it away, so he stood up and took a step closer. "No, leave it," Leo said. "I mean I'm finished with this little game we've been playing."

Corey's heart began beating way too fast. "I'm not sure what you mean, sir."

"I was out on the balcony here yesterday and saw you and Angelique in the garden. The view from up here is really quite something. And then I recalled seeing you two together a few other times, and it all started to make sense." He eased the blanket from his legs, swiveled off the bed and pushed his bare feet into his slippers. "So how long have you two been together? You are dating, aren't you?"

"It's recent, I guess. Really recent."

"I've been dying to know something."

"What's that?"

"What exactly did you hit me with?"

Corey tried to swallow but it felt as though a rock had suddenly wedged in his throat. He stammered, "I—uh, I don't know what you're—"

"Relax, son. You really brained me, and gave me the worst fucking headache of my life, but I admit I had it coming."

The silence hung between them like smoke in a windowless room, each second an eternity.

"Yeah," Corey finally said, his face filling with heat. "You did."

"You think you love her, don't you?"

"Maybe, so what."

"Jesus, I bet you do. You two are so goddamn

young. That's good, though." He paused, his face scrunched in a way that had Corey wondering if he was about to laugh or cry. "We should all be so lucky . . . To find love."

"You all right, Mr. Sheffield?"

"In most ways I can't really answer yes to that. But physically, yes. I'm fine."

"Maybe you'd rather I left you alone so you can sleep."

"He told me he loved me, but I never said it back."

"Sorry, what?"

"Henry, the young man from the pool—" Leo pointed in the direction of the pines. "You're the one Angelique said took photos, right? And you probably saw where he is now, too, thanks to that damn dog."

Corey looked at him, unsure if he should respond.

"Maybe I did love him," Leo said, pausing to breathe deeply. "But even if I didn't, I cared about him, so why couldn't I just say it? I mean, really, would it have killed me to give him what he wanted?"

"I don't—"

"The thing about regrets, Corey—it's much better to regret something you *have* done than something you *haven't* done. Remember that. My biggest regret is not telling Henry that I loved him before he died. Didn't matter if it was true.

For his sake, I should have given him that. I keep going over it and over it, whether he'd still be alive if I'd said it."

"I think you should sit down at least, Mr. Sheffield. You're really not looking so good."

"No!" Leo turned toward the closed door with his fist clenched, then leaned closer with tears welling up and spoke much softer. "This has to happen tonight. I need your help. I need you to move him."

"You can't be serious," Corey said, already flashing to the awful image of Henry's face when he'd leaned over him and then brought the blanket over his head. He backed a step away from his mom's boss, envisioning clips of himself struggling to lift Henry's body from the forest floor, the blanket unfurling, Henry's cold arms out-flung, and then, worst of all, someone seeing him carrying a dead man from the trees. "No," he said. "That's crazy. No way."

"You have to. Please. A detective called a few minutes ago. Your mom answered, and she knows about Henry now, too. The detective already knows he was coming here, because Henry's mother said so when she reported him missing. I can't start answering questions if he's still on the property. And to make things worse, Polly won't leave him the fuck alone. I saw you chase her into the woods. She led you right to him, didn't she?"

"Hey, hey—hey there, Mr. Sheffield. Hold up. Stop crying for a second."

Corey felt his arm rise up with his hand out, but he quickly pulled it back. Through some unexpected reflex he'd nearly placed a hand on Leo's arm to console him.

"As long as you give Angelique the money tonight," he said, "like you promised, we won't tell. I understand that you're in a bad way right now, but I'm not moving a dead body for you. No fucking way. *Sir*."

"Don't worry, I won't renege on the cash I promised Angelique. In fact, you can have some of it now. You keeping quiet about what you saw is more than a fair deal for that money. But if you help me with Henry, I'd be willing to give you a whole helluva lot more than a million, enough to set you and your mom up for life. Name your price."

Corey eyed him for a while, thinking about how much a guy as rich as Leo would be willing to pay in such a desperate position, but then the tape played through to the end and all he could see were his wrists in cuffs and the bars of his cell clanging shut.

"Think about it," Leo said. "Your mom could quit working here if she wanted, start a whole new life for herself and you and your brother. Consider the big picture for a second. Think about what that kind of money would mean for your family."

Leo reached out to the painting on the wall, lifted it from its hook and uncovered the wall safe Corey already knew was there. Turning the heavy dial, Leo told him to go into the closet and bring over the dark blue gym bag.

Corey's thoughts were all jumbled, but he did as he was told and then held the bag open while Leo dropped in banded stacks of hundred-dollar bills, counting them out in pairs until the bag held a hundred grand. Then Leo reached into the safe once more. "Here," he said, and handed Corey a gold watch. "I want you to have this."

Corey felt the weight of it in his palm, then noticed ROLEX etched along the bottom of the clock face. Five minutes ago he had roughly ten bucks to his name, and now he stood with a sack full of cash and, as far as he knew, one of the most expensive watches on the planet. He glanced up at the open safe. There must have been another hundred grand inside, easy, along with a ring box, folders fat with papers, a few other fancy watches, and loose pieces of jewelry. But that wasn't all. A second before Leo swung the heavy safe door closed, Corey nearly choked. He'd seen a box of ammo and the barrel of a handgun peeking from behind the stacks of cash.

Leo turned the dial to relock it and rehung the painting, then placed his hands on Corey's shoulders and looked him dead in the face. "Please. You have to move Henry off the property—the only caveat being that you put him someplace where he won't be disturbed again. How much will it take for you to help me with this? I'm begging you. Please."

Corey held the gun in his mind's eye like an afterimage, saw it pointed at his head, saw the flash as it fired in super-slow-motion. He wondered just how desperate Leo might become if he didn't agree to help him. He had the gym bag in hand. More money inside it than he'd ever conceived of holding. He should find Angelique and just take off. No goodbyes or excuses for Gina—she'd be all right now that she'd decided to get that restraining order on Ray. Just leave now, and then call and apologize after they'd made it far away.

"Leo," he said, feeling he should take Mr. Sheffield down a peg and call him by his first name. "It won't matter how much you agreed to pay me if someone sees me with Henry's body. I'd go to jail, probably for the rest of my life."

"That's just it, though—no one will see you."

"Easy for you to say."

"No, they won't. You know why? Later tonight there's going to be a fireworks show that one of the homeowners across the lake has spent a fortune on. As soon as the first burst hits the sky everyone will already be out here at the party on the lake side of the house, and they'll be staring up for the next half hour until the finale ends.

Meanwhile, you'll have Henry ready at the tree line beforehand and you can take the beginning of the fireworks as your cue to pull your truck across the far lawn with your headlights off. Nobody will be within an acre or two of you, maybe more, and it's plenty dark out there. Five or ten minutes later, well before the show is over, you'll be pulling out the gates. Where you take him from there, that's up to you. You'll be okay. We both will, as long as you say yes."

"I can't believe you're asking me to do this."

"You're my only hope. Say yes, and I'll be forever in your debt."

"Why can't you just do it yourself?"

"People would notice I was missing, and I can't risk someone coming to look for me."

"You're telling me you'd give me whatever I ask? Like a hundred million if I do this?"

Leo paused for no more than a second, then nodded.

"It would take time, but yes. Absolutely. I can afford that."

"This is fucking insane."

"Do this for me, Corey, and I swear on my life and on the lives of my kids, I'll give you and your mother enough money to never have to worry."

# THIRTY-ONE

The musicians had all but set up under the party tent on the lawn, a few of them tuning their instruments while the pianist played a tinkly riff that seemed an improvised response to the lightly falling rain. Heavy clouds had been rolling in and rumbling ever since lunch, accompanied by frequent gusts of wind that matted large swaths of the lawn and rippled patterns along the lake. Some of the guests for the most formal party of the weekend drifted back to shelter through the open tent walls just before a day-worker began unrolling the vinyl sheets and staking them down, while others wandered across the gentle slope toward the lake with raincoats draped over tuxedo jackets and gowns.

Tiffany sat on the porch with a wineglass at her bottom lip, stunned by Angelique's news.

"I guess I sort of get it. Yeah, he's kind of cute, Angel, but he's a small-town guy, though, right? I mean, how well do you even know him?"

"Well enough to know that I want to leave with him."

"Where are you two planning on going?"

"So far, all we've decided is that we want a long road trip before fall semester. He's smart, you know. All you ever see of him is the work he does here, but he actually has a full ride at a school upstate."

"He does?"

"Yeah, he just isn't sure yet if he'll go this fall because of family stuff."

"So you're gonna just hop in his run-down pickup truck and drive, with no idea where you're going. Sounds kinda nutso, Angel-fish . . . But then again, what the hell do I know."

"I promise I'll call."

"I can't change your mind? I wish you'd stay here with me like we planned. What am I going to do here without you? Make fun of my parents' hideous guests by myself? Go to the beach with my tight-ass banker brothers and their idiot friends? You're really leaving me here alone all summer with my crazy family?"

Angelique took her friend's hand and squeezed it. "You'll be fine," she said, and just then Clayton's dog loped past with muddy steps across the porch, distracting her for a second. She let go of Tiffany's hand and leaned closer from her chair. "As much as I appreciate you and your parents offering to have me here all summer, with everything that's happened over the past few months with my mom and all, I just need to be somewhere totally new."

"I get it, this place will be full of awful people all summer. But it still sucks you're leaving me here."

"I know, but I'll be back. And we'll meet up in the city before school starts. I just have to go now."

"What-the-fuck-ever."

"You can stop with the guilt trip now, right? I really like Corey, Tiff. He's got a good heart, and I trust him. Can you be happy for me?"

Tiffany rolled her eyes and angled her head forward, motioning with her finger in her mouth and making a quick vomit sound. "Fuck's sake," she said, grinning and shaking her head. "I'm happy if you're happy, whore-face. You just better call me from the road, though, like every few hours, so I know you're not, like, in a Dumpster somewhere."

"You have my solemn oath, slutty-pie. It shall be done."

They stared out at the lake and the two swans waddling beside the bulkhead with their heads down, a gust of wind spreading the lake water behind them and raising it like ribs.

Tiffany smiled and placed her hand on Angelique's shoulder. "So now I suppose we'll have to find me a big-hearted townie, too. Huh?"

They laughed together until a stinging sensation spread into the corners of Angelique's jaw and her eyes watered over. Despite Tiff's faults, she would miss her friend terribly. But their friendship could never be the same after what Mr. Sheffield had done, whether Tiff ever heard about it or not. They'd been friends for as long as she could remember, but even if this insane weekend hadn't blown so much certainty away, she'd already wondered if this summer might be the last they spent together out here by the lake. During her first two semesters at Brown and Tiff's at NYU, their friendship involved so much more distance, much more time apart. They'd spoken less, barely met up when they both spent their breaks in the city. In the coming years they'd likely see even less of each other. Tiff had already started an internship in some plush Manhattan art gallery with other trust fund teenagers and twentysomethings who didn't actually need to work, and for her, staying in the city—aside from summers out here—made total sense. Angelique had no clue where she wanted to go once she and Corey had the money, but with her mother gone and her sister estranged, the idea of living in New York held no appeal. She needed to get far away. She needed to see all the places between here and someplace new.

The sky grumbled over the lake, the rain falling harder when Michael stepped out to the right of their chairs, held the screen door open and clanged a large metal triangle with a large metal spoon to signify that dinner was about to be served. Looking like the cast of a Samuel Beckett play, the hooded guests turned in unison and plodded toward the porch.

The girls stood and hugged, and after holding much tighter and for much longer than her best friend normally would, Tiffany asked if she was okay.

"Fine, darling. I just love you is all."

"Right back at you, sweet cheeks. But don't you go getting all blubbery on me. Let's find us a glass of vino, huh? How about it? It's a special occasion, right? So you'll finally have a drink with me?"

Angelique deflected her question by saying she just realized she hadn't eaten all day, and placed a hand on her stomach to emphasize how ready she was for dinner. They walked through the living room and into the hall, where Tiffany intended to pull a bottle from one of the wine chillers, but then they both paused beside the nearest bathroom door, which was open a crack.

Someone sounded like they were battling a demon in there, in pain and praying whole-heartedly from their gut, either suffering from food poisoning or regretting having drunk way too much. Tiffany tapped lightly on the door, nudging it open, and as she did Angelique got a full view of Corey's mother there on her knees— her hair matted on one side, her hands gripping the toilet seat, drool dangling from her chin—an expression of abject defeat as she turned and saw the two girls watching her.

# THIRTY-TWO

After dinner, the party hit full swing. Once again, tiny white lights had been strewn around the porch rails and mini chandeliers hung at intervals above the heads of a few dozen guests with martinis and wine and champagne glasses in hand. Despite the darkening shelf of clouds over the lake, everyone had settled in with their cocktails, more animated than ever due to the rising energy of the storm. They, along with Sheila and the Sheffield sons, socialized in their formal wear along the porch and within the party tent's thick water-resistant walls, sheltered from the wind and rain, all of them still blissfully oblivious that Leo's dead lover lay a few acres from them in the woods.

Corey had been surveying the scene for a while now, psyching himself up to sneak off and make his way over to the opposite side of the property. He hadn't seen his mother since Angelique told him what she and Tiffany witnessed when they pushed open the bathroom door. He worried about her. Gina's drinking had always concerned him, but so much more lately, especially since her trip to the hospital this week. There wasn't much he could do for her now, though, except to follow through with Leo's request. It would be a thousand times easier to help pull Gina from her downward spiral once he had all that money. He thought back to Leo begging him to move Henry, and how Leo kept pressing him until he'd finally blurted out, "Alright, fine. If you're seriously going to give me a hundred million bucks, I'll do it." Stunned by how genuine Leo seemed when he agreed, he'd left the bedroom a minute later in a daze, amazed that the sorry fuck hadn't even hesitated, and instead had thanked him. But would Leo really hold to his promise? Should he have gotten that in writing? Would he give a fortune to the kid who'd nearly killed him a few nights ago? With the cops closing in and a handful of people already aware of Henry, Leo was desperate enough to say anything. Still, maybe it was worth the risk. Gina needed to go to rehab, a good one, an expensive one, and once he held up his end of the deal and moved Henry, whatever other money changed hands, Leo would pay for it—the best rehab they could find.

The sun had nearly set, though most of the fire colors at the horizon lay obscured by the rain clouds laced in gray and black and indigo. The edges of the lawn had already been swallowed by shadows. Soon night would fall completely. Not much longer now before all the acres outside the party lights and tiki torches would be dark enough for Corey to get started.

He walked backward off the porch steps and discreetly slipped out of sight past the corner of the house, spun on the wet lawn and hustled through the rain to the garden, where he found Angelique waiting for him, crouched inside the archway. The rain tapered to a drizzle while they hugged and fatter drops of water dripped on his neck from the flowery arch overhead. She said over his shoulder, "I wish we could just go right now."

Hoping to protect her, he'd kept her in the dark about his part with Leo and Henry. He'd also kept her from questioning his upcoming absence by saying that's when he'd get the rest of the million himself. "I just have to take care of a couple other things before the handoff," he said, longing to get the whole thing over with. "But I promise, we'll leave soon. Meet me at the gates right after the fireworks end."

"Are you okay?"

"Yeah, I'm fine. Could you do me a favor, though? Check and see if my mom's still around? Her car's still here, but I haven't seen her for a while."

"The last I saw her after we found her in the bathroom, Tiff's mom was with her and it didn't look like things were all too friendly. I'll look for her, though."

"Thanks," he said, releasing his arms. "A couple hours from now, I promise, we'll be done with this place forever."

She took a step back, half turned and grinned. "I was thinking about where we could go."

"Oh yeah? Where?"

"We should drive to Bryce Canyon."

"Okay, where's that?"

"It's a national park in Utah, and it looks amazing. All these spires that are different colors, sort of like caves turned inside out, and some of the reddest sand and boulders you've ever seen. I've wanted to go there since my mom first showed me pictures when I was little. We'd planned to go together during my spring break this year—but she was already gone by then."

Corey felt the weight of her statement and breathed deeply before answering. "That's where we'll go, then."

Angelique held eye contact while she continued her slow backpedal toward the house. "Thanks," she said. "Even though I wish I could have gone with her, it'll mean a lot to me to finally be there." About halfway to the door she smiled and ran her hand beneath each of her eyes, calling back to him as she jogged to the door, "Tonight, let's drive all night."

Once she was inside, Corey pulled out his phone and dialed his brother's number. Glancing up at the balcony, he wasn't surprised to find Leo approaching the railing, staring down at him. They locked eyes, and though nothing was said, everything was understood. Time for him to earn his fortune. Time to start walking toward that darkness way out there.

He turned and began trudging across the lawn. The rain returned and he walked faster, trying to ignore the sense that Leo's eyes had begun burning a hole in the back of his head. When his brother answered, he started by asking how he was doing. Casual.

"Not bad," Dylan said. "But Ray came by again, man. I didn't let him in or anything, but he was hammered, shouting all sorts of nasty shit about Mom from the front yard."

"When was that?"

"About an hour ago, something like that?"

"You said she was getting a restraining order, right? You should call the cops, tell them what happened."

"Yeah, alright, I will. Seeing him here like that and his crazy shit with the gun outside Layne's house—the guy's way off the deep end now."

"You should tell her all this when she gets home tonight, too, even the stuff from the other night. I didn't want to worry her with that before, but she should know. And if Ray comes back, definitely call the cops again. Sorry so much of this shit is falling on you tonight."

"It's all right, I'll just be happy when they arrest that asshole."

Corey passed by the last of the bronze chess pieces, still moving as he turned to look over his shoulder, far enough away now that Leo's bathrobe-shrouded body there on the balcony appeared no bigger than an ant. As far as he could tell in the light rain and darkening twilight, nobody else had any idea he'd trekked out here. The rest of the Sheffield family and their guests all lingered on the lake side of the house. Nobody but Leo would be looking his direction. Nobody would see him dragging Henry from the woods, or see his truck when he drove over with the headlights off.

His brother had gone quiet on the other end, waiting for him to say something more.

"We should get off the phone so you can call the cops now," Corey said, "but before we do I wanted to let you know I'm gonna be away for a little while."

"Where are you going?"

"On a road trip with—" He stopped walking. "With someone you haven't met yet. My girl-friend."

"Girlfriend? When the fuck did that happen?"

He imagined his younger brother preparing some snarky comment. He would miss Dylan. His friends, too, but mostly his mother and brother, the two people he'd shared a tiny house with since Dylan was born—the only people he'd ever truly cared about. Tomorrow and each day he and Angelique put more distance between themselves and the estate, he would make sure to call Gina and Dylan to let them know he was okay.

"I'll tell you all about her soon," Corey said. "I gotta go now, though. Just wanted to check in with you before we left, and to give you the heads-up that Mom's had a really rough day, so take care of her as best you can tonight, alright?"

"Sure, man."

"Thanks, Dyl."

He paused, debating whether he should say the three sappy words he had in his head. No need to overthink it, though. He should just say it.

"Love you, man," he said.

Dylan stayed quiet on the other end for a few beats.

"You okay, Core? You sound, I don't know, different."

"What, a guy can't tell his bro he loves him?"

"Alright. Yeah, I love you, too."

The call ended and Corey noticed that the distant violins and cellos had been playing the entire time, but now seemed to be drifting all around and settling over him as a calm blanket of sound, a comforting background when he walked on toward the pines, and while he doubled back to the toolshed, where he grabbed the flashlight hanging from a nail on the plywood wall and then pushed the Sheffields' wheelbarrow with one of their shovels gently clanging inside.

At the spot where he'd followed Polly into the woods he squatted down and stared toward the house once more, straining to decipher any voices amid the party static beneath the music. Squinting hard, he counted to ten and still saw no one out there in the faraway flaps of light from the tiki torches.

*Just wait for the fireworks,* he thought, *then drive over here with the headlights off, load him up, then stick to the speed limit till I get to that spot in the woods in North Sea where Mick said we should grow pot last summer.*

Roughly a two-mile drive across Southampton with Henry rewrapped in the blanket and hidden beneath the wheelbarrow, and then no one would see Corey's truck parked twenty or thirty feet from the road, shrouded by so many trees in that enclosed space where he and Mick and Joey and Dylan used to drink once in a while but had all but forgotten . . . and no one would see him wheeling the body deep into the woods out there, either.

"I can do this," he said, as he started pushing the wheelbarrow into the woods, the flashlight clicked on and beaming, aimed at the trail Leo had left in the pine needles when he'd dragged Henry through.

With the shovel clattering, he approached the body slowly, already aware that Polly had returned and disturbed the blanket much more than when he'd last been here, unfurling it more than halfway. Henry had rolled a bit as well, and now lay on his left side on a bed of pine needles, his chest facing Corey, his head awkwardly turned away.

Corey set down the wheelbarrow and knelt and looked at Henry's face. *What am I doing?* The question struck him just before the smell, which had grown so much stronger since his last visit here. He started to dry-heave. He'd never taken death inside his nose, and now he needed to keep his arm up to block it from seeping in any deeper. He didn't have any gloves. Why hadn't he thought to bring gloves from the shed? Too late to head back to get them. The countdown to the fireworks had already begun ticking loudly in his head. Time to suck it up and take this dead guy by the wrists and flop him into the wheelbarrow. He'd just have to use his bare hands and then wipe down Henry's skin afterward to make sure he left no prints. But easier said than done, because the second his hands touched the cold skin of Henry's wrists, Corey recoiled as though he'd been snake-bit.

His entire body shuddered. His stomach didn't feel right. He wretched while turning his face away from Henry's face, coughing the smell from his lungs, covering his nose with his shoulder. The pine boughs kept him pretty well sheltered from the rain, but the wind gusted some more, the dark canopy of branches high overhead bending and shaking wildly, releasing another spatter of rainwater. The music far off on the other side of the property had been reduced to the thinnest thread of sound and no longer calmed him, but instead penetrated his head like a needle.

He leaned back and sat on his heels, willing

his stomach to relax. How had he ended up here? What had he been thinking to even consider transporting a dead body? A muted flash of light turned his head upward but he couldn't see anything through the dense pine boughs. The flash set him wondering if there would even be any fireworks if the rain started falling any heavier, and without that distraction to keep everyone's eyes fixed to the sky, Leo's plan wasn't much of a plan anymore. Without the fireworks, someone might wander back to this side of the property and see him loading something big and heavy and unexplainable from the woods into the bed of his pickup, or at least witness him driving across the lawn.

For the first time since he'd agreed to help Leo with this horrible task he doubted that he could follow through. Millions of dollars aside, this was just too fucked up, and way too risky. Wasn't it? He tilted his head back and prayed for a sign.

Then he looked down.

The flashlight lay angled in such a way as to illuminate the dead man's face in profile, an image worse than anything Corey had ever imagined seeing in real life—Henry's bluish-purple lips, the gash and trace of dried blood, a thin strip of his skull exposed just above his temple, the pine needles between his teeth, the busted capillaries and violet blotches along his cheekbone, and the worst detail, that sliver of milky-gray eyeball where the wrinkled lids hadn't quite stayed closed.

Corey couldn't breathe as he stood and went stumbling back. He fell to his hands and knees, his backbone arching up like a dog with its hackles raised, coughing until he felt his throat might tear. He couldn't go through with it. No fucking way.

The wind fell away for a moment, which he took as a good omen, a nod from the universe that finally he'd reached a moment of clarity. He'd been insane to consider this, but it had taken only a second to be returned to a familiar sense of himself. He used his T-shirt to wipe off Henry's wrists, thinking as he did that he and Angelique had enough money to leave now and they could be on their way within the hour—and he had to believe Gina would be safe enough for the night with Dylan looking out for her and his call to the cops. Soon, whatever fate decided should happen here with Leo and Henry would come to pass, and all that mattered in the aftermath would be that Corey had had nothing to do with it.

He started heading out of the woods, pushing the wheelbarrow as quickly as he could without it tipping over. The sound of the rain beyond the pines resembled rolling waves. At the tree line he stumbled over a backbone-shaped root, and then tried to hold the flashlight steady while texting Angelique: Meet me at the driveway gates ASAP.

Once he left the canopy of the pines, he jogged

362

the wheelbarrow back to the shed, his head low as the rain came down hard, blowing at him sideways with each swell of wind. Breathing heavily outside the shed door, he stood still for a moment, fine with getting soaked, thinking he'd made the right choice. There wouldn't be any fucking fireworks with it raining like this . . . How could there be?

A sudden blast from above hit him like a cannonball to the chest and whipped his head toward the lake. The first burst of fireworks—streaks of green, branches of red, concussive shots pop, pop, popping along flashing veins of chemical reactions, shimmering, crackling, a bright gold willow-tree-shaped explosion, flecks glittering down and sizzling before they faded. Then another crack, a burst, a series of booms followed by purple and green asterisks tearing open the sky, thunderclaps echoing off the lake, the whole sequence so violent and yet beautiful enough to mesmerize.

Corey stood as still as the chess piece statues beside him. Soon someone would make the horrible discovery out there in the woods, and when they did, he and Angelique needed to be long gone. At least one detective in the city had started retracing Henry's final days, and eventually would come looking for him here . . . and that's if the dog or the smell didn't draw someone to the woods first.

He walked on, shuddering with each new crack in the sky, his palms pressed to his ears. Supernatural flashes of light, shadows dancing, his pace too slow, acid churning in his stomach when his hands dropped and he started running toward the gates, now propelled by the explosions. Never had he been so wide-awake and simultaneously plagued by a voice telling him that this waking life was really all a dream. If not for her, he'd be wishing for nothing more than to wake up. If not for her, he may have been so blinded by the money that he would have forced himself to follow through with Leo's plan and moved the body, which he knew now would have been a huge mistake.

He kept running, but the gates off in the distance seemed no closer than they had a minute ago when he'd been walking, so he ran harder. The next series of fireworks flashed like artificial stars and lit up the driveway enough for him to see Angelique out there crouched beside the hedge, his legs suddenly feeling so much lighter as she stood up and waved and began running toward him with the gym bag full of cash over her shoulder. He couldn't get to her fast enough . . . but she was helping to close the space between them twice as fast as he could have done alone, racing through the bomb blasts and colorful flashes of light to meet him.

# THIRTY-THREE

Leo stood out on the master bedroom's balcony in his robe. Around the house to the left of him, the orchestra music and a cacophony of sounds from the party echoed out over the lake, while to his right, the boy he'd begged and bribed hurried away from the commotion, toward Angelique.

As long as the boy followed through with his end and moved Henry's body, Leo would keep his side of the bargain and hand over the sealed envelope addressed to Gina with bank codes for two of the accounts in the Caymans, and the Halpern family would have all the money they'd ever need. Then he would decide whether to sign the note he'd worked on throughout the evening, which now lay on his writing table in the bedroom. The paragraph explaining his reasons for suicide had taken no effort at all, though his apologies to Sheila and the kids had.

A few minutes ago, he'd returned the scrap of paper with Detective Faraday's phone number to the writing table drawer, spun the dial and opened the wall safe, and now gripped the gun in his silk bathrobe's deep pocket. The signing of the suicide note rather than its burning in the fireplace still depended on whether Leo still felt this empty after knowing Corey had done his

365

part to save him from prison and his family from such inconceivable scandal. If this hollowness remained for any substantial amount of time after Henry had been moved, it would simply be too much to bear; and instead of wallowing in morbid self-reflection throughout yet another sleepless night, he would start the countdown.

First step: sip his final glass of Scotch. Second step: ask once more for Henry's forgiveness, as well as his father's forgiveness, and then God's forgiveness, though he wasn't so sure he believed either of those last two mattered anymore. Third and final step: he would click the safety off and chamber the bullet, breathe one final deep breath and be done.

He regretted not returning Henry's *I love you* so intensely it was as though his spine had begun cracking, his body crumbling in on itself. He still couldn't begin to reconcile his failure to give him that one act of kindness before he died, after he'd so recently slashed his wrists. He stared down at Corey and Angelique with his right hand clutching the wet balcony railing, watching the young lovebirds hug and then the girl hurrying off out of sight.

Corey looked up and saw Leo perched above him. They stared at one another for longer than either could have held his breath. Then the boy turned with his cell phone pressed to his ear and started heading toward Henry through the sculpture garden, and Leo sighed, believing he would follow through, not out of any sense of duty or kindness or even pity for his mother's boss, not even out of any personal greed. He would do it for his family.

The boy's frame grew smaller and fainter in Leo's vision as he entered the darker distance beside the old-growth oaks roughly halfway to the pines, and soon enough he vanished altogether, along with the last hints of daylight, as if he'd been absorbed by the branches swaying and bowing in anticipation of the encroaching storm. Leo exhaled and removed his hand from his pocket. Despite the vague hope that Corey might actually save him, the desire to live still eluded him. He ran through his countdown once more, thinking afterward that he might have put his pistol to his head and pulled the trigger right then and there, but he still needed to sign his note to Sheila and the kids.

*No,* he thought, *better to do this right.* Planning to pour his final drink, or possibly his second to last, he turned to walk inside, feeling . . . peculiar.

*Peculiar?*

It seemed the most accurate word to describe this purgatorial state he'd been trapped in all weekend long, especially *peculiar* to have made up his mind that this was to be his final night on earth—after his biggest fear only a few days ago had been that Henry might try to kill himself again. *Peculiar.* The word kept ringing out as he considered the fact that he hadn't truly contemplated killing himself since he was younger than Corey was now, back when Leonard Sr. had fallen ill and suddenly spent all his time at home, so much more time spent berating Leo for his subtle affectations, the violence of his words all too often evolving to violence from his shaky hand. And even so, back then, if Leo had been honest with himself, he would have admitted to fantasizing far more about homicide than suicide. He'd loved his father, though there had been no one else on earth he'd ever hated so much, either during his youth or since. The therapists and psychiatrists over the years had encouraged him to let go of his anger through a slew of so-called cathartic exercises. He should try his best to forgive, they'd said. But the suggestions had been too abstract, the therapy more akin to picking a scab than healing. He'd never felt anything change.

*Peculiar,* as well, that his existence had suddenly been distilled to such simple desires. His only two wishes now boiled down to resurrecting the dead—two people, each for very different reasons. Most of all he would give anything for Henry's death to have been a dream, to then have the second chance to grant Henry's wish and return the sentiment he'd offered a week ago. But almost as much as this, he wished his father hadn't died all those years ago—because then, if he were still alive now, he could finally kill him.

Daydreaming had kept him on the balcony for an extra minute or two while raindrops pattered all around and the nearby oak branches seemed to sway, not from the wind but along with the rhythms of the orchestra's interpretation of Beethoven's *Moonlight Sonata*. Lulled momentarily into a thoughtless space by the soft sound of the rain, Leo then swiftly fell to Earth, as he noticed Gina down below, staggering toward the garden with her face in her hands and then falling to her knees.

He removed his palm and fingers from the gun butt and let it rest in his bathrobe pocket, thinking he could wait a few more minutes to pull the trigger. Come to think of it, it might be better to pull the trigger outside, anyhow. Yes, better to do it in the garden instead of leaving behind a slasher-movie scene in the bedroom. Gina shouldn't have to clean up after him anymore, especially not any mess as gruesome as that.

*That poor woman,* he thought, leaning over the rail to get a better look at her kneeling in the rain. She'd been a friendly presence in the orbit of his fractured family for so many years. She'd been trustworthy all along. He should try to help her, if for no other reason than she'd kept his horrific secret for the past two days.

He'd wait to pull the trigger. And by waiting a few extra minutes he might even feel there had been the slightest silver lining to this miserable goddamned weekend, a brief bright spot in his altogether dark and unfulfilled life. He could leave this all behind with less guilt—if, and only if, when he held the barrel to his temple sometime later, he could at least look back on his final hour and know that he'd helped her up first. If he could say to himself that he'd done at least one small, good thing.

# THIRTY-FOUR

Kneeling on the wet grass, Gina hunched forward to shield her phone from the rain and dialed her sponsor. It rang three times, and then she felt as though a shard of glass had wedged in her throat when the voice-mail recording kicked on. She squeezed her eyelids closed, breathing in deeply. She didn't want to leave a message, sure as hell didn't have any idea how to sum everything up in thirty seconds or less, but then her phone buzzed right when the recording ended with a beep, and she pressed the icon to answer the call-back from Maryanne.

"Glad you called, hon. How'd the rest of your day go?"

Gina responded with a half snort, half shriek sort of exhausted laugh. "Well," she slurred, "the biggest news is that my boss just fired me." She couldn't keep from sobbing into the phone as she went on. "But there's a lot more that's happened since I talked to you aside from being let go from the job I've had for the past twelve years. It's all gone to shit. Sheila had every reason to fire me."

"Calm down, hon. What happened?"

"It's a lot to catch you up on, but basically I got drunk and took a bunch of pills during the past two days here. I'm drunk and stoned on their

371

property right now and I can't even decide how I'm going to get home. I guess I'll ask my son to drive me. At least the rain just stopped, but I'm already wet."

"It's good that you called. We can figure this all out together."

"I'm sorry to be bothering you with this, and sorry I didn't call before I drank. I'm sorry to you and to everyone else who's been around me lately for being such a fucking mess. I wouldn't blame you if you fired me, too."

Maryanne said something that Gina sensed was an attempt to comfort her, but she didn't hear the actual words since a man's voice had just called out to her from behind. She turned and fell onto her side, the wet grass slippery as she fought gravity and tried to resituate herself on her knees. With her head angled she squinted up at Leo Sheffield, who for some reason stood a few yards away from her barefoot and bare-chested and dressed in nothing but a loosely tied robe.

He waved at her as he approached and repeated what she thought she'd just heard him say: "You're not fired."

Maryanne had continued talking, but Gina cut her off and said she'd call her back, her own voice sounding so small, as though she were half-asleep and just barely able to piece together her words after awakening from an unsettling dream. She clicked off, lowered the phone from her ear and managed to kneel once more, staring up at Leo while he stared down at her.

"How long were you listening?"

"Long enough," he said, helping her up.

"I deserve to be fired."

"Whether you deserve it or not, you're not going anywhere unless you want to. I need you. Forget what Sheila said. You've got this job for life if you want it for that long. You've looked out for me plenty. I'm glad to return the favor now."

"Mr. Sheffield, I—"

"Save it, I know what you're going to say. But I'm the one who should be thanking you. You have no idea how much of a relief it is to focus on someone else right now. I've been in a very dark place this weekend, as you know, though particularly tonight. I suppose we both have, huh?" He paused to reach out to her and placed his hand on her shoulder. "Strange as it might seem, seeing you so upset and coming down here to see if I could help has just helped me."

"I do need help," she said, and brought both hands to her face.

Leo hugged her while she kept her face covered. "Hey, hey . . . Easy . . ." he said, and after a minute or so she let her hands down and ran a finger under each eye. Leo pushed some wet strands of hair from her face, left his hand where her neck met her jaw and kissed her cheek. "You're going to be okay," he said.

She sniffed, staring up at him with watery eyes before she wrapped her arms around him and rested her head on his shoulder. They hugged like that for quite some time, the unexpected comfort allowing Gina to stand upright, even as they shuddered together and turned toward the lake at the first explosion and the bright flashes in the sky.

Another crack and thunderous boom was followed by a shimmering sound, the two of them standing side by side, speechless during the next few minutes of artillery shell bangs and brilliant colors igniting high above and reflecting off the lake water.

Gina had been lulled into a much calmer state, semi-mesmerized by the streaks and flashes and winking cinders falling all across the sky. But then she looked to the side as she saw something moving, someone running way off in the distance. She strained to focus, realizing as she wiped rainwater from her face that it was Corey. Her eyes followed him racing between the sculptures toward the gates while she stood in the rain like a mannequin, and in the next moment she noticed another figure running the opposite direction. It was Angelique, running toward him with a bag over her shoulder.

Gina muttered, "What the fuck are they doing?" Then everything suddenly telegraphed back, and in the brief space between the next burst of fireworks, she lost sight of her son. A man's voice had shouted her name. She blinked water from her lashes, saw the man moving toward her before she recognized his face. But a moment later it was all too clear.

Ray stomped closer. Shouting like a lunatic. Although his voice had been mostly swallowed by the fireworks bursting overhead, Gina wished she hadn't heard what he'd said.

He'd shouted for her to get her ass over to him, and for her half-dressed boss to turn around.

# THIRTY-FIVE

As far as Leo was concerned, the man was a stranger. Roughly twenty feet away, he approached with uneven steps and kept shouting, but Leo couldn't hear him over the steady procession of fireworks. The longer Leo looked at him the less he believed that he'd ever seen this man before, and yet he couldn't be sure because saturated shades of green and purple and red continued flashing all around, throwing shadows down from the oak branches.

The man moved closer, jabbing his finger at them, accusing one or both of them of some offense, shouting wordless threats that couldn't contend with the bomb blasts over the lake. After a few more steps, he'd closed in enough for Leo to decipher from the movements of his mouth that he was shouting Gina's name. A pause between explosions, and then Leo finally heard what the wild-eyed madman had been so hell-bent on saying to him, finally realized that this was the husband Gina had been borrowing money for and bailing out.

He shouted at him once more to let Gina go. Before Leo could think of how to respond, Gina moved a step away from his shoulder and shouted back, "Goddamn it, Ray, what part of us being done don't you understand!"

Gina's husband continued stomping toward them, the man Leo had heard only bad things about each time Gina had sheepishly asked him for a small loan. Another burst of sound over the lake coincided with phosphorescent streaks raining down, flashing red across Ray's face.

He didn't respond to Gina. Instead, he calmly reached back. And in the next flash, he brought his hand up—and in the next, he leveled the gun at Leo's chest.

# THIRTY-SIX

Leo raised his hand from his bathrobe pocket and squeezed the trigger the same instant that Ray fired at him. As if suddenly immersed in a time-lapse video, through a series of flashing shadows and light, his chest opened on his in-breath. He watched Ray's arms drop to his sides, his eyes filled with pale yellow fire. He'd ceased shouting, and now stood stock-still, gazing with the same expression of surprise that Henry had had just after Leo abandoned the compressions and mouth-to-mouth and cradled him in the pool. Then, as if his bones had suddenly turned to ash, Ray seemed to crumble in the strobing colors.

Gina screamed through another series of explosions overhead, though for Leo the volume of the world had begun rapidly turning down, shrinking finally to a needle-tipped sound, a piercing frequency. Then all went silent. His fingers released the gun to the lawn. The man who'd fired at him, Ray, lay on his side a few yards away, his body contorted, his head lolling. Between lazy blinks, his eyes fixed on Leo.

With his first exhale, Leo coughed. Confused by the way the earth had opened up beneath him, he tasted metal. Warmth spread between his ribs as he looked down. His fingers pressed against his chest, his fingers wet against petals of a blooming rose.

So far to fall. So many words unsaid. Still on his feet, yet falling—shot—time stuttering on now at one one-thousandth its normal pace—eye blinks, camera shutters, one giant aperture closing against the flares of fire—the holiday weekend, the reason for the fireworks, the violins and cellos—heat lightning—silence and light—his father had been wrong—no one survives.

*Say goodbye, Leo—to Sheila, to the kids, to the woman staring down . . .*

"I signed the letter—it's upstairs," he said to Gina, whose screams continued, silenced by the fires raining down. "You won't need—to worry anymore," he said, sinking deeper. Slow, shallow breaths. His lungs filling with blood. Choking, drowning. Exactly this, he believed he deserved. Each of us, he believed now, gets what we deserve. The pain left him. His hand slid from his chest. Floating now, out there on the water, a swan.

He would move Henry somewhere safe, soon. But for now, the sky needed to explode some more. Shatter more stars across his eyes. The light, like a womb, pulsing all around. Light. Pulsing.

His heart beat. Once more.

And then.

Nothing but light.

# MEMORIAL DAY

# THIRTY-SEVEN

Police and fire department vehicles blocked a long section of Gin Lane all morning and afternoon. The guests gone, only the family occupied the house while a slew of police milled about in the vicinity of Leo's murder. The two detectives from the city had planned to arrive midafternoon to question him about Henry, but news of the violent event during the fireworks quickly spread and they'd headed out before dawn, now under the assumption that their investigation into Henry's disappearance aligned with Ray. Leo now lay in the morgue. Ray had undergone emergency surgery and lay heavily sedated in a hospital bed, his wrist cuffed to a rail. Meanwhile, two uniformed officers continued redirecting traffic away from the Sheffield estate, offering no information for the local residents and vacationers who asked what all the commotion was about.

At this point, Gina had answered the detectives' questions to their satisfaction. Corey and Angelique were still the only other two people who knew that a body still lay on the property, and they were long gone, driving west on I-70 and already closing in on another time zone.

Soon enough, though, the detectives would request a K-9 unit on-site. And soon after, the trained dog would lead its human partner toward the far corner of the vast Sheffield property, the detectives and a convoy of officers trailing behind. Soon after that, the dog would yelp and tug on its leash and direct them all into the pines, sniffing over the root-gnarled ground while pulling, seeking to run the rest of the way. And then the mound would appear, Henry's clawed hand and half his face exposed. Detective Faraday would shout for the K-9 officer to hold the dog back, he and his partner would ask the other officers to set up a perimeter and evidence flags beside the scattered debris: the shovel, the bottle, the plastic bag and clothes. Then Faraday would kneel, holding Henry's photo beside the dead man's face, and would finally nod to his partner and say, "Yep, it's him."

Later in the day, even before the detectives had their chance to question Ray about Leo's murder and Henry's death, a widespread Manson-murder-type fascination would then take hold of most everyone in the area, locals and visitors alike, but the wealthy vacationers would be left especially stunned, speaking of the poor Sheffield man while sitting poolside or in deck chairs or in glass-walled rooms with a view of the ocean, too preoccupied by the notion that they themselves could have been the target of such violence to notice their servants—many of whom, with their own drinks in hand, later recalling what their employers had been saying all day long:

*Can you believe it? Murder, in the Hamptons?*

# WEDNESDAY

# 2,400 MILES WEST

# THIRTY-EIGHT

Three days after Corey spoke to Gina on the phone and heard about Leo's death and Ray's hospitalization, he and Angelique continued adding more distance between themselves and the Sheffield estate. Still driving west just after sunrise, after another few hours of sleep in the truck at a roadside rest area somewhere in Utah, Angelique leaned over from the passenger seat and rested her head on Corey's shoulder while he kept both hands on the wheel, both of them looking through the windshield with tired eyes as they wound their way along the curvy two-lane road, the final stretch to Bryce Canyon.

For the past mile or two they'd been the only ones on the road, cruising with the headlights still lit as they faced the fading sunrise colors hovering above alien hills. At the next curve, Angelique sat up and pointed out the window at a crumbling hillside and the rock formations jutting up from the orange sand. Corey slowed and downshifted into first gear, gazing out at three surreal pillars of perfectly stacked boulders looming over the shoulder of the road, each of the massive, fiery-red rocks rounded around the edges but flat, like mammoth skipping stones.

"Let's stop here and get out," she said.

Corey nodded slowly, his eyes still fixed on the martian landscape where she'd pointed.

"Damn," he said, stepping out of the truck and doing his best to rub the sleep from his eyes. "Thanks for suggesting that we come here."

They leaned against the front bumper between the headlights and Corey slung his arm over her shoulder while she leaned into him. He thought about his most recent call with Gina, how she'd put him on the spot about whether he'd been the one who'd knocked Leo over the head. He'd admitted to it, told her the whole story, in fact, and after a pause she'd said, "Promise me you won't ever tell anyone else about that." Although he'd agreed and said he understood why no one else should ever know, she made him promise again after updating him on all the drama, informing him that Leo's funeral would take place later in the week, and that the detectives didn't believe Henry had died in an accident. Ray was their number one suspect, quite possibly their only suspect. They'd questioned her about him, asked if she thought he might have come to the estate earlier in the week to kill Leo but had run into Henry instead. Although he enjoyed hearing that Ray was facing life in prison, now that he and Angelique were thousands of miles away, Corey heard his mother's news from the Hamptons as details from a past life, as an epilogue to a story that no longer had anything to do with him.

He huddled with Angelique against the truck bumper in the chilly morning air. Neither of them spoke for a few minutes. Then he looked up, and Angelique angled her head back as well, as a hawk swooped overhead and screeched on its way over the hill. They turned to face each other at the same time.

"Amazing, huh?" Angelique said. "And this isn't even the actual canyon. It's just the road that takes us there."

"Incredible. Sorry you didn't get to come here with your mom."

She looked at him, seeming to study his eyes, then answered with her head on his shoulder. "She would have liked you."

Corey smiled and stared at the curve in the road as a wave of heat entered his cheeks.

"You ready to drive the rest of the way?"

"Yeah, but since there's a garbage can over there, let's first get rid of some of the trash."

They each opened a door and started collecting the empty bottles and cans, candy bar wrappers and empty plastic bags, and when they were about finished Angelique pulled a crumpled paper from beneath her seat. "What's this?"

It took Corey a second to recognize it. "Oh, that's an essay I wrote just before I graduated," he said, realizing he hadn't read it or thought about it since he'd parked at the ocean the night he broke into the Sheffield estate and had to hide from her under Tiffany's bed.

He jogged over to the garbage can and dropped the trash inside, and when he hopped back into the truck and they each shut their doors, she asked him to wait. She was looking down at the wrinkled paper. "What are these lines on the other side of the page?"

"Nothing, just a poem I started a while back."

"Full disclosure," she said, "I just read it. And I like it a lot."

"Thanks, but it's nothing really."

"How about I read it out loud?"

Without giving Corey a chance to answer, she spoke for him by clearing her throat and snapping the paper taut before her eyes.

*This doesn't even seem real,* he thought as he drove on, watching the landscape change with each curve, and then the hawk returning, soaring high overhead, circling back and diving across both lanes just a few car lengths ahead.

"You ready?" she said.

He nodded and kept driving slowly down the final road that would lead them to the canyon she'd shown him pictures of and spoken so much about during their cross-country drive, the inside-out caves, the sea of spires like thousands of stone cathedrals huddled together, all carved from rain. He couldn't wait to get there, though he also felt they had all the time in the world now that she'd started reading in the voice he'd heard calling out to him from deep within, for all his life. He listened, her voice filling the truck cab with his words.

*There's a quiet voice I have inside
that I can only hear when I sit beside*

*the ocean. This ocean where I hide
is all mine—this moonlight and this*

*midnight tide. Believe me when I say
that this is the only space I'll miss*

*when I leave this place
forever.*

—C. Halpern

# ACKNOWLEDGMENTS

To Sarah Bedingfield, agent extraordinaire and all-around wonderful person—thank you for your belief in me and my work, and your endless warmth and support. I am the luckiest author there is to be teamed up with you.

To my brilliant editor, Liz Stein—thank you for going without sleep (after already being sleep-deprived with a six-month-old at home) when you first read my manuscript, and for championing my work so enthusiastically ever since. To Erika Imranyi—thank you for "devouring" my manuscript early on, and for the thousand things that you and Laura Brown and the world-class team at Park Row have done to bring this book to the world. To the team at Levine Greenberg Rostan Literary Agency, thank you for backing me all the way. To Alice Lawson, thank you for envisioning this story as a film and for reaching out when it was still in development.

To the talented and supportive fiction authors who helped guide me along the way: Claire Davis, Jack Driscoll, John Vernon, Craig Lesley, Jaimee Wriston Colbert, Alexi Zentner, Ben Percy, Brady Udall, Pam Houston, Meg Wolitzer, Bonnie Jo Campbell, Susan Reese, Tony Wolk and Peter H. Fogtdal—thank you all so much. To the faculty and alums of the Pacific University MFA program and the PhD program at Binghamton University, and to the directors of those programs, Shelly Washburn and Maria Mazziotti Gillan—I'm eternally grateful to have connected with each and every one of you. To the lovely and talented Andrea Jurjević, to her sons, Kian O'Rourke and Saoirse O'Rourke; and to all my friends (sorry I can't list you all but the list would be way too long—damn, I'm lucky)—thank you. Special thanks to Liam Costello and Kristi Murray Costello for providing a space to finish the final revisions of the novel, and to Barrett Bowlin and Ben Burgholzer for offering to be early readers. To the Hamptons kids from working-class families and broken homes, to those who survived and those who left us too soon; to all the Friends of Bill—thank you for reminding me that we never need to walk alone.

To my mother, Linda Allen, and my brother, Jesse Allen—thank you for loving me through all the ups and downs, and for always believing in me, even when I didn't.

# ABOUT THE AUTHOR

Jason Allen grew up in a working-class home in the Hamptons, and for some years during that previous life he worked a variety of blue-collar jobs for wealthy estate owners. He writes fiction, poetry and memoir, and is the author of the poetry collection *A Meditation on Fire*. He has an MFA from Pacific University and a PhD in literature and creative writing from Binghamton University, and currently lives in Atlanta, Georgia, where he teaches writing. *The East End* is his first novel.

Books are produced in the United States using U.S.-based materials

Books are printed using a revolutionary new process called THINKtech™ that lowers energy usage by 70% and increases overall quality

Books are durable and flexible because of Smyth-sewing

Paper is sourced using environmentally responsible foresting methods and the paper is acid-free

**Center Point Large Print**
600 Brooks Road / PO Box 1
Thorndike, ME 04986-0001 USA

(207) 568-3717

US & Canada:
1 800 929-9108
www.centerpointlargeprint.com